Blooms of Darkness

Blooms of Darkness

AHARON APPELFELD

Translated from the Hebrew by

JEFFREY M. GREEN

Schocken Books · NEW YORK

Translation copyright © 2010 by Schocken Books, a division of Random House, Inc.

All rights reserved. Published in the United States by Schocken Books, a division of Random House, Inc., New York, and in Canada by Random House of Canada Limited, Toronto.

Schocken Books and colophon are registered trademarks of Random House, Inc.

Originally published in Israel as *Pirkhei Ha'afeilah* by Keter Publishing House Ltd., Jerusalem, in 2006. Copyright © 2006 by Aharon Appelfeld and Keter Publishing House Ltd.

Library of Congress Cataloging-in-Publication Data

Appelfeld, Aron.
[Pirhe ha-afelah. English]
Blooms of darkness / Aharon Appelfeld ; translated from the Hebrew by Jeffrey M. Green
p.   cm.
ISBN 978-0-8052-4280-5
I. Green, Yaacov Jeffrey.   II. Title.
PJ5054.A755P5713 2010   892.4'36—dc22   2009033532

www.schocken.com
Book design by Robert C. Olsson
First American Edition
2 4 6 8 9 7 5 3

In memory of Gila Ramraz Rauch

Blooms of Darkness

1

Tomorrow Hugo will be eleven, and Anna and Otto will come for his birthday. Most of Hugo's friends have already been sent to distant villages, and the few remaining will be sent soon. The tension in the ghetto is great, but no one cries. The children secretly guess what is in store for them. The parents control their feelings so as not to sow fear, but the doors and windows know no restraint. They slam by themselves or are shoved with nervous movements. Winds whip through every alley.

A few days ago Hugo was about to be sent to the mountains, too, but the peasant who was supposed to take him never came. Meanwhile, his birthday approached, and his mother decided to have a party so Hugo would remember the house and his parents. Who knows what awaits us? Who knows when we will see one another again? That was the thought that passed through his mother's mind.

To please Hugo, his mother bought three books by Jules Verne and a volume by Karl May from friends already marked for deportation. If he went to the mountains, he would take this new present with him. His mother intended to add the dominoes and the chess set, and the book she read to him every night before he went to sleep.

Again Hugo promises that he will read in the mountains

and do arithmetic problems, and at night he will write letters to his mother. His mother holds back her tears and tries to talk in her ordinary voice.

Along with Anna's and Otto's parents, the parents of other children, who had already been sent to the mountains, are invited to the birthday party. One of the parents brings an accordion.

Everybody makes an effort to hide the anxieties and the fears and to pretend that life is going on as usual. Otto brought a valuable present with him: a fountain pen decorated with mother-of-pearl. Anna brought a chocolate bar and a package of halvah. The candies make the children happy and for a moment sweeten the parents' grief. But the accordion fails to raise their spirits. The accordion player goes to great lengths to cheer them up, but the sounds he produces only make the sadness heavier.

Still, everybody tries not to talk about the Actions, or about the labor brigades that were sent to unknown destinations, or about the orphanage or the old age home, whose inmates had been deported with no warning, and of course not about Hugo's father, who had been snatched up a month before. Since then there has been no trace of him.

After everyone has left, Hugo asks, "Mama, when will I go to the mountains, too?"

"I don't know. I'm checking all the possibilities."

Hugo doesn't understand the meaning of "I'm checking all the possibilities." He imagines his life without his mother as a life of attention and great obedience. His mother repeats, "You mustn't act spoiled. You have to do everything they ask of you. Mama will do her best to come and visit you, but it doesn't depend on her. Everybody is sent somewhere else. Anyway, don't expect me too much. If I can ever come, I will."

"Will Papa come, too?"

His mother's heart tightens for a moment, and she says,

"We haven't heard from Papa since he was taken to the labor camp."

"Where is he?"

"God knows."

Hugo has noticed that since the Actions his mother often says, "God knows," one of her expressions of despair. Since the Actions, life has been a prolonged secret. His mother tries to explain and to soothe him, but what he sees keeps telling him that there is some dreadful secret.

"Where do they take the people?"

"To labor."

"And when will they come back?"

He has noticed. His mother doesn't answer all his questions the way she used to. There are questions she simply ignores. Hugo has learned meanwhile not to ask, to listen instead to the silence between the words. But the child in him, who just a few months ago went to school and did homework, can't control itself, and he asks, "When will the people come back home?"

Most days Hugo sits on the floor and plays dominoes or chess with himself. Sometimes Anna comes. Anna is six months younger than Hugo, but a little taller. She wears glasses, reads a lot, and is an excellent pianist. Hugo wants to impress her but doesn't know how. His mother has taught him a little French, but even at that Anna is better than he. Complete sentences in French come out of her mouth, and Hugo has the impression that Anna can learn whatever she wants, and quickly. Unable to think of an alternative, he takes a jump rope out of a drawer and starts skipping rope. He is better at hopping than Anna. Anna tries very hard, but her ability at that game is limited.

"Did your parents find a peasant for you already?" Hugo asks cautiously.

"Not yet. The peasant who promised to come and take me didn't show up."

"My peasant didn't show up, either."

"I guess we'll be sent away with the adults."

"It doesn't matter," says Hugo, bowing his head like a grown-up.

Every night Hugo's mother makes sure to read him a chapter from a book. Over the past few weeks, she has been reading him stories from the Bible. Hugo was sure that only religious people read the Bible, but, surprisingly, his mother reads it, and he sees the images very clearly. Abraham seems tall to him, like the owner of the pastry shop on the corner. The owner liked children, and every time a child happened into his shop, a surprise gift awaited him.

After his mother read to him about the binding of Isaac, Hugo wondered, "Is that a story or a fable?"

"It's a story," his mother answered cautiously.

Hugo was very glad that Isaac was rescued, but he was sorry for the ram that was sacrificed in his place.

"Why doesn't the story tell any more?" asked Hugo.

"Try to imagine," his mother advised him.

That advice turned out to work. Hugo closed his eyes and immediately saw the high, green Carpathian Mountains. Abraham was very tall, and he and his little son Isaac walked slowly, the ram trailing behind them, its head down, as if it knew its fate.

2

The next night a peasant came and took Anna away with him. Hugo heard about it in the morning, and his heart tightened. Most of his friends were already in the mountains, and he remained behind. His mother kept telling him that a place would soon be found for him. Sometimes it seemed to him that children were no longer wanted, and that was why they were sent away.

"Mama, why are they sending the children to the mountains?" He can't stop his tongue.

"The ghetto is dangerous, don't you see?" She is curt.

Hugo knows that the ghetto is dangerous. Not a day goes by without arrests and deportations. The road to the railway is crammed with people. They are burdened with heavy packs, so heavy that they can hardly move. Soldiers and gendarmes brandish their whips over the deportees. The miserable people are shoved and collapse. Hugo knows now that his question, "Why are they sending the children to the mountains?" was foolish, and he is sorry he hadn't been able to restrain himself.

Every day his mother equips him with short instructions. She repeats one directive: "You must look around you, listen, and not ask. Strangers don't like it when you ask them questions." Hugo knows his mother is preparing him for life without her. He has had the feeling that over the past few days she has for some reason been trying to keep him at a distance. Sometimes her strength fails her, and she weeps and moans.

Otto sneaks in to play chess. Hugo is better than Otto at the game, and beats him easily. Seeing his defeat, Otto raises his hands and says, "You won. There's nothing to do." Hugo is sad for Otto, who doesn't play well and doesn't even notice a simple threat. He consoles him and says, "In the mountains you'll have time to practice. And when we meet after the war, you'll be well trained."

"I don't have any talent."

"The game isn't as complicated as it seems to you."

"It's complicated for me."

You have to prepare yourself for independent life, it occurs to Hugo to say to him, but he doesn't say it.

Otto is a passive boy. He's like his mother, who keeps saying, "There are some people that the war gives life to. I raise my hands and surrender. I don't have the strength to fight over a slice of bread. If that's what life is, you can have it."

Otto's mother was a high school teacher. People still respect her even now, in these lamentable conditions. In the past she expressed opinions and estimations and presented examples from ancient and modern history. Now she shrugs her shoulders and says, "I don't understand a thing. A different kind of reason has come to the world."

Hugo records in his heart everything his eyes see: the people who enter the house in a panic and spit out a horrifying bit of news, and the ones who sit by the table and don't utter a word. The house has changed beyond recognition. The windows are shut tight and the curtains add to the darkness. Only from Hugo's narrow window, which looks out onto the courtyard, can he see Railroad Street and the deportees. Sometimes Hugo recognizes a parent or a child from his class among the deportees. He knows that his fate will be no different from theirs. At night he burrows under his blanket and is sure that he is now protected.

People come in and out of the house without knocking on the door and without asking permission, like after his grandfather died. His mother greets them, but she can't offer them a cup of coffee or lemonade. "I have nothing to give you," she says, raising her hands.

I'll remember every corner of the house, Hugo says to himself, *but more than the house, I'll remember Mama. Mama without Papa is lost. She tries to do everything necessary; she runs from place to place to find a peasant who will take me with him to the mountains.*

"How can we know that he's an honest peasant?" his mother keeps asking in despair.

"That's what people say," they reply.

Everyone is groping in the dark, and in the end they deliver their children to the unknown peasants who come at night. Evil rumors say that the peasants take the money for themselves and deliver the children to the police. Because of those rumors, some parents aren't willing to let the peasants have their children. "When the child is with you, you can defend it," a panicked parent will say. For some reason, Hugo is not afraid. Perhaps because he used to go to his grandparents in the country in the summer. Sometimes he stayed for a week with them. He loved the fields of corn and the meadows, where spotted cows grazed. His grandparents were tall and quiet. They spoke little. Hugo loved to be in their company. He imagines his life among the peasants as one of great tranquility. He will have a dog and a horse, and he will feed them and take care of them. He always loved animals, but his parents refused to take in a dog. From now on, he'll live in nature, like the peasants who doze under the trees at noon.

For safety's sake, Hugo and his mother go down into the cellar at night and sleep there. At night the soldiers and gendarmes sweep through houses and snatch up children. Quite a few children have already been seized. The cellar is cold, but they wrap themselves in blankets, and the cold doesn't penetrate.

Otto secretly sneaks in and tells Hugo that Anna has reached the mountains safely and that he has already received a letter from her. Every letter that arrives from the mountains is a small victory. The skeptics, of course, keep to their pessimism and say, "Who knows what conditions the letters were written under. The peasants who brought the letters asked for more money. There's no love of mankind with them, just greed."

Hugo hears the skeptical voices and he thinks of telling Otto, *You mustn't be so pessimistic. Pessimism weakens you. You have to be strong and encourage your mother.*

At first the majority were optimists, but in the past weeks they have become a minority. People dismiss their hopes and hold them in contempt.

At night his mother admits that she hasn't succeeded in finding a peasant who is willing to hide him. If there is no alternative, she will take him to Mariana.

Mariana is a Ukrainian woman who went to elementary school with Hugo's mother. While still a young girl, she left school and had fallen low. *What does "fallen low" mean?* Hugo asks himself. A wagon rolls down and tumbles into a chasm, but a person collapses and doesn't make the sound of rolling down.

Hugo likes to listen to words. There are words whose sounds made their meaning clear to him, and there are words that don't evoke pictures but just go past him without showing him anything.

Hugo sometimes asks his mother the meaning of a word. His mother tries to define it, but she doesn't always manage to make a picture out of the word.

Just then Aunt Frieda comes into the house with some

news. Frieda is well-known. Everybody talks about her with a certain smile. She was married twice, and she has recently been living with a Ukrainian man years younger than she.

"Julia, don't worry. My boyfriend is willing to take you to his village. He has an excellent hiding place."

His mother is stunned. She hugs Frieda and says, "I don't know what to do."

"Don't lose hope, my dear," says Frieda, pleased that the family is accepting her again.

Frieda is a pretty woman. She wears unusual clothing, and every once in a while she causes a scandal. Because of her wild way of life, her family kept its distance from her. Even Hugo's mother, who helps the needy, wasn't charitable to her.

Frieda keeps praising her boyfriend, who is willing to endanger himself for her and for her family. "Only Ukrainians can save us, if they want to," she says, glad to be able to help her family, even though it has been estranged from her for years.

Hugo's mother thanks her again and says, "I was already in despair."

"You mustn't despair," says Frieda. It is clear that she has been practicing that sentence for years, and now she can demonstrate that despair is indeed an illusion. "There's always a way out. There's always someone who loves you. You have to be patient and wait for him." Hugo looks at her closely, and to his surprise he discovers features of a little girl in her face.

3

The ghetto is thinning out. Now they are snatching old people and children in houses and in the streets. Hugo spends most of the day in the dark cellar, reading and playing chess by lantern light. The thick darkness plunges him into early sleep. In his sleep he escapes from the gendarmes by climbing a tree, but in the end he falls into a deep pit. When he wakes up, he is glad that the fall didn't hurt him.

Every few hours his mother comes to see him. She brings him a slice of bread spread with fat, and sometimes an apple or a pear. Hugo knows she is denying herself food to give him more. He implores her to eat a portion of the food, but she refuses.

Again, another transport. Hugo stands at the narrow window and watches. There are shoves, screams, and bitter fights. In the pressing crowd, Frieda's colorful figure stands out. She is wearing a flowery dress, her hair is disheveled, and from a distance it seems that the shoving is making her laugh. She waves her straw hat as though she hadn't been caught but was going of her own free will on vacation to a resort.

"Mama, I saw Frieda in the transport."

"Impossible."

"With my very eyes I saw her."

In the evening Hugo's mother finds out that Frieda has been seized and deported without any of her belongings. The great hope that her Ukrainian boyfriend would give them refuge has been destroyed.

Hugo's mother speaks more and more about Mariana. Mariana lives outside of the town, and they will apparently make their way to her through the sewer pipes. The pipes are wide, and after midnight little sewage runs in them. Hugo's mother tries to speak in her ordinary tone of voice, and from time to time she gives it a tinge of adventure. Hugo knows she is doing that to calm him down.

"Where is Otto?"

"I assume that he's also hiding in a cellar." His mother speaks curtly.

Since his mother told him they would make their way to Mariana through the sewer pipes, Hugo has been trying to recall her face from his memory. His efforts evoke only her height and long arms, which hugged his mother at the meetings when he was present. Those meetings were mostly fleeting. His mother would give her two packages, and Mariana would hug her warmly.

"Does Mariana live in the country?" Hugo gropes in this new darkness.

"In a village."

"Will I be able to play outside?"

"I don't think so. Mariana will explain everything to you. We've been friends ever since we were girls. She's a good woman, but fate hasn't been kind to her. You will have to be very disciplined and do exactly what she tells you to."

What is the meaning of "fate hasn't been kind to her"? Hugo wonders. It is hard for him to imagine that tall, pretty woman dejected or humiliated.

His mother repeats, "Everyone has his own fate."

That sentence, like the one before, is inscrutable.

Meanwhile, Hugo's mother takes a knapsack and a suitcase down into the cellar. She places books in the knapsack, and the chess set and the dominoes. She packs clothes and shoes in the suitcase. It is stuffed and heavy.

"Don't worry. Mariana will take care of everything. I spoke with her. She liked you," his mother says with a trembling voice.

"And where will you go, Mama?"

"I'll look for a hiding place in the nearby village."

His mother has stopped reading the Bible to him, but after Hugo puts out the lantern, he hears her calling to him. Her voice is soft, melodious, and penetrating.

"You must behave like a grown-up," his mother says, not sounding like herself. Hugo wants to reply, *I'll do everything that Mariana tells me to do,* but he stops himself.

At night sounds come from outside and shock the cellar. They are mainly the sobbing of women whose children were snatched away from them. The women were daring and ran after the gendarmes, pleading with them to return their children. The pleas drove the gendarmes mad, and they beat the women furiously.

After the kidnappings, silence reigns. Only here and there a suppressed sob is heard.

Hugo lies awake. Everything that happens in the house and in the street affects him. An expression that he heard by chance returns to him at night with intensified clarity. It is hard for him to read and hard for him to play chess. Images and sounds fill him.

"Where is Otto?" he keeps asking his mother.

"In a cellar."

Hugo is sure that Otto, too, has been snatched, thrown into a truck, and is now on his way to the Ukraine.

His mother sits with her legs crossed and describes the place where Mariana lives. "She has a big room and within it is a big closet. In the daytime, you'll be in the big room, and at night you'll sleep in the closet."

"At Mariana's, are they also liable to seize me?" Hugo asks cautiously.

"Mariana will watch over you like a hawk."

"Why will I have to sleep in the closet?"

"For safety's sake."

"Will she read out of the Bible for me?"

"If you ask her."

"Does she know how to play chess?"

"I imagine not."

The short questions and answers sound to Hugo like final preparations for a secret journey. Sitting in the cellar oppresses him, and he is eagerly looking forward to the day when he'll put the knapsack on his back and go down into the sewer with his mother.

"Is there a school there?" he suddenly asks.

"My dear, you aren't going to go to school. You have to be in hiding," his mother says in a different tone of voice.

That sounds like a punishment to him, and he asks, "Will I be in hiding all the time?"

"Until the end of the war."

He is relieved. The war, he has heard, will not be long.

Hugo's questions, asked as he gropes blindly, pain his mother. Usually she answers with a complete sentence or gives half an answer, but she doesn't deceive him. She has a rule: never deceive. But there were times, to admit the truth, when she blurred things, distracted him, and concealed facts from him. For that reason, her conscience bothers her. To overcome her twinges of conscience, she says, "You must be aware, listen to everything that's said, and understand that we're living in strange times. Nothing is the way it was."

Hugo feels that his mother is distressed, and he says, "I'm listening, Mama. I listen all the time."

"Thanks, dear," his mother answers. She has been feeling recently that she has lost control over her words. They slip out of her mouth and don't touch on the main point. For example, she wants to tell Hugo about Mariana and her profession, so that he will know and be careful, but all the words she tries to mobilize don't help her.

"Excuse me," she says suddenly.

"What for, Mama?"

"Nothing. My mistake," she says, and she covers her mouth with a handkerchief.

Again Hugo is ill at ease. It seems to him that his mother wants to tell him a big secret, but that for some reason she is hesitating. That hesitation makes him talk too much and repeat things he's already told her.

"Does Mariana have children?" Hugo tries a different approach.

"She isn't married."

"What does she do?"

"She works."

To conclude the interrogation, she says, "There's no reason to ask so many questions. I repeat, Mariana is a good woman. She'll watch over you like a hawk. I trust her."

This time Hugo is insulted, and he says, "I won't ask."

"You're allowed to ask, but you have to realize that there isn't an answer to every question. There are things that it's impossible to explain, and there are things that a boy of your age can't understand." To console him a bit, she adds, "Believe me, everything will be clear to you. In a short while you'll understand a lot of things. You're a smart boy, and even without answers, you'll understand." His mother opens her eyes wide, and they both smile.

4

The night finally came. It was preceded by a day of house-to-house searches, kidnappings, and cries of dread. The noose was getting tighter, and his mother decided that after midnight they would set out. All the days in the cellar, Hugo didn't feel afraid. Now, as he is on his knees and stuffing the books back into the knapsack, his hands tremble.

"Did we forget anything?" asks his mother, the way she used to ask before they went on vacation.

It's one in the morning, and they walk up the steps in the dark house. Through the darkness Hugo can see his room—the desk, the dresser, and the bookcase. His schoolbag lies at the foot of the desk. *I won't be going to school anymore*—the thought passes through his head.

Hugo's mother hastily puts a few small things in a handbag, and they go out the back door into the street. The street is dark and silent, and they cling to the walls as they walk, to avoid discovery. Near what was once the bakery is the manhole. Hugo's mother pulls up the cover and goes down. Hugo throws her the suitcase and the knapsack. He immediately dangles his legs down, and his mother takes him in her arms. Luckily for them, the sewage isn't deep at that hour, but the stench and the stifling air slow them down. Hugo knows that quite a few people have been caught coming out of the sewers. His mother assumed that on a Sunday night the guards would be drunk, and they wouldn't leave the ghetto to lie in wait for people running away. From time to time the level of the sewage rises, and the air grows more stifling. While they are trudging along, Hugo collapses. His mother doesn't lose her wits. She drags him, and in the end she pulls him out. When he opens his eyes, he is lying on grass.

"What happened, Mama?" he asks.

"It was suffocating, and you felt ill."

"I don't remember anything."

"There's nothing to remember." His mother tries to distract him.

Hugo will think a great deal about that dark night, trying to tie the details together, and he will wonder again and again how his mother had managed to pull him out of the sewer and restore him to life.

But meanwhile, it's dangerous to linger in the open field. They make their way, hunched over, to a nearby grove of trees. Every few minutes they stop, kneel, and listen.

"Mariana works at night, and you have to get used to being alone." His mother reveals another detail to him.

"I'll read, and I'll do arithmetic problems."

"I hope that Mariana has a light in the closet," she says in a trembling voice.

"When will you come and see me?"

"That doesn't depend on me," she says without emphasizing any word in the sentence.

Then they take a break and sit without talking, and it seems to Hugo as if many hours have passed since they left the cellar, were in the sewer, and clambered out of it.

"Will Papa also come and visit me?" he asks, hurting his mother without knowing it.

"It's very dangerous to wander around outdoors, don't you see?"

"And after the war, will you come and visit me?"

"We'll come right away. We won't delay even a minute," she says, and she's glad that this time she's found the correct words.

Then she tells him that she doesn't intend to go back home. She will go to the nearby village. She has a friend thére, someone with whom she'd gone to school, and maybe this friend will agree to hide her until the troubles are over. If that friend doesn't agree, she will go to the village of Khlinitsia, where a woman who was a servant in Hugo's grandparents' house lives, an old woman with a good temperament.

"Why can't you stay with me?"

"There isn't room for me."

Then she speaks in a torrent, as though she were reading out loud or reciting. Hugo doesn't understand anything she is talking about. He only senses that she wants to tell him something that's hard to reveal. It's her voice, but not her usual voice.

"Mama."

"What?"

"And you'll come to visit me?" The words burst from his mouth.

"Certainly I'll come. Do you have any doubt?"

The silence mingles with the darkness, and the smell of the damp grass rises from the soft ground. "Autumn," says his mother, and her voice wipes away the memory of the stifling sewer and the fears of the night. Other sights, silent and enchanting, rise from oblivion.

In the autumn they used to go for a week in the Carpathians, to see the fallen leaves. The autumn lay on the earth in a myriad of hues, and they would step slowly, so as not to destroy the big leaves that floated in bright colors, detached from the trees. Hugo's father would bend over, pick up a leaf, and say, "A waste."

"A waste of what?" His mother's question came promptly.

"Of this beauty."

Other marvelous things were said then, but Hugo didn't take them in, or maybe he didn't retain them. His contacts with his parents at those times were delicate and soft, and what was said sank into him.

For a moment it seems to Hugo that his mother is about to say, *It's late, let's go home. We were wrong, but we can correct the error.* His mother sometimes used sentences like that, expressions of her optimism. His father liked that sentence and would try to adopt it in his own way.

"How do you feel?" she asks, looking at Hugo with her eyes wide open.

"Excellent."

"Thank God. In half an hour we'll be at Mariana's."

Hugo, flooded by memories of the Carpathians, tries to delay the parting and says, "Why rush?"

"Mariana is waiting for us. I wouldn't want to delay her. It's late."

"Just a little."

"We can't, dear. The way was long, beyond what I had thought." Hugo knows that phrase, "beyond what I had thought," but this time it seems as if it has been plucked out of another place and another time.

"What time is it?" Hugo asks.

"It's two-thirty, after midnight."

Strange, the thought flits through his mind, why did his mother say "after midnight"? There was no light in the whole area. Everything was night. Why say "after midnight"? Wasn't that self-evident?

"It's very late. I wouldn't want to bother Mariana too much. But if we make an effort, we'll be there in half an hour," his mother says softly.

5

Hugo's mother was right. Before long, they are standing by a narrow wooden door. His mother knocks, and to the question in a woman's voice, she answers, "Julia."

The door opens, and a tall woman, dressed in a long night-gown, stands at the entrance.

"We got here," says his mother.

"Come in."

"I won't disturb you. Hugo's clothes are in the suitcase, and there are books and games in the knapsack. We came through the sewer pipes. I hope the clothes didn't get dirty. You know Hugo?"

"He's grown since I last saw him," she says, and looks at him.

"He's a good boy."

"I'm sure."

"Mariana will watch over you. She remembers you from when you were very little."

"Mama," Hugo says, as though his lips have stopped him from saying more.

"I have to leave immediately and get to the village before dawn." She speaks with strange haste and takes something shiny out of her handbag and hands it to Mariana.

"What's this?" says Mariana, without looking at the jewelry.
"It's for you."

"Good God. And you?"

"I'm going away from here to Sarina, and I hope to get there before sunrise."

"Be careful," says Mariana, and she hugs Hugo's mother.

"Hugo, dear," she says, "always be quiet and polite. Don't bother with questions and don't ask for anything. Always say please and always say thank you." The words are choked in her throat.

"Mama." He tries to keep her for another minute.

"I have to go. Take care of yourself, dear," she says, kisses his forehead, and separates herself from him.

Mama, he is about to call out again, but the word is blocked in his mouth.

Hugo manages to see her go away. She walks stooped over, making a way for herself through the bushes. When she is swallowed up in the thick darkness, Mariana closes the door.

That is the break, but Hugo doesn't feel it. Perhaps because of the night chill that his body had soaked up, or because of his fatigue. He is very confused and says, "Mama left."

"She'll come back," says Mariana, not meaning it.

"Is it far to the village?" he asks, breaking the first rule that his mother drilled into him.

"Don't worry about your mother. She's experienced. She'll find a way."

"Sorry." He tries to fix things.

"You're surely tired," Mariana says, letting him into the closet, a long, narrow space without windows. At first sight it looks like the roomy pantry in Hugo's house. But the strong smell of sheepskins immediately reminds him of the shoemaker's cellar, where his mother brought shoes to be repaired every few months.

"This will be your bedroom. Can I bring you something to drink?"

"Thanks, there's no need."

"I'll bring you some soup."

Hugo surveys the closet, and on his second look he discovers colorful nightgowns suspended from hangers, a few pairs of shoes, and, on a surface like a bench, scattered silk stockings, a corset, and a brassiere. Those women's things amuse his eyes for a moment.

Mariana brings him the soup and says, "Eat, dear. You've had a hard day."

Hugo eats the soup. Mariana looks at him and says, "You're a big kid. How old are you?"

"Eleven."

"You look older. Take off your shoes and go to sleep. Tomorrow we'll sit together and talk about how to make your days with me pleasant," she says, and closes the closet door.

It's still dark outside, and through the cracks in the closet wall the shrieks of birds of prey filter in, as does the clear cry of a rooster that has woken up. For a moment it seems to Hugo that the door will open soon and his mother will come in, stooped over, the way she was in the habit of walking during the past weeks. She will tell him that she has found a marvelous hiding place and that they will go there together now. Her voice and expression are clear, and he awaits her arrival intently. But in the end fatigue overcomes him, and he falls asleep.

It is an uncomfortable sleep that presses on his chest and binds his feet. Several times he tries to slip out of the oppression. In the end he wakes up and feels better.

Now he can see the closet. It's narrower than he imagined. Through the cracks between the boards light filters in and brightens the back. The front remains dipped in thin darkness.

Sleep, it seems, has wiped the expectation away from his

heart. He sees his mother standing at the counter in the pharmacy with his father at her side, as though time had frozen them in their places. The panic of the last few months is not visible on them. They look quiet and settled, and if they weren't frozen into mummies, there would have been no change in them.

While he is still wondering about their frozenness, the door opens, and Mariana stands in the doorway, dressed in a colorful nightgown, with a cup of milk in her hand.

"How did you sleep?"

"Well."

"Drink, and I'll show you my room."

Hugo takes the cup and drinks. It is sweet, fresh milk that seeps into him and warms him up.

"Where's Mama?" He can't control himself.

"She went to the village to find refuge."

"When will she come to me?" Again he makes a mistake and asks.

"It will take a little time. Come, I'll show you my room."

Hugo didn't expect such a surprise. It is a broad room, well lit and wrapped in curtains. All the slipcovers in the room are pink, as are the chairs. Colorful jars and flasks are scattered on the dressers.

"Do you like the room?"

Hugo doesn't know what to say, so he answers, "It's very beautiful."

Mariana chuckles, a kind of suppressed laugh that is hard to figure out.

"The room is very beautiful." He tries to correct himself.

"In the daytime you can play here. Sometimes I sleep in the daytime, and you can watch over my sleep."

"I'll play chess," it occurs to him to tell her.

"Sometimes I'll have to hide you, but don't worry, it will be for a short time, and then you'll come back here. You can sit in the armchair or on the floor. Do you like to read?"

"A lot."

"You won't be bored with me," Mariana says, and she winks.

6

Mariana goes out and leaves Hugo by himself. The room isn't like a room where a person lives. The pink slipcovers, the fragrance of perfume, give it the look of a beauty parlor. Not far from their house was a beauty parlor. There, too, the furniture was pink. In the corners they shampooed the hair of full-figured women and did their finger- and toenails. Everything was done there with a lazy ease, with laughter and open enjoyment. Hugo liked to stand and look at the scene, but his mother's feet never crossed the threshold of the beauty parlor. Every time they went by it, her lips would curl into a smile whose meaning he couldn't fathom.

For a long time Hugo stands still, wondering about the nature of this roomy place. Finally he sums it up for himself: it's not a beauty parlor. There isn't a broad bed in the middle of a beauty parlor.

Meanwhile, Mariana comes back with a tray of little sandwiches and says, "This is for you. Sit in the armchair and eat as much as you want."

Hugo remembers that at weddings the waitresses would serve sandwiches like that. At home the sandwiches were simple and served without a paper wrapping. "These are sandwiches for a wedding, isn't that right?" The sentence slips out of his mouth.

"We eat that kind of sandwich here. Are they tasty?"

"Very."

"Where were you recently?"

"In the basement of our house."

"If they ask you, don't say that you were in the basement."

"What should I say?"

"Say that you're Mariana's son."

Hugo doesn't know what to say and hangs his head.

Hugo senses that he is now standing at the threshold of a new period in his life, a period full of secrets and dangers, and he has to be cautious and strong, as he promised his mother.

Mariana keeps staring at him. Hugo feels uncomfortable, and to evade her gaze, he asks, "Is this a big house?"

"Very big," she says, and laughs. "But you'll only be in my room and in the closet."

"Am I allowed to go out into the yard?"

"No. Children like you have to be inside."

He has already noticed: Mariana speaks in short sentences and, unlike his mother, she doesn't explain.

After he finishes eating the sandwiches, she says, "Now I'm going to tidy up the room and take a bath. You'll go back into the closet."

"Am I allowed to play chess with myself?"

"Certainly, as much as you please."

Hugo goes back to his place, and Mariana closes the closet door.

Three weeks earlier, when the Actions became fiercer, his mother started talking about great changes that were about to take place in his life, about new people that he would meet, and about an unknown environment. She didn't speak in her usual, simple language, but in words with many meanings, words that bore a secret. Hugo didn't ask. He was bewildered, and the more she explained and warned, the more bewildered he became.

Now the secret bears the face of Mariana.

Hugo had met Mariana several times in the past, mostly in dark alleys. His mother would bring her clothes and groceries. The meetings between them were emotional and lasted only a few minutes. Sometimes they wouldn't meet for a while, and the image of Mariana's face would depart from his eyes.

Hugo curls up in his dark corner, wrapped in one of the sheepskins, and the tears that were blocked in his eyes burst out and flood his face. "Mama, where are you? Where are you?" He whimpers like an abandoned animal.

He cries himself to sleep. In his sleep he is at home. Rather, in his room. Everything is in its place. Suddenly, Anna appears and stands in the doorway. She has grown taller, and she is wearing a traditional Ukrainian dress. The dress suits her.

"Anna," he calls out.

"What?" she answers in Ukrainian.

"Have you forgotten how to speak German?" He is alarmed.

"I haven't forgotten, but I'm trying very hard not to speak German."

"Papa says that you don't forget a mother tongue."

"I assume that's correct, but in my case, the effort was so powerful that it drove the German words from my mouth." She speaks in a torrent of Ukrainian.

"Strange."

"Why?"

"Strange to talk with you in Ukrainian."

Anna smiles the restrained smile he knows well: a mixture of shyness and arrogance.

"Is it also hard for you to speak French?"

She smiles again and says, "In the mountains people don't speak French."

"When you come back, after the war, we'll speak German again, right?"

"I assume so." She speaks like an adult.

Only now does he see how much she has changed. She has grown taller, and her body is full. She looks more like a young peasant girl than the Anna he knew. True, some features still remain, but they, too, have filled out and grown wider.

"Anna," he says.

"What?"

"Until the end of the war, you won't come back to us?" he asks, and is surprised by the question.

"My spirit is here all the time, but my body, for now, must be in the mountains. And you?"

"I just got to Mariana's now."

"To Mariana's?"

"My impression is that she is a good woman."

"I hope you're not wrong."

"Mama also told me that she was a good woman."

"Be careful, in any event."

"Of what?"

"Of those women," she says, and disappears.

7

A moment before awakening, Hugo manages to see Anna shrink down to the dimensions familiar to him. He is so glad that she hasn't changed, that in his excitement he claps his hand and shouts, "Bravo."

Without meaning to, he surveys the closet. A broad-brimmed, colorful hat, hanging on a nail, catches his eye. It looks like a magician's hat. Mariana is a magician, the thought flashes through his mind. At night she entertains the audience at the circus, and in the daytime she sleeps. The circus suits her. He immediately imagines her uttering bird calls, throwing balls up very high, and, with marvelous balance, carrying three brightly colored bottles on her head.

The door opens, and once again Mariana stands in the doorway. Now she is wearing a pretty floral-print dress, her hair is up, and she holds a bowl of soup in her hand. "Straight from our kitchen," she announces. Hugo takes the bowl, sits down, and says, "Thank you."

"What's my sweetie been doing?" she asks in a slightly artificial tone.

Hugo immediately notices the new tone and says, "I was asleep."

"It's good to sleep. I also like to sleep. What did you dream about?"

"I don't remember," he says, not revealing any secrets.

"I dream, and, to my regret, I remember," she says, and laughs with her mouth open.

At home, neither his father nor his mother had called him "honey," "sweetie," or other common words of endearment. His parents were repelled by those verbal caresses.

Hugo is hungry and eats the soup eagerly.

"In a moment I'll bring you the second course. Did you manage to play chess?"

"I fell asleep. I didn't even open the knapsack."

"After the meal you can play in my room."

"Thank you," he says, and he is glad he is following his mother's instructions diligently.

Only a day has passed since Hugo parted from his mother, and the new place is no longer strange to him. Mariana's arrivals and disappearances seem to him, perhaps because of their regularity, like his mother's appearances in the cellar. A few hours ago, he felt as if his mother was about to enter the closet. Now he sees her moving farther into the distance, gliding on waves of darkness.

Meanwhile, Mariana comes back and brings him a meatball and some potatoes, saying, "I have a greeting from your mother. She reached the village, and she'll stay there."

"When will she come and visit me?"

"The roads are dangerous, you know."

"Maybe I can go to her?"

"For boys the road is even more dangerous."

Now his day is a stretch of naps, sometimes soaring high and sometimes on a gloomy cruise. The sudden separation from his parents and friends has left him feeling cut off on this strange floor covered with long carpets embroidered with giant cats that look out at him.

It's strange—he doesn't receive the news that his mother has reached the village safely as a good omen. In his eyes, his mother always belonged to him. She sometimes disappeared but always returned on time. Now, too, he takes the news that she exists as self-evident. He does not yet know that every movement outside that ends well is a miracle.

Hugo takes the chess set out of his knapsack, arranges the pieces on the board, and immediately starts to play. Reading books and having long conversations until late at night—that was an area that belonged to his mother. Chess and walks in the city and outside it—that was his father's realm. His father did not talk a lot. He listened and responded with a word or two. His parents were pharmacists, but each was a world unto himself. Chess is a game of great strategy, and Hugo's father was excellent at it. Hugo knows the rules of the game, but he didn't always use proper caution. He took unnecessary risks and lost, of course. His father didn't reproach him for his haste and risk-taking, but he laughed softly, as if to say, *Everyone who takes unnecessary risks is bound to lose.*

When his father was seized and sent to the labor camp, Hugo cried for days on end. His mother tried to persuade him that his father hadn't been snatched away but had been sent with many other men to work, and that he would return soon, but Hugo refused to be consoled. He visualized the word "snatched" as being taken by wolves. No words could uproot the wolves from his mind. From hour to hour the pack grew, dragging away the people they had snatched with their mighty teeth.

After a few days, he stopped crying.

Hugo raises his eyes from the chess board and the strange, pink room perplexes him. On the dressers pictures of Mariana shine in gilded frames. She is dressed in exotic bathing suits. Her waist is narrow, and her breasts bulge like two melons.

This is an odd room, he says to himself, and tries to imagine a similar room, but he can see only the beauty parlor, which was called Lili's Hair Salon, where rich and spoiled women came to recline on chaises longues, and his mother was disgusted by everything that was there.

While Hugo is immersed in the game, he hears a woman laughing. He is still unfamiliar with the house, and he can't tell if the laughter comes from the adjacent room or from the yard.

He senses that his life is surrounded by many secrets. What is their nature? He can only grope for answers, and the groping leads him to strange and unusual places. This time it seems to him that his physical education teacher was the one who laughed. She was entirely unrestrained, spoke loudly, and laughed at the janitor and at the pupils. She was the omnipotent ruler of the school yard.

Hugo rises to his feet, goes over to the window, and pushes the curtain aside, revealing a small, neglected courtyard, fenced in with thick stakes. Two brown hens stand in the middle of the courtyard.

He remains where he is and listens. The laugh keeps ringing, but now it is restrained, as though someone put a muzzle on the laughing woman, or she herself stifled her laughter. Strange, he says, surprised by the quiet courtyard left to itself.

The sky grows redder, and Hugo sees his friend Otto before his eyes. A defeated expression has crystallized on Otto's face and is very obvious, especially on his lips. Now Hugo clearly remembers how Otto would wave his hand when he lost at chess. Because he waved that way every time he lost, the gesture was engraved in Hugo's memory—a frozen motion.

Hugo's mother used to say, "Otto is hiding in a cellar," but Hugo sees him crammed into one of the trucks that take the captured people to the railway station.

For a moment it seems to him as if Otto were standing at the door.

"Otto," he whispers, "is that you?"

There is no response, and Hugo understands that he was mistaken. Mariana's instructions were unequivocal: "Don't answer if somebody knocks on the door."

He curls up in a corner of the room and doesn't move.

8

The hours pass. The evening lights pour into the windows and change colors. The dangers that were lying in wait for Hugo seem to have withdrawn, and the pink room is not only pleasant but also protected. Great desire draws him to enter the wide, soft bed and cover himself with the quilt, but his instincts tell him that it is Mariana's domain and forbidden to him.

Again he sees his house—the living room, his parents' bedroom, and his room. The house was neither spacious nor fancy, but it was comfortable. Otto's and Anna's parents would come every Sunday. Hugo would entertain his friends in his room, serving them lemonade or fruit. On weekends his parents used to buy dates and figs. That exotic fruit would bring the distant, warm lands where they grew into the house.

During the visit coffee and cake would also be served. The fresh fragrances would fill the house. Everything was handled smoothly and pleasantly. After the visit a sudden melancholy would settle on those remaining. His parents would immerse themselves in reading, and Hugo would sit in his room and call up the faces of his guests in his memory.

. . .

The lights in the windows become gray and a small cloud descends on the bushes next to the fence. Hugo sees that they are lilac bushes, like in his yard, and happiness floods over him, as if he had seen someone he knew.

When he was five or six, he became sad and cried about the lilac flowers that suddenly withered. His mother, seeing his sorrow, promised him that in the spring they would blossom again, and everything would be as it was. He loved his mother's optimism. She always knew how to make a gray color into a bright one, pleasant to the eye.

Hugo's father, by contrast, did not know how to prettify situations, or how to reverse or change them. Beneath the veil of his silence dwelled a quiet skeptic. He didn't spread gloom about him, but it was clear that he would not beautify reality. Hugo loved his father, but he was not drawn to his spirit. In his mother's presence, he always felt elated. His mother sweetened every sorrow, as if to say, *Why sink into melancholy when it's possible to help people?*

Now he sees his father again. For some reason it seems that he's grown older since he was snatched away. His hair has turned gray, and many wrinkles have been plowed into his face. Hugo is sad that his father has suddenly changed, and, as his mother used to do, he says, *This is an illusion, a thought that's out of place. At the first opportunity it will go away, and everything will again be the way it was.*

While he is exchanging one thought for another, the evening descends. From Mariana's room the closet looks dark, and even the colorful gowns draped on hangers are enveloped with gravity. Hugo is sorry he has to be alone, far from his father and mother and his friends.

While he is mired in self-pity, Mariana appears. She is wearing the same dress she wore in the afternoon, but now she is gayer, her lips are red, and her hair is done up, showing off her long neck.

"How is my young and darling friend?" she asks in a hoarse voice.

"I played chess with myself." He rushes to apologize.

"Too bad I don't know how to play. I would gladly play with you."

"I'll teach you. It's not so hard."

"Mariana's head is already blocked up. A head that doesn't study gets blocked up. Since I finished school, I haven't studied."

"You can try." Hugo speaks in his mother's tone of voice.

"It would be a waste of time," says Mariana, making a dismissive gesture with her hand.

The light in the room is dim. Nevertheless, he senses that Mariana has drunk too much and apparently forgotten that Hugo is a boy, calling him "my young and darling friend." Now she suddenly changes her tone and says, "Honey, in a little while you'll have to go into your closet."

"I'm ready," says Hugo, and holds on to the box in which the chess set is stored.

"Good night. Sweet dreams."

"Do you perhaps have a lamp?" Hugo asks, forgetting that he is under the protection of strangers.

"A light!" She laughs. "In the closet, you mustn't light a lamp. In the closet, you close your eyes and go to sleep. If only I could sleep at night."

"Pardon me," says Hugo.

"Why are you asking to be pardoned?"

"Because I asked for a lamp."

"You don't need to beg pardon for little things like that. Come over to me and I'll give you a good-night kiss." Mariana kneels down and Hugo approaches her. She hugs him fully against her breasts and kisses his face and lips.

The smell of brandy strikes him.

"Don't I get a kiss?"

Hugo kisses her cheek.

"That's not how you kiss. You kiss hard."

Hugo holds her face again and kisses her.

"I'll have to teach you how to kiss," she says, and closes the closet door.

Hugo stands there as though he'd been struck: he has never known contact like that.

The transition from Mariana's room to the closet is an uprooting from a world full of colors to a world of darkness laden with the smell of sheepskins. He has already gotten slightly used to the smell, but not to the darkness. When Mariana locks the closet door, he feels more heavily stifled. When the suffocating feeling grows stronger, he rises to his feet and stands near the cracks.

In daylight hours Hugo can see the meadows where horses and cows graze, the gray fields, and two houses covered in vines. He has already seen children carrying schoolbags, on their way to school. How strange—all the children are going to school, and only I am forbidden to study. Why was that punishment imposed on me?

Because I'm a Jew, Hugo answers himself.

Why are we Jews punished? he asks again.

At home they didn't talk about it. Once he had asked his mother how people knew who was a Jew and who wasn't.

His mother answered simply: "We don't differentiate between Jews and non-Jews."

"Why are they kicking out the Jews?"

"It's a misunderstanding."

That incomprehensible answer stuck in Hugo's mind, and he tried to understand where that misunderstanding lay, or who had caused it.

"Is it the Jews' fault?" he asked once.

"You mustn't speak in generalizations," his mother answered softly.

Ever since Hugo could remember, he had tried to take sentences apart and understand words. Those efforts brought him no joy. His father encouraged him to think in an orderly way. His mother, by contrast, taught him to blend into whatever was happening and not to ask unnecessary questions, because not every question has an answer. You have to greet people warmly and not seek a reward for every deed.

"Hugo, you have to be generous. A generous person isn't miserable." That was his mother's great rule, and she lived by it. In the pharmacy, poor people received medicine without paying, but his mother wasn't satisfied with that. She helped poor people on her own. She would visit them in their homes and bring them a hot meal or some cash. To Mariana she used to bring fresh food and warm clothing.

Not only poor people came to the pharmacy, but also the mentally ill, petty thieves, and even criminals. The pharmacy had been surrounded more than once by policemen and detectives. Hugo's parents were united in the opinion that if a person comes for medicine, you shouldn't examine him too closely. Several times they had been accused of helping lawbreakers. His mother kept saying, "We aren't saints, but we can't ignore people in need."

9

Hugo wraps himself in the sheepskins, and it seems to him that he will fall asleep right away. But that good sleep, which he already felt at his fingertips, withdraws and leaves him awake in the empty, silent space. Again he sees the way he got here. His mother is carrying the suitcase in one hand and the knapsack in the other. The knapsack is heavy, and it is too hard for Hugo to carry it.

Another life, he says to himself, and doesn't know what he is saying.

After they took his tonsils out, he hadn't known what was taken from his body and how many days he would have to suffer from pain. The people around him, two nurses and a doctor, looked to him like severe and cruel creatures. His mother and father stood behind them helplessly. They looked at him with eyes full of mercy, as though saying to Hugo, *You aren't alone. We'll protect you with all our strength. In a little while the medical team will leave you, and you'll come back to us. We know, it's not an easy experience, but in a few days it will all pass, and you'll be with us, as always.*

Hugo sees his parents very clearly. The distant past that hides within him removes its veils and stands before him, face-to-face. He is sad that he has been separated from his loving parents and that he has to lie under the cold and stinking sheepskins.

While he is sunk in that frightening vision, Hugo hears a voice in Mariana's room. It is the voice of a man who isn't satisfied and who expresses his dissatisfaction with blunt words. The man speaks in German, but a German different from his. Hugo doesn't understand most of the words. At first it amuses him to eavesdrop, but as the disagreements grow stronger, a clear threat is heard in the man's voice.

Mariana, whose voice he definitely recognized, tries to mollify the man, but he sticks to his opinion. In the end Mariana says a few things that make him laugh. The differences of opinion die down, and there are whispers that Hugo can barely catch.

Sleep has been stolen from him. He is awake, with an alertness that grows steadily sharper. Sounds of scraping come from Mariana's room, as though they are trying to move a heavy piece of furniture. The sounds of movement intensify, and it is clear that the words have stopped and only the unseen movements are doing what they are doing.

Then he hears Mariana say, "If I'm not what you want, you can pick another woman. I'm not the only girl in this house." Hugo doesn't catch the man's answer. They argue, but there isn't any anger. In the end he hears the man say, "You know very well what my conditions are."

"I try, but I don't always manage."

"That's your problem."

"I've always drunk, and you just started complaining recently."

"Because you overdo it. A drunken woman is a damaged woman."

"You're wrong. A drunken woman is a woman liberated from all restraints, who knows how to love right."

"I don't like it when people mix things up. Drinking is one thing and love is another."

"And I actually think that it's a good idea to mix them. Love without a drink is dull love, full of inhibitions and tasteless."

"I understand you," he says, but it is clear that he doesn't agree with her.

"What can you do? That's how I am. It's clear I won't change."

Though he is tired, Hugo catches the whole conversation. The words "drunk" and "brandy" are no strangers to him. His uncle Sigmund, his mother's brother, was addicted to brandy, and in Hugo's house that subject was constantly discussed. Hugo loved his uncle even when he was drunk. When he came to their house drunk, his mother kept Hugo out of the living room and ordered him to go up to his room. Uncle Sigmund was a happy drunk. He would joke about his drunkenness and make everyone laugh. Only Hugo's mother wouldn't laugh. Sigmund's drunkenness made her sad, and sometimes she would cry.

Meanwhile, Hugo falls asleep.

In his dream he is with his parents, and they are swimming in the Prut River. Suddenly Uncle Sigmund appears, and he is drunk and dirty. His mother, in her despair, tries to hide the shameful sight from Hugo. Because her hands can't do it, she throws a big bath towel over his head, and it covers him completely. Hugo is suffocating and tries to throw the towel off, but his mother tightens it with both hands and refuses to heed his shout. Then her hands weaken, and Hugo falls into the waters of the Prut, which suddenly change color and become black and sticky.

His mother grabs him with both hands and picks him up, shouting, "The boy has drowned, the boy has drowned, help!" Because of the suffocation, or perhaps because of the scream, Hugo wakes from the nightmare.

The first morning light filters into the closet. From Mariana's room merry voices can now be heard, as if Mariana and a man were rolling around in the bed, throwing pillows at each other. Clearly this isn't the same man who grumbled before. This is a cheerful man, who is amusing Mariana.

"You're funny," she keeps saying.

"I don't mean to make you laugh."

"But you do make me laugh. You're good to me."

"I'm going to eat some of you."

"And I'll eat some of you, too."

The laughter grows stronger, and it is obvious they are happy with each other.

Later he hears the man's voice. "It's late. I have to go."

"And when will you come back?" she asks right away.

"I don't know. My unit is going north."

"If you come back here, don't forget me."

"Of course not."

"I was good to you, right?"

"Excellent."

After a short silence the man says, "They're probably sending my unit to the front."

"I hope not," says Mariana.

"Pray for me that I won't be wounded. Better to die than be wounded. A wounded man is as good as dead. I've taken care of a lot of wounded men."

"I'll pray, I promise you."

"Do you go to church?"

"Sometimes."

"My whole name is Johann Sebastian. My parents named me after the famous composer. They hoped I would become a musician."

"I'll pray, I promise."

"Is that a strange request?"

"No, why?"

"I've seen too many wounded men in the past two years."

"Don't be scared, dear."

"I'm not afraid of death. I'm afraid of being wounded."

He leaves, and Mariana leaves right after him. The silence returns.

Hugo lays his head on the sheepskins and says to himself, *Strange things happen here. I don't understand a thing.* He closes his eyes, and again Uncle Sigmund appears to him. Because of his alcoholism, Uncle Sigmund never finished his medical studies. He kept promising his sister that he would soon dry out and return to them. That went on for years.

Not only was his drinking shameful. Sometimes he would bring a woman with him, usually from the lower classes, who was also addicted to drink. She would cling to him, hugging and kissing him in front of everybody and declaring, "Sigmund is a prince. Sigmund is a king." Seeing such a woman, Hugo's mother's eyes would turn saffron yellow. His father was less sensitive, and during Uncle Sigmund's strange appearances, he would sit and talk with him, sometimes for hours, about medicine and literature. Hugo didn't understand a thing from those conversations, but he enjoyed watching the men. Even then he would say to himself, *Everything I see, I'll lock up in my heart.* The thought that life passes by and that the dead will not come back to life pained him even then.

10

Hugo has apparently been forgotten, because it is ten o'clock before Mariana stands at the closet door with a cup of milk in her hand.

"How's Mariana's sweet little puppy?"

"He's okay." Hugo is drawn into her way of speaking.

"Soon Mariana is going to tidy up the room and you can move over into it. Mariana won't sleep this morning. She has to go to town and buy some things for herself. You can amuse yourself quietly."

"Thank you."

"Why do you say thank you for everything? Mariana's not used to being thanked. You only have to say thank you for big things."

Like what? he wants to ask, but he doesn't ask.

Hugo drinks the warm milk, and he feels that every sip eases the thirst that has tortured him since he woke up. Meanwhile, Mariana tidies her room, puts on makeup, changes her blouse, and when she comes back to him, she is already different: her face is open. The smile of a contented woman lights it.

"Sweet puppy, Mariana's locking the door. If somebody knocks, don't answer."

Mariana's way of referring to herself in the third person

amuses his ear for a moment. He has never heard anyone talk about himself that way. Mariana repeats her instruction: "If someone knocks on the door, don't answer. You mustn't make a mistake, do you hear?"

Sometimes Mariana talks to him in German—faulty German, a little like children's speech. Several times he wants to correct her mistakes, but in his heart he knows that Mariana won't like that.

Before going out, she says to him, "If you're hungry, eat the sandwiches that are on the dresser. They're tasty." And without another word, she leaves and locks the room.

Hugo stands in place without moving, and for a moment it seems to him that his previous life has sunk into the world of dreams, that it is far away and unattainable. Now reality is the closet, Mariana's room, and Mariana herself.

That thought seeps into him, and sharp longings flood him. Self-pity quickly follows.

Soon Hugo collapses and bursts into tears. The crying fills him, and he feels the cold walls of loneliness. He whimpers for a long time, and in the end the weeping becomes the broken whine of a dog thrown out of a warm house into a kennel.

Hugo cries so much that he falls into an exhausted sleep on the floor and notices nothing. Not even Mariana's arrival wakes him. Only when she touches him with her foot does he rouse and realize he has slept.

"My puppy took a nap."

"I slept," he says.

"Now we'll bring you hot soup. Why didn't you eat the sandwiches?"

"I was asleep," he repeats, trying to recover his wits.

"Did anyone knock on the door?"

"I didn't hear a thing."

"Darling, you were sleeping like a log," she says, and chuckles.

Mariana immediately leaves and returns with soup and two meatballs. Hugo sits on the floor and eats. Mariana sits on the bed and observes him.

"How old are you, darling?" she asks, apparently forgetting that she has already asked him that.

"I'm eleven. A little while ago I had a birthday."

"You look older than your age."

"When will Mama come and visit me?" The question escapes his mouth.

"Outdoors is very dangerous for Jews. She's better off sitting inside."

"I'm protected, right?" he asks.

"You're in Mariana's house. It's a bit strange, but you'll get used to it. If somebody asks you whose you are, tell them out loud, 'I'm Mariana's.' Do you hear?"

That instruction astounds him again, but he doesn't open his mouth.

"I've thought about it a lot. You'll have to improve your Ukrainian. You look a lot like Mariana. Your hair is dark blond, and your nose is small. If you improve your Ukrainian, they won't identify you. We'll do everything slowly. You don't do things like that hastily," she states without explaining.

Mariana remains seated on the bed, following his movements. It's hard to know what she's looking for in him. Hugo feels pressured. He finishes the meal quickly and hands the bowl to Mariana.

"Mariana's tired. Now she'll sleep for an hour or two. And you, darling, you'll go back to your kennel."

Hugo gets up and goes to the closet. He has acquired a hunched-over way of moving here—the way animals hang their heads when they are ordered to leave the house.

Hugo takes the chess set out of the knapsack. He arranges the pieces and starts to play right away. The game goes well. He remembers his father's warnings about the opening. A small mistake in the opening, and the game is lost. As he plays, his father appears. He looks like a man who has stayed in a mildewed hideout for many days. His face is pale, yellowish, and a tired gaze emanates from his eye sockets.

"Where were you, Papa?" Hugo raises his eyes from the board.

"Don't ask," he answers, having forgotten, apparently, that he is speaking with his son and not with an adult.

"You're very pale, Papa."

His father bows his head and says, "For many days I was in a closed place."

"Will I become as pale as you?" Hugo's question is not slow in coming.

"You, dear, won't stay in the closet for a long time. Mama and I will come and get you immediately at the end of the war. You must be patient," he says, and withdraws into the darkness.

"Papa," Hugo calls out.

His call remains unanswered.

Later Hugo's father appears to him again, and Hugo holds a long, silent conversation with him. Hugo tells him that he is now under Mariana's protection. Mariana is very busy and hardly sees him. But the meals she serves him are tasty. Life is a riddle, and every day the riddle gets bigger. Sometimes Mariana seems like a magician and sometimes she sounds like the owner of a restaurant. People visit her in her room, but the meetings aren't always pleasant. Hearing that information, Hugo's father smiles and says, "Mariana is Mariana. You, in any event, must be careful."

"Of what?"

"You'll see for yourself."

That was his father's way of talking. Always a single word or a short sentence. He always mixed reservations into his speech.

One morning Hugo dares to ask Mariana, "What is the name of this place?"

"The Residence," she answers clearly.

"I never heard that name before."

"You'll hear it, don't worry," she says, and smiles.

11

The days pass, and autumn makes its mark on everything Hugo's eyes take in. Clouds descend from the sky and spread out over the meadows. Wrapped in the last darkness of the night, children saunter to school. Here and there is a wagon laden with beams, a peasant carrying a long scythe on his shoulder.

Hugo stops counting the days. If he read or did arithmetic problems, as he'd promised his mother, his days would have been clear of twinges of conscience. He has not yet opened a book or notebook. Everything that was in his house, in school, in their yard, or in the playground now seems detached from his life.

He is heedful of what Mariana says, dependent on her daily schedule, on her occupations and moods. When her mood is foul, her face changes. She mutters, curses, tears papers, and breaks bottles. He prefers her drunkenness. In her drunkenness she is merry, speaks about herself a lot in the third person, and kisses him hard.

Every day Hugo promises himself he will read tomorrow, do arithmetic problems, and write in his journal. He promises but doesn't keep the promise. He doesn't even manage to finish a single game of chess. All his attention is given over to Mariana. He looks forward to her arrival, and when she is late, he worries. Sometimes it seems to him that she is standing outside and guarding him, but sometimes he has the feeling that she doesn't care about him. She is totally occupied with herself, with her dresses, her makeup, and her perfumes. "Mariana is cursed. Everybody sucks her blood and nobody gives her anything." That's what she mumbles when she is angry or in a bad mood. Hugo feels guilty and wants to go to her and tell her, *I don't want anything, it's enough for me that you're with me.*

Once she said to him, "Don't be afraid. Mariana is guarding you like a lioness. If anyone tries to touch you, I'll rip him to shreds. I swore to your mother that I would watch over you like a hawk, and I'll do it. Julia is dearer to me than my sister."

"Do they want to catch me?" Hugo couldn't keep from asking.

"Certainly. They're going from house to house and looking for Jews. But you have nothing to fear. You're mine. You look like me, right?"

Her words, meant to calm him down, sowed disquiet in him. He immediately saw many soldiers before his eyes, swarming over the houses and dragging out the people who were in hiding.

"Will they look here, too?" Hugo asked cautiously.

"They wouldn't dare look in my room and in my closet."

Mariana's speech is simple and unadorned. But every word of hers quickly becomes a picture that stays with him for a whole day, sometimes for two days.

"It's hard for me to understand why they're persecuting the Jews," she said once. "There are good people among them, not to mention your mother, Julia, who devoted her whole soul to humanity. Not a week passed that she didn't bring me fruit and vegetables."

When she said, "devoted her whole soul," Hugo saw his mother as a long, thin bird gliding over the town's streets, landing here and leaving a parcel of food, landing there and giving a bundle of clothes to a poor woman. His father used to say, "Language is a tool for thought. You have to express yourself clearly and precisely." "Clarity" and "precision" were key words for him. Hugo's mother wasn't precise the way his father was. But every word that came from her mouth quickly became a picture. And that, amazingly, was what happened with Mariana. It's strange, but a spare way of speaking can also be colorful. This thought flashed through his head.

But on the days when Mariana is despondent, a cloud covers her face, and she neither asks for nor promises anything. She hands Hugo a cup of milk and immediately throws herself down on the bed and sleeps for hours. Sometimes the sleep soothes her dejection. She gets up another woman, tells him about her dream, and hugs him against her body. Such an hour is an hour of grace, and Hugo knows how to appreciate it.

But sleep doesn't usually free Mariana from the bonds of depression. What oppressed her before she went to sleep continues to oppress her. She stamps her feet and breaks bottles, announces that in the coming days she will run away from here. These desperate declarations always sow disquiet in Hugo's soul, but one smile from her is enough to scatter the clouds of fear—he is immediately certain that Mariana won't sell him or abandon him.

Thus the days pass. Sometimes he sees Otto and sometimes Anna. When they are revealed to him, he is so happy that he wants to kiss them hard, the way Mariana kisses him. Once both of them appeared, and Hugo called out in astonishment, "Darlings!" Hearing that strange appellation, they opened their eyes wide but didn't say a thing.

Anna told Hugo about her village in the mountains, and Otto disclosed to him that he, too, had found shelter in a village. For a moment it seemed to Hugo that in a short time the war would be over, and everyone would return to where they had come from and to their ordinary lives. But in his heart Hugo knows that what had been would never be again. The time in the ghetto and in hiding is already embossed on his flesh, and the power of the words he would use has faded. Now it isn't words that speak to him, but silence. This is a difficult language, but as soon as one adopts it, no other language will ever be as effective.

12

One night, angry voices are heard from Mariana's room. Mariana is speaking in German, and the man corrects every mistake. The corrections drive her crazy, and she says angrily, "We're here to have a good time, not to study grammar."

"A loose woman remains a loose woman."

"I may be loose, but not for any price."

The man responds to that with shouts, insults, and, apparently, a slap in the face. A broken sound comes from Mariana's throat, but she doesn't surrender. In the end he threatens to kill her, but Mariana is daring and shouts at him, "You can kill me. I'm not afraid of death."

The fight stops all of a sudden, and for a moment it sounds to Hugo as though Mariana is choking and having convulsions. He rises to his feet and presses his ear against the wall. No sound can be heard. The silence grows thicker. Hugo trembles with fear and curls up on his couch again.

At home, they insisted on proper speech. Only Uncle Sigmund, when he was drunk, would utter a naughty word or a curse. Hugo's mother would silence him and say, "The boy can hear," and the boy did indeed listen and wondered about the nature of the dirty words that were forbidden to be used.

Later, a woman's voice is heard in Mariana's room. The

woman speaks to Mariana softly. "You mustn't quarrel with a customer. The customer comes to enjoy himself and relax. He doesn't like it when you make a comment to him or contradict him."

"He corrected every word that came out of my mouth, and I felt like he was whipping me with his tongue."

"What do you care? Let him correct you."

"What kind of behavior is that, to correct every word you say. It's worse than a beating. I might be loose, but I'm not a slave."

"Our profession, dear, demands a lot of patience of us. Every customer's got his own quirks. Don't forget, the whole thing doesn't last more than an hour, and you get rid of him immediately."

"I'm fed up. Let him do what he wants, but not correct my German."

The other woman speaks softly, with a country accent. She asks Mariana to go to Madam and apologize. "If you don't apologize and express remorse, she'll fire you. It would be a shame to lose a job."

"I don't care."

"You mustn't say, 'I don't care.' Anyone who says 'I don't care' is desperate. We believe in God, and we don't despair easily."

"I don't go to church." Mariana persists in her rebellion.

"But you believe in God and in His Messiah."

Mariana doesn't respond. From her silence, it is evident that her obstinacy is softening slightly. In the end, she asks, "What should I say to her?"

"Tell her, 'I apologize, and in the future I won't make comments to customers.'"

"It's hard for me to get a sentence like that out."

"It's like spitting and going on. Enough."

Hugo listens intently and catches every word.

Hugo understands Ukrainian. He learned the language from their maid, Sofia. Sofia used to say, "If you learn Ukrainian well, I'll take you to my village. In my village there are lots of animals, and you can play there with the colt and with the calf." Sofia was always happy, and she used to sing and chatter from morning till the end of her work at night.

When Hugo began first grade, Sofia said to him, "Too bad you have to go to school every day. School is a prison. I hated school and the teacher. The teacher used to shout at me. She insulted me and called me 'stupid.' True, I had trouble with arithmetic, and I wrote with mistakes, but I was a quiet girl. She liked the Jewish children, and she used to say, 'Take an example from them. Learn how to think from them. Clear the straw out of your heads and put in some thought.'

"I hope you won't suffer. I suffered all the years I was in school and I was glad to leave the walls of that prison. Oh, I forgot, dear," she said, slapping her forehead, "I forgot you were a Jew. Jews don't have trouble with arithmetic. You'll raise your hand. You'll raise your hand all the time. Whoever raises his hand has the right answer."

Hugo loved Sofia. She was plump and merry, and she peppered her words with proverbs and sayings. She was pleased with whatever came her way. When his parents weren't home, she used street language, like "bitch," whore," or "son of a bitch."

Once he asked his mother, "What's a whore?"

"It's a word we don't use. It's a dirty word."

But Sofia uses it, he was about to say.

Every time Hugo heard that word, he would envision Sofia washing her body with a stiff sponge, because anybody who used that word was dirty and had to wash his body very well.

Now, in the last darkness of the night, Hugo sees Sofia's whole body, and she, as always, is singing and cursing, and that obscene word is rolling around in her mouth. The familiar, clear vision restores his house to him all at once, and, amazingly, everything is in its place—his father, his mother, the evening, and the violin teacher, who used to close his eyes in protest every time Hugo played out of tune.

Hugo's progress in playing was very slow. "You have an excellent ear, and you even practice, but your desire isn't strong, and without a strong desire, there's no real progress. Music has to be in your fingers. Fingers that don't have music sunk into them are blind fingers. They'll always grope and always make a mistake or play out of tune."

Hugo understood what was demanded of him. But he didn't know exactly what to do. Sometimes he felt that the music really was in his fingers, and with more effort, they would do what they were ordered to. But in his heart he knew that the mountain called "correct playing" was very steep, and it was doubtful that he would be able to climb it.

Anna was better than he in this, too. She had already performed at the end of the school year, and her future in this field was not in doubt. Hugo would make efforts not to fall behind, but his achievements were mediocre, and in his report card there were no "excellents."

Anna had only one competitor for the title of "Outstanding Pupil of the Year"—Franz. Franz was also good in every subject. He solved arithmetic problems easily, wrote fluently, and quoted poems and famous sayings by heart. He was thin, and his hair stood up, which was why they called him "hedgehog." But don't worry, there wasn't a pupil in the class who came up to his ankles. His head was full of dates and the names of cities, national leaders, generals, poets, and inventors. He devoured books and encyclopedias. More than once he shamed the teacher with his knowledge. Once, full of envy, Anna said, "He's a machine, not a human being." Franz heard her and retorted, "Anna is knowledgeable up to a certain point."

So the competition went. Not even the war and the ghetto

halted it. Franz made sure that Anna got word of his achievements. Anna examined every one of them, and in the end she
said, "In French, I have no competitor."

From the dark corner of the closet, Hugo's earlier life suddenly seems like petty busyness. His mother used to say, "Why
compete? Why degrade yourself? What good are competition
and envy? Let everyone make an accounting with himself, and
that's enough." Back then he didn't understand the meaning of
"make an accounting with himself," but now he pretty much
understands: *I have to immerse myself in listening and observing
and to write down everything my eyes see and my ears hear. Many
secrets surround me. I must write down every secret.* In saying this,
it was as if light flooded the dark closet, and Hugo knows that
his mother, who pulled him out of the sewer and restored him
to life, has done it again.

13

All night long Hugo trembles with excitement. The thought that from now on he will record precisely everything that his eyes and ears absorb, and that at the end of the war he will have five full notebooks, fires his imagination. His handwriting is usually clear, and with a certain effort he can improve it.

His mother had a notebook bound in suede in which she used to record the events of the day—about the family, about pharmacists and the pharmacy, and of course about help to those in need. Sometimes she would sit and read out loud from the notebook. It was hard for Hugo to imagine his father sitting and writing in a notebook.

Only at the chess board did Hugo's father's heart open, but not excessively. His mother would say, "Hans's thoughts are orderly, the papers are in place, and every day he knows what is in stock and how much. What would I do without him? He saves me and redeems me." Hugo's father's response usually took the form of "You're exaggerating."

Some people loved and admired Hugo's mother. Others honored his father and would order a prescription only from him. As for help for the poor, there were no differences of opinion between them about this, or about Uncle Sigmund. His mother loved her brother because he was her admired big brother. His father loved him because he was his absolute opposite. He would stand in wonderment at the flow of Uncle Sigmund's language and his ability to entertain people. Unlike his mother, his father never tried to persuade him to stop drinking brandy.

When Uncle Sigmund wasn't drunk, Hugo was allowed to listen to the conversation and even to ask him a question or two. Hugo's questions amused Sigmund. Sigmund claimed that the Jews were a strange nation, that they had hooked noses and dreadful ears, and he would immediately point at his nose and ears, make his eyes bulge, and say, "Look at Sigmund. You can say whatever you want about him, but handsome he's not. From that point of view, he is an outstanding representative of his tribe." Hugo's mother didn't agree with her brother. If it weren't for the brandy, women would stand in line to ask for his hand. He was tall and handsome, and German poems and proverbs flowed from his mouth. He even knew Ukrainian folk songs by heart. When he wanted to shock or impress people, he would speak in Latin. Hugo's mother was proud of him, and at the same time ashamed of him. He had been the family's hope. Everyone used to say, "Sigmund is meant for greatness. You'll hear of him."

The hopes had not lasted long. Even while he was a student, his eye was on drink. At that time, brandy added charm to his charm, but as he grew older and drank more and more, his looks deteriorated. People kept their distance from him, and he plunged into his fantasies.

Uncle Sigmund was seized and deported along with Hugo's father. Now Hugo saw him at his full height. A broad, mischievous smile filled his large face. He was telling jokes and singing, and every time he used a dirty word, Hugo's mother would silence him.

Most of the images that Hugo brought with him to the closet have evaporated from his mind, but not the figure of

Uncle Sigmund. Day by day it grows larger. His mother kept saying, "It isn't Sigmund, but what remains of him. If he stopped drinking, he would be what he once was. His place is at the university and not in a tavern."

Indeed, Uncle Sigmund was a favorite customer in the tavern, where he frittered away most of the allowance his family gave him. Toward the end of the month, he would ask his friends for loans. He begged at his acquaintances' doors and caused great pain to Hugo's mother. Every time she would hand him a banknote or two and beg him not to ask for loans from strangers.

When Uncle Sigmund came into the house, Hugo's father would put on a special face to greet the amiable guest. Sometimes, when Sigmund was reciting a poem, he would forget a line. Hugo's father would come to his assistance and immediately blush. His father blushed whenever he was forced to point out an error or exaggeration made by his partner in conversation. But now Hugo sees them together. Now his father doesn't admire his brother-in-law. Rather, the brother-in-law admires his father's silence.

During the night, clear and focused visions come to Hugo, and he doesn't close his eyes. He waits for the morning so he can open the notebook and write down the day's events, as he promised his mother. It seems to him that the writing will come easily.

The morning light filters into the closet, drop by drop, and the darkness remains untouched. The hours pass slowly, and hunger oppresses him. This time, too, Mariana is late in coming, and all his attention is focused on his distress, wiping away the clear visions that had moved him during the night.

It isn't until eleven that Mariana, her face rumpled, appears in a nightgown and hands Hugo a cup of milk.

"I fell deeply asleep, darling," she says. "You're probably thirsty and hungry. What have I done, dear?"

"I was thinking about my house."

"Do you miss it?"

"A little."

"I would take you out, but everything is dangerous. Soldiers are looking from house to house, and informers are swarming in every corner. You have to be patient."

"When will the war be over?"

"Who knows?"

"Mama told me that the war would end soon."

"She's suffering, too. It's not easy for her, either. The peasants are afraid to hide Jews in their houses, and the few who do are living in great fear. You understand that, don't you?"

"Why are they punishing the Jews?" he asks, and he immediately regrets his question.

"The Jews are different. They were always different. I like them. But most people don't like them."

"Because they ask when they shouldn't?"

"Why did you think of that?"

"Mama told me not to ask questions but to listen, and I'm always breaking that rule."

"You can ask as much as you want, sweetie," Mariana says, and hugs him. "I like it when you ask me. When you ask me, I see your father and mother. Your mother was my angel. Your father is a handsome man. What luck your mother has, to have a man like that. I was born without luck."

Hugo listens and senses that envy has sneaked into her voice.

A few days earlier he heard Mariana conversing with one of her friends. "I miss the Jewish men," she said suddenly. "They were good and gentle. Contact with them was mild and correct. Do you agree?"

"I completely agree."

"And they always bring you a box of candy or silk stockings, and they always kiss you as if you were their faithful girl-friend. They never hurt you. Do you agree?"

"Absolutely."

For a moment it seemed to Hugo that he understood what they were talking about. Mariana's speech was different from anything he had heard at home. She spoke about her body. Rather, she spoke about the fear that her body would betray her.

"Honey, soon we're going to have to take a bath. The time has come, right?"

"Where?"

"I have a secret bathtub. We'll talk about it soon," she says, and winks.

14

Every few days Mariana forgets about Hugo, and this time she has forgotten about him for many hours. At twelve o'clock she stands at the closet doorway, dressed in a pink nightgown, and looks at him guiltily, saying, "What's my darling puppy doing? I neglected him. All morning long he's had nothing to eat, and he's certainly hungry and thirsty. It's all my fault. I slept too much."

She quickly hurries to bring him a cup of milk and a slice of bread spread with butter. The warm milk is quickly swallowed.

"Have you been awake for many hours? What were you thinking about?"

"I was thinking about my uncle Sigmund." Hugo doesn't hide it from her.

"Poor guy, a good man."

"Did you know him?" Hugo allows himself to ask.

"Since my childhood. He was handsome, and a genius, too. Your mother was sure he'd become a professor at the university, but he became enslaved to drink and destroyed his life. Too bad about him. He was a good uncle, right?"

"He always brought me presents."

"What, for example?"

"Books."

"Sometimes he would come to me, and we would talk and laugh. He always made me laugh. Where is he now?"

"He's in a labor camp with Papa," Hugo answers quickly.

"I liked him very much. I even dreamed about marrying him. You're still hungry. I'll bring you some sandwiches."

Hugo likes the food that Mariana brings him. In the ghetto food was scarce. His mother did everything possible and even the impossible to prepare meals from nothing. Here the food is tasty, especially the sandwiches. Because of the sandwiches, the place seems to him like a big restaurant where people come from all over the city, like Laufer's restaurant, where his parents went on his birthday and on his mother's birthday. His father refused to celebrate birthdays.

After eating the sandwiches, Hugo asks, "Is there a school here?"

"I already told you. There is one, but not for you. You're in hiding now with Mariana until the end of the war. Children like you have to hide. Are you bored?"

"No."

"In the afternoon, we'll take a bath. The time has come to take a hot bath, right? But meanwhile I brought you a little present, a cross to wear around your neck. I'll put it on you right away. That will be your charm. The charm will protect you. You mustn't take it off either by day or by night. Come here, and I'll put it on you. It suits you very well."

"Do all the children here wear crosses?"

"Certainly."

Hugo feels the way he felt on the day he was called up to the blackboard to get his report card from the teacher. The teacher said, "Hugo is a good pupil, and he will improve."

It turns out there is a bathroom behind the cupboard in Mariana's room. The bathroom is wide and luxurious, with little cupboards, a dresser, a mat, soap bars of every color, and bottles of perfume.

"I'll bring two pails of boiling water. We'll add cold water from the faucet, and we'll have a bath from paradise," Mariana says in a festive tone.

Hugo is stunned by the colors. It is a bathroom, but different from any he's ever seen. The ostentatious luxury says that here people do more than take baths.

In a few moments, the bathtub is full. Mariana touches the water and says, "Marvelous water. Now get undressed, my dear." Hugo is astonished for a moment. Since he was seven, his mother had stopped washing him.

Mariana, seeing his embarrassment, says, "Don't be ashamed. I'll wash you with perfumed soap. Plunge in, dear, plunge in, and I'll soap you down right away. You start by plunging in, and only afterward you soap yourself."

The embarrassment evaporates and a strange pleasantness envelops his body.

"Stand up now, and Mariana will soap you from your feet to your head. Now the soap will do wonders." She soaps him and washes him hard, but it's a pleasant hardness. "Now plunge in again," she orders. In the end she pours tepid water on him and says, "You're good. You do everything Mariana tells you to do."

She wraps him in a big, fragrant towel, puts the cross around his neck, looks at him, and says, "Wasn't it nice?"

"Excellent."

"We'll do it often."

She kisses his face and neck and says, "Now it's night. Now it's dark. Now I'll lock you in your kennel, honey. You're Mariana's, right?" Hugo is about to ask her something, but the question slips out of his mind.

Mariana says, "After a bath, you sleep better. Too bad they don't let me sleep at night."

Why? he is about to ask, but he stops his tongue in time.

That night is quiet. Though he does hear voices from Mariana's room, they are muffled. He can feel the chilly darkness and the thin night lights that filter through the cracks between the boards and make a grid on his couch.

The bath and the cross that Mariana put around his neck seem to mingle into a secret ceremony.

Both gestures gave him pleasure, but he doesn't understand what is visible here and what is a secret.

That night Hugo dreams that the closet door has opened, and his mother is standing in the doorway. She is wearing the coat she wore when they parted, but now it looks thicker, as though she has filled it with wadding.

"Mama," he calls out loud.

Hearing his voice, she puts her finger on his mouth and whispers, "I'm also in hiding. I just came to tell you that I think about you all the time. The war is apparently going to be long. Don't expect me."

"When approximately will the war be over?" Hugo asks with a trembling voice.

"God knows. Do you feel well? Mariana isn't mistreating you?"

"I feel fine," he says, but his mother, for some reason, narrows her shoulders in disappointment and says, "If you feel well, that means I can go away quietly."

"Don't go." He tries to stop her.

"I mustn't be here. But there is one thing I want to say to you. You know very well that we didn't observe our religion, but we never denied our Jewishness. The cross you're wearing, don't forget, is just camouflage, not faith. If Mariana or I-don't-know-who tries to make you convert, don't say anything to them. Do what they tell you to do, but in your heart you have to know: your mother and father, your grandfathers and grandmothers were all Jews, and you're a Jew, too. It's not easy to be a Jew. Everybody persecutes you. But that doesn't make us inferior people. To be a Jew isn't a mark of excellence, but it's also not shameful. I wanted to say that to you, so that your spirits won't fall. Read a chapter or two of the Bible every day. Reading the Bible will strengthen you. That's all. That's what I wanted to say to you. I'm glad you feel well. I can go away in peace. The war will apparently be long, don't expect me," she says, and goes away.

Hugo wakes up in pain. For many days he has not seen his mother with such clarity. Her face was tired, but her voice was clear and her words were orderly.

Several days ago he had promised himself that he would write down the events of the day in a notebook, but he didn't keep his promise. His hand refused to open the knapsack and take the writing implements out of it. *Why aren't I writing? Nothing could be easier. I only have to put out my hand and immediately I'll have a notebook and a fountain pen.* Thus Hugo sat and spoke, as though he weren't talking to himself but to a rebellious animal.

15

Meanwhile, the days are growing shorter. Cold filters through the cracks and freezes the closet, and the sheepskins don't warm Hugo. He wears two pairs of pajamas and a woolen hat, but the cold penetrates every corner, and there is no escape from it. At night, when no one is in her room, Mariana opens the door, and the warm air from her room flows into the closet.

Sometimes a vision from the past flashes by, but it quickly dies away. Hugo is afraid that one night the cold and the darkness will form an alliance and kill him, and when the war is over, when his parents come to get him, they will find a frozen corpse.

Mariana knows how cold the closet is at night, and every morning she says, "What can I do? If only I could move the porcelain stove from my room to the closet. You deserve it more than I." When Mariana says that, he feels that she does indeed love him, and he wants to cry.

But the mornings in her room are very pleasant. The blue stove roars and gives off heat. Mariana rubs his hands and feet and orders the cold to leave his body. Amazingly, the cold does indeed go away and leave him alone.

Sometimes it seems to him that Mariana has assigned an important role to him, because she keeps saying, "You're a big fellow. You're one meter and sixty centimeters. You're like your father and your uncle Sigmund, handsome men, as everyone agreed."

That talk encourages him, but as to reading or writing, it doesn't get him that far.

One morning he asks Mariana, "Do you read the Bible?"

"Why do you ask?"

"Mama liked to read from the Bible to me." He tells her some of what he has on his mind.

"When I was a little girl, I would go to church with my mother every Sunday. Then I loved the church, the hymns and the priest's sermon. The priest was saintly, and I was in love with him. He apparently sensed my love for him, and every time I came close to him, he would kiss me. Since then lots of water has flowed under the bridge. Since then Mariana has changed a lot. And did they take you to synagogue?"

"No. My parents didn't go to synagogue."

"The Jews aren't religious anymore. Strange. Once they were very religious, and suddenly they stopped believing." After a few minutes of silence, she says, "Mariana doesn't like it when they preach morality to her or ask her to confess. Mariana doesn't like it when they mix into her life. Her parents mixed in more than enough."

Every day Mariana tells him something about her life, but the hidden part is still greater than the visible part.

When she gets drunk she mixes things up and says, "Your father, Sigmund, would spend hours with me. I loved him. Why don't the Jews marry Christians? Why are they afraid of the Christians? Mariana's not afraid of the Jews. On the contrary, she likes the Jews. A Jewish man is decent and knows how to love a woman."

Hugo knows that in a little while a man will come to her room and scold her for drinking. He has already overheard many quarrels, curses, and blows. When men hit her, she shouted at first, but soon she fell silent, as though she were choking or who knows what. Hugo was very frightened by those sudden silences.

However, there were days when she came back from town happy: she had bought a dress or a pair of shoes. She would apologize for being late, bring him a good meal, hug him, and say, "Too bad I can't heat the closet." Hugo would be perplexed and tell her what he had thought about during the day. He wouldn't talk about his fears.

Some nights bad dreams persecute him, and in the morning he gets up and can't remember a thing. He has already learned that a dream forgotten in the morning has not disappeared. It is hiding and secretly burrowing. There are forgotten dreams that break out and rise up in the middle of the day.

Some days Hugo's father and mother are so distant that even in a dream they seem strange to him. His mother tries to approach him nevertheless. He looks at her and is surprised that she doesn't understand that from such a great distance it's impossible to draw near. *Mama,* he calls out, to share her sorrow more than anything. It is clear to him: the distance between them is steadily growing, and in a little while he won't see her anymore.

It isn't always that way. There are days when his parents appear to him in a dream and remain with him all day long. They haven't changed. They are exactly as they were. That they are unchanged is felt every step of the way. For example, the way his mother hugs the coffee cup in the morning, and his father puts a cigarette in her mouth. When he sees that picture, he is certain it will be that way forever. He has to be patient. The war will end soon, and the trumpets of victory will sound all over the city.

16

One day Mariana comes back from town drunk and angry. Her face is rumpled, and lipstick is smeared on her chin. "What happened?" asks Hugo, rising to his feet.

"People are bastards. Just to steal from Mariana. Just to take from her. Whatever she gives them is never enough. They want more and more, the leeches."

Hugo doesn't understand why she is angry, but he isn't afraid. In the months he has been with her, he has learned her moods. Now he knows that in a little while she will curl up in her bed and sleep till the evening. Sleep is good for her. When she gets up, her face will be peaceful. *Darling*, she will ask, *what did you do?* And it would be as if all her anger had never been.

This time it is different. She sits on the floor and doesn't stop muttering: "Bastards, sons of bitches." Hugo approaches her, sits next to her, takes her hand, and brings it to his mouth. That gesture seems to move her, because she hugs him and says, "Only you love Mariana. Only you don't want anything from her."

For a moment it seems to him that she is about to say something else. *Now Mariana is going to sleep, and you, darling, will sit next to her and guard her sleep. Mariana is quieter when you watch over her.* This time she surprises him, turns to him with a wink and says, "Come and sleep with me. I don't want to sleep alone."

"Should I put on my pajamas?"

"No need. Just take off your shoes and your trousers."

Mariana's bed is soft, the covers are pleasant to the touch, and perfumed. Hugo immediately finds himself embraced in her arms. "You're good. You're sweet. You don't want anything from Mariana. You pay attention to her." Hugo feels the warmth of her body flow to him.

His mother used to sit next to him before he went to sleep. She would read to him, she would answer his questions and look in his eyes, but his legs had never touched her knees.

Now he is embraced in Mariana's long arms and close to her body.

"How is it to be with Mariana?"

"Fine."

"You're really delicious."

In a few minutes, she falls asleep. Hugo remains awake. Images of the day he came to Mariana flash before his eyes. Now it seems to him that even her drunkenness is beautiful. The lipstick smeared on her chin adds to her charm. *If Mama comes, what will I say to her?* The thought passes through his mind. *I'll tell her that I was cold, that the closet froze my legs.* That sudden thought casts a shadow over his coziness.

The day grows darker. Mariana wakes up in a panic. "Darling, we slept too long." She speaks to him as if to a member of her household, not someone who has slept in her bed for the first time. "Now we've got to get dressed. Mariana has to start working in a little while."

Mariana quickly puts her clothes on, makes herself up. Remembering that Hugo hasn't eaten lunch, she rushes to bring him soup. There isn't any more soup, but she brings thin sandwiches decorated with vegetables. "I starved my darling. Now let him eat his fill," she says, kneeling down and kissing him on the face. Mariana kisses hard, and sometimes she also bites.

"I'm sorry you have to go back into the closet. Don't worry, Mariana won't forget you. She knows it's very cold there, but what can she do? She's got to work. Without work, she has no food, she has no house, she can't support her mother. You understand Mariana, right?" She kisses him again. Hugo doesn't restrain himself this time. He takes her hand and kisses it.

Soon a man's voice is heard in Mariana's room. The voice is stern. Mariana is ordered to change the sheets, and she does it in good spirits, joking with him and saying, "You're wrong to suspect me. I change the sheets and pillowcases after every customer. That's the basis of all trust. My job is to give enjoyment, not unpleasantness. I'm changing them so you'll feel good."

The man doesn't stay in Mariana's room for long. When he goes, she opens the closet door, and the heat of her room comes into the cold closet. Hugo wants to get up and thank her, but he restrains himself.

The two pairs of pajamas he is wearing, the hat, and the heat that comes from Mariana's room finally warm him, and he waits for sleep to come and gather him up. He manages to hear another man come in, who immediately announces that it is very cold outside. He has been on watch for five straight hours, and it's a good thing that's over.

"Did you always keep guard?" Mariana asks.

"I've already been on all sorts of disgusting missions. Guarding an installation isn't the worst thing of all."

"Poor guy."

"A soldier isn't a poor guy," he corrects her. "A soldier does his duty."

"Right," says Mariana.

Then he tells her about funny letters that were sent from home, about the strange packages that reach the soldiers from parents and grandparents, and about a soldier who received a pair of slippers. It's clear he needs someone to listen to him, and he has found a ready ear.

Hugo eavesdrops and eavesdrops, gets tired, and falls asleep.

17

In Hugo's dream he sees Otto. At first sight, no change has taken place in him. The same skepticism and the same pessimism that he inherited from his mother are spread across his face. Only the pale pink of his narrow cheeks has turned brown, gotten thicker, giving him the look of a farmer.

"Don't you know me?" asks Hugo.

Hearing his question, Otto smiles, and suntanned creases spread across his forehead and cheeks.

"I'm Hugo, don't you recognize me?" He makes an effort to emphasize the words.

"What do you want from me?" Otto shrugs his shoulders. Hugo recognizes that gesture very well, but at home it was accompanied by a few swallowed words of pessimistic justification. Now it's a silent twitch.

"I have come from far away to see you. I miss you." Hugo tries to rouse him from his forgetfulness.

What do you want from me? Otto's gaze rejects any further approach.

Hugo sits and observes him: a peasant lad, with loosely fitting clothes, shoes made of coarse leather, and leggings wrapped around his calves. "If you deny me, I'll go on my way." He finds the words to say to him.

Otto responds to this appeal by lowering his head, as though he has grasped that it's a question of bad manners.

"Otto, I didn't come to bother you. If you decide to ignore me, or to forget me, or I don't know what, I'll clear out right away. You're allowed to choose your friends as you please, but there is one thing I want to say to you. You're deeply embedded in my soul, no less than Anna. You may forget me, but I won't forget you."

Hearing Hugo's words, Otto raises his head, looks at him as if to say, *Don't waste your time, I can't understand a word you're saying.* Clearly it isn't denial or ignoring or contempt. Otto has changed completely. From his earlier incarnation nothing remains.

Hugo looks around again: the mountains are covered with trees, and on the broad plains peasants are harvesting golden grain, working together at a steady rhythm. In a moment Otto will join them. In these areas there is apparently no need for words. Otto is happier than he was at home. Here he blends into the seasons. There are no exceptional events. There is no mother to proclaim, morning and night, "If this is what life is, I'll give up my share." Here everyone eats full meals, and the animals submit to the discipline of the working people. No one argues or contradicts anyone, and in the evening, they gather up their belongings and return to their huts.

Suddenly Otto gives Hugo a look that says, *Take me out of your thoughts. Your thoughts are no longer my thoughts. I belong to this place. This isn't a land of wonders. It's a difficult country, but whoever clings to it is cured of pessimism. Pessimism is a serious disease. My poor mother bequeathed it to me.*

"And what will become of all of us?" Hugo asks.

Otto gives him the practical look of a peasant, as if to say, *That's no longer my concern.* "The Jews and their pessimism tried to send me to hell. Now, thank God, I'm rid of them," he says, and then vanishes.

Hugo wakes up, apparently because of the commotion taking place in Mariana's room. Mariana is shouting at the top of her lungs, and a man is threatening, "I'll kill you if you don't shut up. I'll kill you. Don't forget that I'm an officer. With an officer, you don't argue. You do what he orders you to do." That threat doesn't silence her, either.

In the midst of it all, a shot is heard. The sound pierces the house and the closet. Mariana's room freezes for a moment. There is no response to the shot from the corridor or from the yard, either. Only later does Mariana burst into loud sobs, and a few women enter her room. "Are you wounded?" one of them asks.

"I'm not wounded," she murmurs.

"That's a relief." The same woman goes on to ask, "What did he want from you?"

Mariana, still sobbing, tells the woman what the officer demanded of her. She speaks in detail, and graphically. Hugo doesn't understand anything she says. The women agree with her that they mustn't give in to demands like those. There is sisterhood and much talk, which slightly diffuses the shock.

After that everybody leaves Mariana's room. There is silence. Not a sound can be heard—just the dripping of the faucet in the yard. Through the cracks in the closet, the first rays of morning light filter in. They are long and touch Hugo's feet. For a moment he forgets the shot and the shock. The wonder of light captures his attention.

Later Hugo hears a woman say, "He didn't intend to kill her. He wanted to frighten her."

"He was afraid that his shame would be revealed to his fellow officers." The voice of an older woman is heard.

"If so, he meant to kill her."

"What can you say? Our profession is dangerous. They should pay us a risk allowance."

Laughter is heard, and the voices mingle with one another.

Hugo knows there will be accusations, clarifications, threats, and, finally, Mariana will have to apologize and promise that in the future she won't shout and will do exactly what the customer demands of her.

It's strange that this knowledge calms his fears and that he is comforted in his heart. In a moment the white morning will be revealed, and everything will be as it was. In the afternoon Mariana will stand in the doorway of the closet with a bowl of soup in her hand.

18

The winds die down and snow falls without letup. Hugo stands next to the cracks in the closet wall and watches the thick snowflakes slowly floating down. The white sight reminds him of home on Sunday mornings: Sofia went to church to pray; his father, dressed in casual clothes, prepared a festive breakfast; his mother put on a new housecoat. The gramophone played Bach sonatas, and the blue porcelain stove roared and gave off pleasant heat.

Hugo loved that relaxed atmosphere, with none of the tension of rushed weekday mornings. On Sunday mornings worries were erased, the pharmacy was forgotten, and his mother didn't even talk about all the poor people she took care of. The music and the quiet enveloped the three of them.

When Sofia returned from church, she would be all covered with snow. Hugo's mother would help her shake off the snowflakes, and then prepare a cup of coffee and a piece of cake for her. Everybody would sit down beside her. Sofia would tell them about the service and the sermon, always bringing back a parable or proverb that had impressed her. One time she recited, "For man does not live by bread alone."

"What impressed you about that verse?" asked Hugo's father.

"We sometimes forget why we're alive. It seems to us that making a living is the main thing. Or that physical love or property is the main thing. That's a great mistake."

"So what is the main thing?" Hugo's father tried to draw her out.

"God," she said, opening her eyes wide.

Sofia was full of contradictions. Every Sunday she would make sure to go to church, and sometimes also in the middle of the week, but in the evenings she liked to pass the time in the tavern. True, she didn't get drunk, but she came back merry and a bit tipsy. Some of the men she had spent time with promised to marry her but changed their minds in the end. Because of those false promises, Sofia decided to return to her native village. In the village, no man would dare to promise marriage and not keep his promise. If a man promised marriage and didn't keep his promise, they would lie in wait for him and beat him till blood flowed.

Hugo liked to listen to Sofia's stories. She spoke to him in Ukrainian. She loved her mother tongue and wanted Hugo to speak it without an accent, too, and without mistakes. Hugo tried but didn't always succeed.

Sofia was so different from his parents and his friends' parents, as if she had been born on another continent: she spoke loudly and with broad gestures, and when it seemed to her that people didn't understand her, she used her large face to imitate her neighbors and suitors. She sang, too, kneeling on the floor and making everyone laugh.

The cold in the closet is unrelenting. Mariana often comes late with Hugo's cup of milk in the morning, and sometimes she goes into town and forgets him all day long. But sometimes she says, "Come to Mariana, and she'll hug you, darling," and so she brings him from the cold darkness to her vibrant breast. In the hours he spends in her bed, embraced in her long arms, marvelous oblivion envelops him. For whole days he looks forward to those hours. When they come, he is stricken, or paralyzed, and he doesn't know what to say or do. But this doesn't happen every day. Most days Mariana is drunk, grumpy, and she falls on her bed in a stupor.

So it is, day after day. There are gloomy days when Hugo sees only the closet walls and Mariana's faded housedresses hanging on hooks. The narrow cracks in the closet walls reveal only the fence and the gray bushes that have shed all their leaves. *This is a prison,* Hugo says to himself. In prison it's impossible to read. It's impossible to do homework. It's even impossible to play chess. Prison stifles thought and imagination. That realization has come to reside within him over the past few days. Since then he has been afraid that his head will slowly empty. He will no longer think or imagine. One day he will fall over like the tree in the yard of their house did last winter. But when Mariana finally remembers him, opens the closet door, and says, "What's Mariana's darling doing?" Hugo's fears evaporate all at once, and he rises to his feet.

19

One day, when they're still asleep in the broad bed, wrapped in each other's arms, Mariana wakes up in a panic.

"It's very late, my darling," she cries out. "You have to go into the closet immediately." When that happens, Hugo feels his body shrink, and he hunches over and walks to the closet without saying anything.

It's quiet. Not a sound can be heard from Mariana's room. For a moment it seems that in a little while the door will open, and Mariana will call out, as she sometimes does, *Darling, come to me.*

Hugo listens expectantly.

He soon realizes that Mariana and her partner are pleased with each other, and whispering. From the few words he catches, it's clear that this time there are no arguments, no accusations, and everything is happening quietly, and with consent.

The thought that Mariana has sent him out of her bed so she can sleep with a grown man suddenly fills Hugo with envy and anger.

He feels so angry and sorry for himself that he falls asleep.

In his dream he sees his mother. She is young and beautiful and dressed in the poplin gown she loved.

"Don't you love me anymore?" she asks with a provocative smile.

"I?" He is stunned, like someone whose secrets have been bared.

"You prefer Mariana to me," she says, pretending to be insulted, the way she sometimes did.

"I love you very much, Mama."

"You're saying that to be polite," she says, and disappears.

When Hugo wakes from that nightmare, he knows the dream's meaning. If his mother were near him, he would try to console her. But since she isn't there, her words remain suspended in the darkness, like an accusation supported by evidence.

In the meantime, the man has been replaced by someone else. Now unpleasant voices come from Mariana's room. The new man speaks sternly, and Mariana tries in vain to get him to understand her. Again the old accusation: alcohol. The man reminds her that she promised not to drink the last time, too. Once again she has failed to keep her promise. After that the storm calms down.

The first morning lights filter into the closet and fill it with stripes of brightness. In a little while Mariana will bring Hugo a cup of warm milk, he comforts himself. But Mariana, as she sometimes does, forgets him. He's so thirsty that he calls out in a whisper, "Mariana." Mariana hears his call, opens the closet door, and bursts in. "You mustn't call me. I warned you not to call me. Never call me." Anger floods her face and darkens it.

For a long time Hugo lies curled up in a corner. In the afternoon Mariana stands in the doorway of the closet with a cup of milk. "How does Mariana's darling feel? How did the night go? Was it cold?" she says, as though nothing has happened.

"I slept."

"It's good to sleep. You don't know how good it is to sleep. I'm going to town to visit my mother. My mother is very sick, and she's alone. There's no one to take care of her. My sister doesn't bother to come and help her. I won't be back until evening. I'll bring you some sandwiches and a pitcher of lemonade. If anyone knocks on the door, don't answer."

Mariana brings Hugo a plate of sandwiches and a pitcher of lemonade.

"Have a pleasant time, my darling," she says. And without another word, she locks the door and goes on her way.

20

Hugo remains standing in Mariana's bedroom. Three months have passed since his mother left him here. Everything has changed in his life. How much it has changed, he doesn't know. Hugo's heart torments him because he hasn't kept his promises to his mother. He doesn't read, he doesn't write, and he doesn't do arithmetic problems.

While he's standing there, Hugo realizes that the room hasn't changed since he first arrived: the same pink slipcovers, the same vases with paper roses stuck in them, the same dresser with its drawers full of little bottles, cotton, and sponges. But that afternoon the room looks to him like the clinic where he was brought to get injections. Anna had a sweet little dog, and Hugo liked to play with him whenever he went to visit her. One morning word spread that Luzzi had rabies. All the children who had played with him or touched him were brought to the clinic.

Some of the children, seeing the hypodermics and hearing the patients cry, slipped out of their parents' grasp and fled. The startled parents tried to catch them, but the children were quicker. They escaped to the cellar and hid there. But their hiding didn't last long. The tall and cunning hospital watchmen closed the doors to the cellar and went from room to room, trapping them. The sight of the children being led back to the clinic stayed in Hugo's mind for many days.

Later, Hugo sits on the floor and begins a chess game. Everything he used to like to do at home is hard for him to do here. Even to open a book is a task beyond his powers. He thinks a lot. Memory keeps bringing up his classmates, his teachers. But to take out a notebook and write isn't in his power.

Hugo is sorry that Anna and Otto have changed so much. Every time he thinks about that change, a chill grips his arms and legs. Thinking about all the delicate embroidery that was spun between him and Anna, between him and Otto—the visits to their houses, the trips and the long conversations about themselves and about what was going on around them—the thought makes him so sad that he chokes. To prevent them from disappearing from his memory, he brings them back up in his mind and says to them, *True, you've changed, but in my head you live as you were. I'm not willing to give up even a single feature of your faces, and for that reason, as long as you're in my memory, your disappearance is only partial, and to a large degree abolished.*

Suddenly, illuminated by the cold afternoon lights, the path Hugo had taken every day to school arises in his memory. It began on the long, shady boulevard with the chestnut trees, and it branched off among narrow, twisting alleys perfumed with the smells of coffee and fresh cakes. In the morning the taverns were closed, and the smell of beer and urine rose from the dark corners.

Sometimes he would stop at a bakery and buy a cheese pastry. The fresh, crisp taste stayed with him until he arrived at the school's front steps. The way to and from school is now imprinted in Hugo's mind with sharp clarity.

He usually walked back home with Anna and Otto, and

sometimes Erwin would also join them. Erwin was Hugo's height, and it was hard to know whether he was happy or sad. A restrained look of surprise was usually spread across his face, and he hardly spoke. The other children didn't like him, and sometimes they picked on him. But Hugo had a feeling that Erwin held a secret within him. Hugo expected that one day Erwin would reveal his secret. Then it would be known to everyone that he wasn't an indifferent creature, limited or lacking in feelings. Once, Hugo discussed this with Anna. Anna didn't think there was any secret in Erwin. She believed he had closed himself off because he had trouble with mathematics and had a feeling of inferiority. A feeling of inferiority wasn't a secret. Anna was smart. She knew how to express her thoughts like an adult.

Once, when they were on their way home from school, Hugo carelessly asked Erwin, "What do your parents do?"

"I don't have any parents," Erwin answered softly.

"Where are they?" asked Hugo, stupidly.

"They died," Erwin said.

For many days Hugo regretted his questions; he felt as though he had been stricken. After that, he was careful not to be in Erwin's company, and if he found himself with Erwin, he spoke little or not at all.

Hugo refused to think about what had happened to Erwin in the ghetto. One night they sealed off the orphanage on all sides, took the orphans out of their beds, and loaded them onto trucks while they were still in their pajamas. The orphans wept and cried out for help, but no one did anything. Anyone who opened a window or went outside would be shot. The shouts and weeping pierced the empty streets, and they could be heard even after the trucks had driven away and disappeared from view.

·   ·   ·

Thus Hugo sits on the floor and dreams about his friends and his school. The chess pieces are arranged on the board, but apart from the opening, he hasn't made a move.

Mariana arrives toward evening and asks, "What did Mariana's shut-in puppy do?" The smell of brandy wafts about her mouth, but she isn't angry. She hugs and kisses Hugo, saying, "You're better than all of them. What did you do today?"

"Nothing."

"Why didn't you eat the sandwiches?"

"I wasn't hungry."

Every time Mariana comes back from town, Hugo wants to ask her, *Did you meet Mama? Did you meet Papa?* But he remembers that Mariana doesn't like him to ask about his parents. Only when she's in a good mood, she's willing to say, "I didn't meet them. I didn't hear from them." Once, in a moment of anger, she said, "I've already told you. They'll only come at the end of the war. The Jews are shut in and locked up in hiding places."

Then she tells him, "My mother is very sick. I don't have any more money for the doctors and medicines," and she bursts into tears. When Mariana cries, her face changes and becomes a child's face. This time she isn't angry at the bastards but at her sister, who lives right near her mother but doesn't take the trouble to go to her and bring her bread or fruit. She ignores her completely. The doctor who came to see Mariana's mother told her they had to buy medicine immediately, because without it she would expire in a few days.

Now Mariana is about to sell the jewelry she received from Hugo's mother. The jewelry is beautiful and very valuable, but it's doubtful that she can sell it for its full value. "They're all cheats," she says, and there's no one she can trust.

After a short pause, she adds, "My mother is still angry at me. She's sure I'm neglecting her. What can I do? I work all night long to bring her food and firewood. A week ago I bought her fruit. What more can I do? I'm willing to sell the jewelry if the medicines will save her. I don't want my mother to be angry at me."

"Your mother knows you love her."

"How do you know?"

"Mothers have a special feeling for their children."

"In my childhood she used to beat me a lot, but in recent years, since my father died, she's calmed down. She suffered a lot all those years."

"Everyone has his own portion." Hugo recalls that sentence.

"You're smart, darling. All the Jewish children are smart. But you surpass even them. It's good that God sent you to me. What do you say? Should I sell the jewelry?"

"If that will save your mother, you should sell it."

"You're right, sweetie. You're the only one I can depend on."

21

That night no sound is heard from Mariana's room. She is alone, and her sleep is punctuated by sudden snorts and mutterings that sound like stifled speech. Hugo expects her to call him to her, but she is immersed in deep slumber.

In the last darkness of the night they wake her. Hugo hears Mariana get dressed and hurry out. When she returns, it is already daylight. She bursts into tears. Hugo has heard her cry more than once, but this time it's a different sort of crying, a choked weeping that comes up from within her in heaves.

Mariana goes out and returns several times. Finally, she stands in the closet's doorway with a short woman and says, "Last night my mother died. I have to set out right away. Victoria will watch over you. She's a woman who can keep a secret. She's our cook, and I'm sure you won't go hungry."

"Don't worry. I'll watch over you," says Victoria in a heavy, foreign accent.

Hugo doesn't know what to say, so he says, "Thank you."

Now he sees Victoria from close up: short, plump, older than Mariana. Her flushed face expresses tense surprise, as if Hugo were different from what she imagined. Mariana repeats, "Hugo is a good boy. Watch over him."

After the door is locked, a curtain falls over his eyes, and he doesn't see a thing. Just yesterday it seemed as if Mariana loved him, and it would not be long before he slept with her again. Now she is gone and has left this miserable creature in her place. Sorrow chokes Hugo's throat, and it is clear to him that until her return he will know no peace. He rises to his feet and stands next to the boards of the closet. If it weren't for the slivers of light that filtered through the cracks, the darkness and the cold would devour him in one gulp. *Mama,* he wants to call out, but he immediately grasps that his mother is far from him, and, like him, she is imprisoned in a closet. His father is even farther away. He no longer appears even in Hugo's dreams.

In the afternoon Victoria brings him soup and meatballs. She looks at him again and asks, "Do you speak Ukrainian?"

"Certainly."

"I'm glad," she says, and her face smiles. She immediately adds, "You're lucky."

"How?" Hugo asks.

"They've already sent away all the Jews, but the Germans aren't satisfied with that. They're going from house to house and making careful searches, and every day they find another five, another six. Whoever tries to run away is shot. Also if anyone is caught hiding Jews, they kill him."

"Will they kill me, too?" He is panicked for a moment.

"You're not like the Jews. You're blond and speak Ukrainian like a Ukrainian."

It's hard to know what's going on in Victoria's head. When she speaks about the Jews, a sort of smile with many meanings spreads across her mouth, as though she were speaking about things one mustn't talk about.

"The poor Jews, they don't leave them in peace." She changes her tone.

"After the war, won't life again be the way it was?" Hugo wants her to confirm that.

"We'll probably live without Jews."

"Won't they come back to the city?" he asks in surprise.

"That's God's will. Who gave you the cross?"

"Mariana."

"And do you believe in Jesus?"

"Yes," he says, without removing all the doubt from her heart.

"The Jews don't believe in Jesus." She wants to put him to the test.

"I like the cross. Mariana told me it was my charm." He avoids her direct question.

"You're doing the right thing," she says, bowing her head.

Toward evening she brings him sandwiches and a pitcher of lemonade and asks, "Do you pray?"

"At night, before closing my eyes, I say, 'God, watch over me and over my parents and over all those who call Your name and seek Your help.' "

"That isn't a prayer," she says quickly.

"What is it, then?"

"It's a request. Prayer has a set wording that we say."

"I'll ask Mariana to teach it to me."

"You're doing the right thing."

"Do you know my mother?" He delays her.

"Certainly I know her. Who doesn't know Julia? Every poor person in the city goes to her pharmacy. She smiles at them all and is never angry. Usually pharmacists are irritable. They scold you or show you that you're ignorant. Your mother greets people kindly."

"Maybe you know where she's hiding?"

"God knows. It's dangerous to hide Jews. Whoever hides Jews gets killed."

"But they're hiding my mother."

"I believe so," she says, and bows her head.

At night, in his dream, Hugo hears a loud noise in Mariana's room, like somebody drilling. Suddenly the closet door collapses and in the doorway stand Victoria and two soldiers. Victoria points at his corner and says, "There he is before you. I'm not the one who hid him. Mariana hid him."

"Where's Mariana?"

"She's mourning for her mother."

"Get to your feet, Jew," one of the soldiers orders him, and blinds him with his flashlight.

Hugo tries to get up, but his legs are attached to the floor. He tries again and again but doesn't succeed.

"If you don't get up, we'll shoot you."

"Jesus, save me!" Hugo shouts, and clutches the cross.

Hearing his cry, Victoria smiles and says, "It's all a pretense."

"Should we kill him?" the soldier asks her.

"Do what you want," she says, and moves aside.

A shot is heard, and Hugo falls into a deep pit.

When he wakes up he knows he's been saved again, and he is glad.

Toward morning Hugo hears voices in Mariana's room, and fear rivets him to his place. One is the voice of a man complaining that the bathtub isn't clean and the sheets are dirty. In her defense, the woman claims that it isn't her room but another woman's. The conversation, as always, takes place in brusque German.

In the end the voices fall silent, and only grunts can be heard. Hugo doesn't fall back to sleep. The visions of the night and the first lights of the morning merge, and he's sad that Mariana is mourning alongside her mother's coffin. The sorrow gradually melds to the remainder of his fear, and they stay within him, becoming one.

22

It is eleven o'clock, and Victoria is late in coming with the cup of milk. Hugo stands at the cracks in the closet wall and listens intently to the cawing of the crows and the barking of the dogs, which rise from the snowy fields.

The winter is now at its height. It now seems as if Hugo has been separated from his mother for a long time, a time crammed with events he doesn't understand. His dreams remain clear, but not with a clarity you can touch. They are accompanied by a strange geometrical dimension. At first that seemed like a prank to him, but soon he realized that the forms were indeed repeated. His mother, for example, wore a triangular hat. He was surprised by that form, but he thought only of a general statement: "People aren't shaped in geometrical forms. The dreams have become confused for me."

But his memory is clear and palpable. In the winter, over Christmas vacation, Hugo's family used to travel to the Carpathian Mountains. That was a joy unlike any other joy. His parents skied with elegant grace. His father was faster, but his mother didn't lag far behind. Hugo learned the sport without difficulty. At the age of nine he already skied easily, without stumbling.

Hugo had always loved trips. It was too bad that his parents didn't have time to take long vacations. During vacations, the daily routine changed according to the weather. There was no sign of haste or rush. Every morning, the peasant woman from whom they rented the cabin would bring them a pitcher of milk, a loaf of bread, a wedge of cheese, and a packet of golden butter. They were vegetarians, and the peasant woman found it hard to absorb that. She repeatedly expressed surprise. "Why abstain from salt pork or a little beef?" When his mother told her, "Vegetables and dairy products are enough for us," the peasant woman would make a strange gesture with her head, as if to say, *Even so, without meat a person isn't satisfied.*

During winter vacation his father appeared at his full height. When he spoke with people back home, he usually stooped. For that reason he sometimes seemed to be the same height as Hugo's mother. During winter vacation, it became clear to everyone that he was a head taller.

Winter vacation was always accompanied by a feeling of soaring—perhaps because of the splendor of the snow, or the long and bright nights. They would drink punch and read until late at night. They spoke little, but sometimes his mother would recall memories from her student days at the university.

The cabin, the horse and sleigh that were at their disposal, the blankets they wrapped themselves in while riding, the thermos bottles and sandwiches, the little bells that hung around the horse's neck—all that earthiness seemed marvelous to Hugo. All fears were erased. Just he and his parents, just he soaring on skis over the glowing snow. School, tests, obligations, and frictions were all erased, as if they had never existed, and Hugo and his parents were what they wanted to be: lovers of nature and lovers of books.

The vacation would end abruptly. At night his mother would pack the suitcases and at first light they would mount the sleigh and go to the railroad station. That cold sundering, which took place early in the morning, would make Hugo shudder and cry. His mother would say, "You mustn't cry about transitory things. Mama and Papa would also like to stay here longer, but it's impossible to close the pharmacy for longer than a week."

Suddenly, that bright life is revealed to him in the closet, appearing before his eyes as it did while it was actually happening.

At noon the door to Mariana's room is opened cautiously, and then the closet door. Victoria tells Hugo right away that soldiers are making house-to-house searches. He must lie still and not make a sound.

"Here are sandwiches and milk. If the searches stop, I'll bring you something else at night, but don't expect me."

"What should I do?"

"Nothing. Lie down as if you didn't exist."

"And if they break in?"

"Don't worry, we won't let them," she says, and shuts the closet door.

Victoria's words don't calm Hugo. He lies on his couch as though paralyzed. All the captivating visions that had raised his spirits just a short time ago have vanished. The thought that in a moment soldiers will break in, arrest him, and bring him to the police station fills him with dread and weakens his knees.

That evening the twilight is long between the cracks in the closet wall, and it gets dark slowly. There are no noises, and for a moment it seems to him that the night will pass without an incursion from outside. Everything will be accomplished quietly, with whispers and grunts. But that's only an illusion. As the night begins, the pounding of hammers is heard, as is the noise of furniture being moved. The commotion continues for a long time. Suddenly, with no warning, as though to contradict everything that was threatening him, an accordion breaks into song. A saxophone joins in immediately. Hugo is astonished. Now Victoria's sowing of fear sounds like an empty threat.

For a long time Hugo lies still and listens. The merry music grows louder and louder, feet stamp, voices shout. Above the din, women's laughter is heard. It sounds as though someone was tickling them. This mysterious place, which encloses him on all sides, suddenly seems like Mr. Herzig's banquet hall, where weddings and parties were held, and where Uncle Sigmund had been married.

When he was drunk, Uncle Sigmund would often present Mr. Herzig's banquet hall as a prime example. Mr. Herzig's hall, disgustingly splendid, was the palace of the Jewish petite bourgeoisie. In it they would get engaged, marry, celebrate circumcisions and bar mitzvahs, and of course silver and golden wedding anniversaries. Uncle Sigmund loathed the Jewish petite bourgeoisie ensconced in large houses, in gigantic department stores, in fine restaurants, and in splendid catering halls. In his drunkenness, he would shout, "They're empty, they're overblown, they're golems whose souls have departed." He was particularly angered by Mr. Herzig's palace, where the men would compete among themselves as to who could provide the most splendid meals and at whose party they served the fullest plates. His former wife embodied them fully. Uncle Sigmund constantly wondered how he could have been caught in that net. He said repeatedly, "In the world to come, if there is such a thing, they'll thrash me because I was blind and didn't see what any sensible person can see. I deserve it. I deserve it."

The music and debauched laughter last until late at night and then suddenly fall silent, as though the dancers have collapsed.

In the last darkness of the night, Mariana's door is opened, and then the closet door. Victoria stands in the doorway and immediately tells Hugo, "You're lucky. All around us they made careful night searches. Apparently because of the big party that was here, they didn't come in, but who knows?"

"What am I supposed to do?" Hugo asks with a trembling voice.

"Pray."

"I don't know how to pray."

"Didn't your parents teach you?"

"No."

"That's strange. You didn't go to synagogue?"

"No."

"Every hour, say, 'God Lord, save me from death.' "

"Should I kiss the cross?" Hugo asks.

"That's desirable. In a little while I'll bring you a cup of milk and some sandwiches. But don't expect me later today. The soldiers are going from house to house and looking for Jews, and it's not a good idea to wander around here. Do you understand me?"

"I understand. Thank you."

"Don't thank me, pray to God," Victoria says, and shuts the closet door.

23

The next morning Victoria again comes late with the cup of milk, and she tell Hugo that searches are still going on in the nearby houses. In one house they found a Jewish family with three children. They arrested the family and the owners of the house who gave them shelter, and all of them were taken to the police station.

Seriousness has clouded Victoria's eyes, and it's evident that she has more news, but she keeps it to herself.

"What should I do?"

"I've already told you, pray."

"And if they discover me?"

"You'll stand up and say you're Mariana's son."

Not noticing what he's doing, Hugo reaches for the knapsack and removes the Bible from it. In the middle of the book lies an envelope. He quickly opens it and reads:

Dear Hugo,
I don't know when and in what circumstances this letter will find you. I imagine that you're not having an easy time. I want you to know that I had no choice. The peasants who promised to come, didn't come, and danger was lurking in every corner. It was not with light thoughts that I decided to

place you in the hands of my childhood friend Mariana. She is a good woman, but life has not been kind to her. She is prone to moods, and you have to be considerate of her. If she's bitter or angry, don't be annoyed with her and don't answer anything. Restraint is always desirable. Moods have a way of passing. Also, suffering has a limit, and in the end, we'll be together again. I think about you all the time. I hope that you have something to eat and that your sleep isn't disturbed. As for me, I don't know where I'll end up. If only I can, I'll visit you, but don't expect me. I'm with you all the time, day and night, and if it's hard for you, think about Papa and me. Your thoughts will join us together. You aren't alone in the world, dear. Grandpa used to say that parting is an illusion. Thoughts join us even when we are far from one another. Recently I've felt that Grandpa is with us, too. He passed away two years before the war. You remember him.

I'm writing these lines about three hours before our departure. For a moment it seemed to me that I didn't equip you with enough instructions. Now I see that in fact we've discussed everything. I imagine that adaptation isn't easy for you. I have one request of you: don't despair. Despair is surrender. I believed and still believe in optimism even in these dark hours. That's how I am. You know me, and apparently I'll stay like that.

I love you very much,
Mama

Hugo reads the letter again and again, and the two sheets of paper tremble in his hands. He loves his mother's clear handwriting. Her world shines from every line: openness, clarity, cordiality, and a willingness to give. She believed that if a person gave, he would also receive, and if he didn't receive, giving was its own reward and joy. More than once reality had slapped her in the face. Even then she hadn't said that there is no way to reform people. Instead, she put her head down and absorbed the insult.

Now Hugo envisions the way she would tilt her head to listen. He sees how her arms would go limp when she was unable to help, and the joy she radiated when the medicine she had given was helpful.

He reads the two sheets again. The more he reads, the more he knows that his mother's situation is worse than his. She bears a heavy knapsack on her back, struggles against harsh winds, and every time she falls to the ground, she calls out, *Hugo, don't despair. I'm on my way to you. I'm sure that soon the winds will weaken, the war will end, and I will overcome the obstacles strewn in my path. Don't despair, promise me.* Her face glows as it did on their way to Mariana's house.

Later, Hugo takes the notebook out of his knapsack and writes:

Mama dear, the letter that you wrote to me only reached me today. I'll carry out your request with great precision. Compared to you, my situation is better. I'm living in a closet in Mariana's room. Mariana watches over me and takes care of my meals. Most of the day I think and imagine things. For that reason I didn't yet start reading and writing, as I promised you. Everything that surrounds me is so intense, and sometimes shocking, that it's hard for me to open a book and follow the plot. Sometimes it seems to me that I am living in a fairy tale. I expect that in the end things will be good.

Mariana's mother died, and she went to her village, but don't worry, the cook Victoria brings me my meals and tells me what's happening on the outside. Your letter brought me many visions of light and much hope.

Take care of yourself,
Hugo

He places the notebook in the knapsack, and the tears that were locked in his eyes roll down his face.

Once again Victoria brings him horrible news. That night they caught more Jewish families. They were taken together with the people who hid them to the town square, where they were all lined up and executed, so that everyone would see and hear and not be tempted to hide Jews.

"What should I do?" Hugo asks cautiously.

"We'll see." Her answer comes quickly.

Saying nothing more, Victoria closes the door, and Hugo takes the notebook out of the knapsack and writes:

Dear Mama,

I don't want to hide the truth from you. For more than a week, soldiers have been going from house to house and making searches. Mariana is mourning for her mother in the village, and I have been placed in the hands of the cook, Victoria. Before, she was sure that they wouldn't search here. Now fear has fallen upon her. I'm not afraid. I'm not saying that to calm you down. The months in hiding have blunted my feeling of fear. I live our life at home every day. The house, the pharmacy, and mainly you and Papa are with me from morning to night. When I'm cold or my sleep wanders, I see you with great clarity. Recently I saw our ski vacations in the mountains once again, and the feeling of soaring came back to me. Mama, the loneliness doesn't hurt me because you taught me how to be by myself. I won't conceal from you that from time to time a feeling of uncertainty attacks me, or despair, but those are passing moments. You equipped me with much belief in life. I'm so glad that you and Papa are my parents that sometimes I want to break down the door of the hiding place and run away to you.

I love you,
Hugo

24

The next day Victoria doesn't appear. Hugo eats leftover sandwiches and listens constantly. Not a sound is heard from Mariana's room. From the neighboring rooms the usual voices are
heard: "Where is the pail?" or "Did you mop the room yet?"
Several times Victoria's voice is heard. It's hard to know, with
her voice, whether she's conversing or arguing. In any event,
there are no quarrels. Between one bit of talk and another,
waves of laughter arise, flood the corridor, fall, and shatter.

Where am I? Hugo suddenly asks himself, as he sometimes
does in his dreams. He already sensed the secret that surrounded this place during the first weeks after his arrival, but
now, perhaps because of dour Victoria, it seems like a prison to
him. Every time he asks Mariana about it, she evades the question and says, "Let that foulness be. It would be a shame to
dirty your thoughts."

Hugo very much wants to take out the notebook and write
about everything that's happening to him, and about his
thoughts. But fear and excitement prevent him from doing
that. All morning long he sees Mariana's face, and it is darkened
by grief. She is muttering incomprehensible words, and from
time to time she raises her head and calls out loud, "Forgive
me, Jesus, for my many sins."

Toward evening men's voices can already be heard. First they sound familiar, but in a short time he catches a military tone of voice.

"Are there Jews here?" The question comes soon.

"There are no Jews. We work in the army's service," a woman answers in German.

"In what service?" the military voice keeps asking.

The woman says something Hugo doesn't understand, and everybody bursts out laughing.

The atmosphere changes all at once. The men are served soft drinks, because one of them, apparently the commander, says, "We're on duty. Alcoholic beverages are forbidden while on duty." They praise the coffee and the sandwiches, and to the woman's invitation to stay and enjoy themselves, the military voice answers, "We're on duty."

"A little entertainment never hurt anyone," the woman's voice cajoles.

"Duty first," answers the military voice.

And then they leave.

Silence returns to the place, but the dread doesn't release Hugo's body. It's clear to him that this time, too, his mother protected him, the way she guarded him during the first days of the ghetto and afterward, when danger lurked in every corner, and especially at the end, in the cellar. He always believed in his mother's hidden power, but this time it is fully revealed.

When it first gets dark, Victoria brings Hugo a bowl of soup and some meatballs.

"You were saved this time, too," she says.

My mother saved me, he's about to say, but he doesn't. "Thank you," he says instead.

"Don't thank me, thank God." She rushes to teach him a lesson.

"I'll give thanks," he quickly replies.

Without another word, Victoria goes out and locks the closet door.

That night it's merry again. The accordion bellows and people dance and shout in the hall. The wild laughter rolls loudly and shakes the closet walls. Hugo is so tired that he falls asleep and dreams that Mariana has abandoned him and Victoria doesn't hesitate to turn him in. He tries to cover himself in the sheepskins, but they don't cover him.

Toward morning the accordion falls silent. The people scatter, and no one enters Mariana's room.

At nine o'clock the closet door opens and Mariana stands in the doorway. It's Mariana, but it is also not her. She's wearing a black dress, a peasant kerchief is on her head, and her face is pale and sunken. For a moment it seems she's about to kneel, put her hands together, and pray. That's a mistaken impression. She stands there, and it's clear that she doesn't have the power to utter a word.

"How are you?" Hugo gets to his feet and approaches her.

"It was difficult for me," she says, and bows her head.

"Come, let's sit down. I have sandwiches," he says, and takes her hand.

A glum smile spreads across Mariana's face, and she says, "Thanks, darling, I'm not hungry."

"I can tidy up your room, mop the floor, whatever you tell me to do. I'm so glad you came back."

"Thanks, darling, you mustn't work. You have to be in hiding until the troubles pass. My poor mother was very sick and died in great pain. Now she's in the good world, and I'm here. She suffered a lot."

"God will watch over her," Hugo quickly says.

Hearing that, Mariana goes down on her knees, hugs Hugo to her heart, and says, "Mama left me alone in the world."

"We're not alone in the world." Hugo remembers what his mother wrote to him.

"I have had some very hard days. My poor mother died in agony. I didn't manage to buy the medicine for her. I'm guilty. I know."

"You're not guilty. The circumstances are guilty." Hugo remembers that phrase, which they used a lot at home.

"Who told you that, darling?"

"Uncle Sigmund."

"A marvelous man, an extraordinary man. I'm nothing compared to him," she says, and she smiles.

25

After Mariana's return Hugo's life changed beyond recognition. Mariana still forgot him sometimes, returned from town drunk and abusive, but in her moments of sobriety she fell to her knees, hugged and kissed him, and promised him that nothing bad would befall him. She would watch over him no less than his mother. Closeness to her was so pleasant for Hugo that he forgot his loneliness and the fears that surrounded him.

The baths were especially pleasant. Mariana soaped him down, washed and rinsed him, and she no longer said, "Don't be embarrassed," but whispered, "A proper young man, in a year or two the girls will gobble you up." When she was depressed, her tone changed, and she turned things around: "If only they washed me like you. Believe me, I deserve it. They crush me every night like a mattress. Not even one word of love."

"But I love you." The words slipped out of Hugo's mouth.

"True, you're good, you're loyal," she said, and hugged him.

After her mother's death, fear of God came over Mariana. She kept repeating that they would roast her in hell because she hadn't watched over her mother, hadn't called the doctor in time, hadn't bought her medicine, hadn't sat by her bedside. And not only that: instead of working in the fields or in a

factory, she was working here. For that God would never forgive her.

Once Hugo heard her say, "I hate myself. I'm filthy." He
wanted to approach her and say, *You're not filthy. A good smell of
perfume comes from your neck and your blouse.* But he didn't
dare. When Mariana was sunk in depression, she was unpre-
dictable. She didn't talk but, rather, spat out harsh words like
pebbles. Hugo knew that at times like that, he mustn't talk to
her. Even a soft word drove her out of her mind.

Hugo takes out his notebook and writes:

> *I'm trying to keep up continuity in my diary, but I'm not
> managing. The place is feverish. Since Mariana returned,
> her moods rise and fall, and sometimes several times a day.
> I'm not afraid. I feel that behind her suffering hides a good
> and loving woman.*
>
> *Mama, sometimes it seems to me that what once was
> will never be again, and that when we meet after the war,
> we'll be different. How that difference will be expressed I
> have no notion. Sometimes it seems to me that we'll speak in
> a different language. Things that we didn't used to talk about
> or ignored will concern us. Each of us will tell what hap-
> pened to him. We'll sit together and listen to music, but it will
> be a different kind of listening.*
>
> *Before I yearned for this meeting, and now, God forgive
> me, as Mariana says, I'm afraid of it. The thought that at the
> end of the war I won't recognize you and you won't recognize
> me is a very hard thought for me to bear. I'm trying not to
> think it, but the thought won't let me be.*
>
> *There's no doubt I've changed a lot in these months, and
> I'm not what I was. For a fact: it's hard for me to write and
> hard for me to read. You remember how much I loved to*

read. Now I'm entirely immersed in listening. Mariana's room, my eternal riddle, is a house of pleasure for me, and at the same time I feel that evil will come from there. The tension that pervades me most of the day has apparently changed me, and who knows what else will be.

By the way, Mariana always complains that everybody exploits her all the time, wrings her out, and crushes her. I often want to ask her, Who's oppressing you? But I don't dare. I mainly observe your instruction not to ask but to listen, but what can I do? Listening doesn't always make you wiser.

The nights are cold. Hugo wears two pairs of pajamas, wraps himself in one of Mariana's cloaks, and covers himself with sheepskins. Even that heavy covering doesn't keep him warm. Sometimes in the middle of the night Mariana opens the closet door and calls him to come to her.

For a long time Hugo's body hurts him from the piercing cold, but gradually sensation returns to his arms and legs, and he feels her soft body. That pleasantness is unlike any other, but, sadly, it doesn't last for long. Suddenly, with no warning, a feeling of guilt breaks out within him and spreads over him like a searing flame. *Mama is suffering on the cold roads, and you are embraced in Mariana's arms. Mariana isn't your mother. She's a servant, she's like Sofia.* But amazingly, that sharp twinge of the heart is quickly swallowed up in feelings of pleasure, and there is no trace of its having entered him. Sometimes Mariana whispers in her sleep, "Why don't you kiss me? Your kisses are very sweet." Hugo does her bidding gladly, but when she says, "Bite, too," he hesitates, afraid to hurt her.

26

Thus February passed. In early March the snow melted, and Hugo stood at the cracks in the closet wall and listened to the burble of the rushing water. The sound was familiar to him, but where exactly he had first seen a spring with rushing water he couldn't remember. His earlier life was gradually slipping away from him, and he no longer saw it with the same clarity. Sometimes he sat on the floor and cried about his former life, which would never return.

Mariana doesn't conceal from Hugo that the searches for Jews haven't stopped. Now they're not made from house to house but based on reports from informers. The informers swarm everywhere, and for trivial sums they turn over Jews and the households that concealed them.

A few days earlier Mariana showed Hugo an opening near the toilet, so that in an emergency he could squirm out through it and hide in the woodshed adjacent to the closet. "Mariana is always on watch. Don't worry," she said, and winked at him.

"And won't Victoria inform on me?"

"She won't do that. She's a religious woman."

But meanwhile the nights have changed and aren't the way they were. Mariana receives two or three men one after the other. From eavesdropping he knows that the reception is harsh and tense, without any laughter. During the day she stays in bed until very late, and when she appears at the closet doorway, her face is rumpled and bitterness is spread across her lips. Hugo goes over to her, kisses her hand, and asks, "What's the matter?"

When Mariana says, "Don't ask," Hugo knows that the night was cursed. She tries to be pleasant to the guests, but they aren't considerate of her. They make all kinds of comments to her and ask her to do things that disgust her. In the end they complain about her to the management.

Apparently that's how it always was, but now the demands have increased, and there are many complaints about her. Almost every day a woman comes into her room and scolds her. "Things can't go on this way for much longer. You have to accept the guests' demands. Don't quarrel with them and don't contradict them. Do exactly what they ask of you. You have to be more flexible."

Mariana promises but doesn't keep her promise. She's devoted to Hugo, though, bringing him sandwiches decorated with vegetables, and if she has no guests, she invites him into her bed. Those hours are his most beautiful ones.

Sometimes Hugo manages to get her to talk, and she tells him about her life and about what she calls "work." Her work, so she says, is the most contemptible in the world, and one day she plans to begin her life again. If she could stop drinking brandy, she could return to ordinary work.

One evening she says to him, "Pamper me now."

"How?"

"Wash me the way I wash you. Mariana needs some pampering."

"Gladly," he says, not knowing what it involves.

Before long, she has filled the bathtub with hot water and taken off her clothes. She says, "Now I'm in your hands. Pamper me."

He begins to wash her neck and back. Suddenly she raises her upper body and says, "Wash everything, my breasts too." He washes her, and it's like a dream: a mixture of pleasure and fear.

Now he sees how big and full she is, and how long her legs are. After he dries her, she puts on a nightgown and says, "Don't tell anyone. This is a secret between you and me."

"I'll keep it, I swear."

"I'll teach you some other things that will be pleasant for you."

All night he sleeps embraced in Mariana's arms. It is quiet and pleasant, but his dreams are nightmares. Soldiers burst into the closet, and he tries to slip out through the opening that Mariana had shown him, but the opening is narrow and he doesn't manage to crawl through. The soldiers stand there and laugh, and their laughter is roiled with contempt. In the end a soldier walks up to him and steps on him with his boot. He feels the heel digging into him and wants to scream, but his mouth is blocked.

The next morning Mariana goes into town and forgets to bring Hugo a cup of milk. Thirst and hunger torment him, but he is so replete with pleasure from the night before that the hours pass with pleasant visions. Now he remembers clearly the tall chestnut trees along the streets, their thick leaves and their flowering branches, the fruit that would fall from them at the end of the summer, their green skin cracking on the damp pavement. To touch the shiny brown chestnuts always made him happy. Once he talked about it with his mother. She, too, thought that all fruit, even fruit that we don't eat, had something marvelous about it. It was no wonder that people who observed the traditions blessed fruit before eating it.

While Hugo is consoling himself with memories of having

slept with Mariana the previous night, the closet door opens and Victoria stands in the doorway. He has already removed her existence from his mind, and there she is, short, round, her face flushed, her short fingers looking as if they have been soaking in red water.

"What are you doing?" she asks, as though he has been caught doing a misdeed.

"Nothing," Hugo answers, trying to evade her gaze.

"Do you pray?"

"Yes."

"You don't look like it."

"I kiss the charm," he says, and touches the cross on his neck.

"It's not a charm, it's a holy crucifix."

"Thank you for the correction."

"Don't thank me. Do what you're supposed to."

Without another word, Victoria locks the closet, and it's clear to Hugo that at the first opportunity she will turn him in.

27

Mariana tried to stop drinking brandy, but without success. On a day without brandy, she confessed, her head felt as if it had been split and her body felt as if it had been raked over. Without brandy, the world was hell. Better to die.

"You have to stop drinking," the woman with the authoritative voice coaxed her. "You're a pretty and attractive woman, and the men like you. But they don't like it when you're drunk. You have to stop drinking and do what the guests ask of you. That's our profession. That's our livelihood."

Mariana promised, but she didn't keep her promise. The guests shouted at her and hit her. Hugo saw blue spots on her body, and his heart felt bitter.

"You're 'the only one who understands me," Mariana says, and hugs him. "You're the only one who doesn't hit me or abuse me, and you don't call me bad names, and you don't order me to do disgusting things." The compliments that Mariana showers on Hugo embarrass him, but he knows that she needs some encouragement now, and he says, "You'll get yourself out of this. You're beautiful, and everybody loves you."

"You're wrong, darling. Everybody wrings me out, abuses me, and then they complain about me."

"We'll run away from here." Hugo tries that stratagem.

"Where will we run to? My late mother's house is about to collapse, and my sister stole what was in it."

"We'll work together in a kitchen." Hugo utters that sentence without knowing how it could be done.

"My darling, no one would hire me. This profession is the mark of Cain not only on your forehead but on your whole self, on your whole life."

Mariana is frightened, but Hugo, for some reason, isn't frightened. Mariana feels that and says, "What would I do without you?"

Once she said, in a moment of distraction, "The Jews are more delicate."

"Than who?"

"Than other people. If you thought that the Germans were polite, you're mistaken. They fall upon a woman like wild beasts. Only the Jews approach a woman cautiously, hug her and kiss her gently, buy her a bottle of perfume, a pair of silk stockings, give her some extra cash so she can pamper herself."

"Did you have many Jewish friends?" he asked, and he immediately regretted asking.

"Mainly students. They were attracted to me, and I was attracted to them. One student even proposed marriage. I was afraid. I said to myself, he's educated, he'll be a lawyer, and what about me? I'm nothing. Aside from that, non-Jews don't marry Jews."

'Why not?"

"Because each one believes in something different."

"We're not religious."

"I know."

One night, a warm, quiet night, angry voices are heard from Mariana's room. Mariana swears by God and His Messiah, "Today not even a single drop of brandy entered my mouth. All day long I struggled with myself not to drink, and I didn't."

Mariana's oaths are of no use. The man claims that she stinks of brandy, and he won't lie with a stinking woman. The man's words push her over the edge. She screams and shouts. The man slaps her face and leaves the room.

Before long the woman with the authoritative voice arrives, and without first coaxing or trying to persuade her, announces that Mariana has been fired, and that she must leave the room within two days.

Hearing that bitter news, Mariana raises her choked voice and says, "Why?"

"You know exactly why." The woman's voice cuts like a knife.

"I didn't drink, I swear to you."

"Why didn't you change clothes? Your clothes stink."

"I didn't know."

"I'm fed up with you," the woman says, and leaves the room.

Hugo knows exactly what that means, but he sympathizes with Mariana and ignores the anger of the woman in charge. *No matter,* he says to himself, *we'll find a better place.*

The hours pass, and Mariana doesn't come into the closet.

Toward morning, defeated and humiliated, she opens the door and says, "They fired me."

"You've suffered more than enough here."

"I don't know what to do." Despite the shock, she grasps the gravity of her situation.

"I'm willing to go anywhere."

"Darling, don't forget that you're a Jew."

"Can you see it on me?"

"Not right away, but people have evil eyes, and they'll discover it very quickly. I thought all day about what to do. It occurred to me to ask my friend Nasha, who works here, to keep her eye on you until I find a hiding place."

"And I won't go with you?"

"Honey, I really love you, but you can't walk around with me in broad daylight. They'll simply kill you. They kill Jews without mercy. Nasha is a good woman, my age. She's different from me. She's not excitable like I am. She always has a plan."

"And she won't turn me in?"

"Perish the thought. She's a very good woman. Her grandpa was a priest."

"I'm afraid," Hugo says, without meaning to say it.

"Don't be afraid. I'll talk to Nasha. Just for a short time, until I find the right place. I swore to your mother that I would watch over you, and I'll keep that promise under any condition. Come to me, and I'll give you a kiss. Now you give me a kiss, harder. We'll always be together," she says, and then locks the closet door.

28

Hugo suddenly feels that danger is approaching. He checks the opening near the toilet that Mariana spoke of, and it's a good thing he does, because it's full of boards and rags. After cleaning it, he crawls through it easily and finds himself close to the woodshed. The thought that in an emergency he can escape makes Hugo glad, and he sits and writes in his notebook:

Mama dear,
Mariana was fired, and she is about to pass me on to her friend Nasha. The contact between people here isn't soft. Everyone demands the impossible from others. Don't worry, it's not aimed at me. Mariana was fired because she drinks, and she really does drink a lot. Mariana promised me that she would look for a hiding place somewhere. I'm sure she'll do it. I won't conceal from you that there are days when I'm scared. In my heart I know that most of the fears are groundless. Everything around me here captivates my heart, and I forget the dangers. Most of the time I'm busy listening and making efforts to understand what I hear. The conjectures, I must truthfully confess, don't lead me far.
I feel that I'm changing. Mariana says that I'm matur-

ing. It's hard for me to know what's happening in my body. I've grown taller, it seems to me.

A few days ago the thought crossed my mind, and it's hard for me to get rid of it: What harm did the Jews do that everyone is persecuting them? Why do they have to take shelter in hiding places? Mariana says that the Jews are more delicate, and that, too, is something I can't understand. Are they persecuted because of delicacy? You and Papa always told me, "People are people, there's no difference among them, the same thoughts and the same pains."

At home we never talked about what it means to be Jewish. What do we have in us that makes us enemies of humanity? Several times I've heard people here saying, "The Jews are a danger to the world, and they have to be destroyed." I also heard one of Mariana's guests say, "Our war isn't against the Poles or against the Russians, but against the Jews." Opinions like that don't raise my spirits. I hope that those malicious intentions will never be carried out.

I think about you all the time,

Hugo

The next day the closet door opens, and Mariana stands there with a woman at her side.

"This is Hugo." Mariana introduces him.

Hugo rises to his feet, as though exposed and with no choice but to admit that he has been in hiding.

"This is my friend Nasha. Nasha will be your new friend from now on. She will watch over you and make sure you're not hungry. As soon as I get settled, I'll come and get you. I won't forget you, honey. Do you like him?" She turns to Nasha.

"Very much."

"He's not only sweet and lovable, he's also smart."

"Like all the Jews." Nasha chuckles in a thin, restrained voice.

"Nasha can keep secrets, and you can rely on her. Her grandpa was a priest."

"Don't remind me of that."

"I'm leaving my things with you, dear. When I make the right kind of arrangement, I'll come and get you."

Hugo feels more and more frozen with every passing minute. The words he intended to say are erased from his mind. Finally he asks, "Where are you going?"

"God knows."

"Take care of yourself," he says, and tears pour out onto his face.

"Don't cry, honey." Mariana draws Hugo close and hugs him. "You're a hero, and you're brave. Heroes don't cry. Heroes say, Mariana has to go, but she'll come back soon. Meanwhile, you'll fall in love with Nasha, and you won't want to come with me."

At first sight it's hard to figure out the new woman, but Hugo immediately notices: she is better groomed than Mariana.

"Goodbye, and we'll be seeing each other very soon," Mariana says, and kisses his face. That is the end of the transfer ceremony.

Hugo sits down and cries. He cries so much that he falls asleep and doesn't hear the closet door open. Nasha is standing at the doorway.

"I brought you soup and meatballs."

"Thank you." Hugo quickly rises to his feet.

"Did you sleep?"

"Yes."

"Your name is Hugo, right?"

"Correct."

"That's an unusual name. It's the first time I've heard that name."

"In my class there was another boy named Hugo."

"That's a Jewish name."

"Maybe. I don't know."

Nasha looks at him attentively, and Hugo feels her gaze surveying him.

"How is it to be in the closet? Aren't you cold?"

"Not anymore. It's spring, right?"

"And it's not boring for you?"

"I think or imagine things." He doesn't hide it from her.

"And that relieves boredom?"

"Apparently," Hugo says, using a word that his mathematics teacher used to use.

"And do you know what we do in this place?"

"Not exactly."

"Didn't Mariana tell you?"

"No."

"We'll talk about that later," Nasha says, and a thin smile spreads across her face.

Hugo knows that was a test. Did he pass? He has already noticed that Nasha is restrained. The words that come out of her mouth are few. Usually they are questions that reveal nothing about her. Mariana, by contrast, spat out words like boiling water.

29

Spring is at its fullest. Through the cracks, the smells of mown grass and flowers filter into the closet. Outside a great sun shines. The cows are brought out to pasture, and the pure tranquility heightens Hugo's longing for Mariana. Only now does he sense how close he was to her. At ten o'clock Nasha stands at the doorway to the closet with a cup of milk in her hand. "How did you sleep?" she asks in an impartial tone of voice.

"I slept well. It wasn't cold."

"What did you do?"

"I thought."

"What did you think about?"

"I thought about Mariana's fate."

"Her fate?" Nasha is surprised.

"I don't have any other word for it."

"You miss her?"

"Indeed."

"In that case, why not say, I miss her."

This is the first personal comment Hugo has heard from her.

Nasha shuts the closet door and begins tidying the room. Hugo can hear her movements, measured and restrained. Mariana hated mopping the floor and changing sheets. She usually neglected cleanliness, and people commented on that more than once.

Hugo soon notices that at night Nasha's guests don't make comments to her or get angry at her. Her voice is hardly heard. The visits conclude in a businesslike way, without ceremonies, and without the shouting that he was used to hearing with Mariana.

Since Mariana left, it has been hard for Hugo to write in the notebook. It seems to him that he doesn't have enough words, that he's concealing the truth. He wants very much to write everything that is happening in his soul, especially his longings for Mariana, but he's afraid his mother won't like that.

Hugo hasn't been in Mariana's room since she left. Now the domains are separate: Nasha is in the bedroom, and he is in the closet. Her way of speaking is moderate, and sometimes indifferent. Every once in a while a slight laugh breaks out, but there is no raising of the voice. Nevertheless, Hugo finds something that Mariana and Nasha have in common: at times Nasha also talks about herself in the third person.

"Today Nasha's going to inspect the room and her body," she announces. Hugo wants to ask what that means, but he withstands the temptation and doesn't ask. This time, in any event, she goes out of her way and reveals a bit to him, perhaps more than a bit. Unlike Mariana, she tidies the room thoroughly and washes for a long time.

Toward evening she brings him soup and meatballs and asks, "What did you do?"

"Nothing," Hugo says, and that's the truth. Since Mariana left him, he has been assailed by fear. It's hard for him to sink into thoughts or imaginings. All his thoughts are cut off. And the images in his memory aren't as clear as they had been. In the morning, Frieda appears before his eyes, trapped in the transport, waving her broad-brimmed hat as though parting from the world with a sarcastic laugh. Hugo wants to go back and examine that image more closely, but fear snatches the picture from before his eyes, and he can see only the transport now, and the people crammed into it. They have no faces, as though they are about to be swallowed in thick fog.

"Why don't you read?" Nasha stabs him without intending to.

"It's hard for me to concentrate." Hugo doesn't hide the truth from her.

"Have you tried?"

"I haven't even tried."

"Jews like to read, isn't that so?"

"Papa and Mama loved to immerse themselves in reading."

"My grandfather was a priest. He used to say, 'Learn from the Jews, they are the people of the book. There isn't a Jewish house without a library.' "

"In our house there's a big library." For a moment the pride of past days returns to him.

"And what happened to the books?"

"There's no one in the house."

Nasha speaks slowly, listens cautiously, and chooses her words carefully. Her gaze is concentrated, so as not to lose a movement or syllable. Sometimes it seems to Hugo that she is spreading traps around her so that he will be caught or fall.

He tries to learn her gestures, the rhythm of her words, but his efforts achieve nothing. *Nasha is a strange creature,* he concludes. *Who knows what secret she keeps in her soul?*

"Isn't it hard for you to live in the closet?" Nasha surprises him again.

"I've gotten used to it."

"You're a strong kid."

"I haven't done anything to justify that description."

"You have."

Every day she leaves him with a loaded word or an incomprehensible sentence. Hugo catches them, and for a long time he turns them over and over, until he becomes weary.

30

Hugo has already noticed that Nasha doesn't speak about her parents or about her sisters. Sometimes she mentions her grandfather, and it's clear that her connection with him was long-standing and close. Every time she mentions his name, she adds, "May he forgive me."

Hugo listens to Nasha so closely and observes her so intently that Mariana's face is erased, but not her scent. At night he sees her in the middle of a field of flowers, and she's drunk and happy, raising her hands to heaven and giving thanks out loud: "Thank you, God, for freeing me from prison. Now Mariana is on her own, just on her own, and no one can tell her what to do." She immediately kneels down, places her hands together, closes her eyes, crosses herself, and prays.

While she's praying, Hugo's mother appears, wearing a long coat that makes her look shorter, her face white and wrung out. For a moment she observes Mariana's prayers, kneels beside her, and waits for her to finish. When she has finished, his mother asks her, "Mariana, what are you doing here?" Hearing that question, Mariana shrinks down and says, "It wasn't my fault that they fired me."

"And where is Hugo?"

"Don't worry, he's in good hands, better hands than mine."

"Are they still searching for Jews?"

"Now the informers are digging in every hole. They are paid for every Jew."

"The Jews are a desirable commodity, I see. How is Hugo?"

"He's developed a lot since you left him. He's a young man in every sense. It's easy to fall in love with him."

"Good God." A shout bursts from his mother's breast.

"Why are you worried? The school of life is an institution that shouldn't be underestimated."

The dream breaks off, and Hugo awakens. Unlike Mariana, Nasha knows how to run her life with strict order. After a night of guests she sleeps until late afternoon. Then she tidies the room, showers, rubs her body with fragrant lotions, and when she appears toward evening she looks calm. She makes no complaints. Sometimes Hugo notices a few wrinkles of dissatisfaction on her face, or a smile mixed with repressed pain, but usually she's quiet or indifferent. Unlike Mariana, she doesn't hug or kiss him, doesn't praise him to the skies or use exaggerated endearments.

Sometimes she asks Hugo to mop the floor and clean the bathroom. The room that he continues to call "Mariana's room" has changed beyond recognition. It is without pictures, without the little decorative bottles on the dresser, and without the small marks of carelessness that indicate poor housekeeping.

The short time Hugo spends in Mariana's room, no longer free and on his own but as a servant, reminds him of Mariana's open face and of the nights he lay close to her. Sharp longings fill him. The day before, Nasha told him, "You have to tidy up the closet. You mustn't live in such disorder." Most of the objects in the closet are Mariana's clothes: robes, dresses, blouses, shoes, corsets, brassieres, and silk stockings. Mariana's clothes are also her. They continue to breathe without her in the thin darkness of the closet.

Every piece of clothing gives her a different form. The colorful garments brighten her face and arouse the joy that was in her. The gray and black clothes add gloom to her gloom. More than once she complained about the corsets and brassieres that constricted her. She used to stretch her leg forward while putting on her silk stockings, a gesture he loved from the first time he saw it. There are clothes she hadn't worn for a long time, and the odors have faded from them. But most of the clothes retain the smells of her body. Hugo brings them up to his nostrils, and Mariana's full being comes to life.

For a long time he sits and sorts. If there were a cupboard, he could arrange the clothes on shelves, but since there isn't one, he places them folded on the bench.

Hugo shows the arrangement to Nasha, and she's pleased. But her satisfaction isn't enthusiastic. When she's pleased, she says, "Acceptable" or "Fine." Unlike Mariana, she guards her emotions and doesn't reveal them. When Hugo compliments her clothes or her hairdo, she isn't moved but says, "Nice of you to notice."

One evening she turns to Hugo and says, "I have a request of you. Help me cut my toenails. It's hard for me to cut them and hard for me to put polish on them."

Hugo is surprised. He didn't imagine she would address such a request to him. "With pleasure," he says.

Nasha's feet and ankles are pretty and delicate, and he cuts her toenails carefully and gently, as she instructs him.

"In our profession, our feet are the front," she says with a guarded smile. Hugo doesn't understand the exact meaning of that sentence. The contact with her, in any event, gives him no pleasure, maybe because she doesn't thank him but says, "Very good," and immediately adds, "Beyond the demands of the profession, it's a good idea to look presentable. Did your parents insist on looking well?"

"My parents are pharmacists."

"Untidiness drives me crazy, and here no one insists on order and cleanliness."

"Why?" Hugo asks carelessly.

"Because everybody is only concerned with himself."

That night he hears one of the guests say, "Now there are no more Jews here. They've all reached their destination, and we'll pull out those who are in hiding one by one. We managed to cleanse the region of Jews. Now it's possible to breathe."

"Have they all gone away?" asks Nasha.

"Without an exception."

"And now there won't be any more Jews?"

"We did our duty, once and for all."

Hugo understands most of what the man says, and what he doesn't understand, he guesses. But he consoles himself with the thought that his mother is hiding in a distant, unknown village. There her childhood friend is watching over her, the way Mariana and Nasha are watching over him.

31

In the morning, Hugo awakens in a panic: Mariana's room is in an uproar. It's hard to know what the commotion is about. For a moment it seems to him that soldiers are making searches, and the women are trying to block their way to the closet. Hugo gets to his feet and is about to slip out through the opening alongside the toilet. Meanwhile, the commotion becomes weeping. From the weeping arises Nasha's name.

Hugo hears, and his body shrinks. For a long time the weeping continues, but gradually it goes somewhere else. A few women remain in the corridor and speak with strange practicality. From what they say he understands that a disaster has befallen Nasha. They don't talk about its nature.

Hugo sits in his place and sees before him Nasha's long, white legs and the toenails he trimmed and painted with nail polish. He had noticed then that, unlike Mariana, Nasha didn't bare her legs easily. It was as though she was afraid of being hurt. All the while Hugo was cutting her nails, she bit her lower lip, and when he finished putting on the nail polish, she folded her legs with a motion that showed fear of pain that might come.

Later he hears one of the women say breathlessly, "After she finished her work, she left her room. She was wearing a warm coat, her hair was neat, she was wearing makeup, and she showed no sign of anything bad to come. The guard was sure she was going to town to visit her cousin and buy a package of chocolates in the bakery, the way she sometimes did."

"Still, who witnessed her drowning?" the woman is asked.

"A fisherman. He saw her jump into the water and tried to pull her out, but he didn't manage to. The current was too strong."

"Where is she now?"

"Have you any more questions like that?" the woman replies angrily.

Suddenly the voice of another woman is heard. She speaks deliberately but not without emotion, telling how Nasha had begun to work there more than a year earlier, and how she had adapted to the place. "A modest woman and loyal to her friends. If a friend didn't feel well, or needed help, Nasha was the first one to help her. She helped without expecting anything in return. She never said, I gave to you, I helped you, you're ungrateful.

"Her grandfather was a priest, and she apparently inherited her virtues from him. She never complained, not about her friends and not about the clients. She suffered in silence, with nobility. She didn't go to church, but God was in her heart. Too bad we didn't know how to watch over her. She gave to everyone, and no one gave anything to her."

"Why did she take her own life?"

"She was apparently very lonely. Lonelier than the rest of us. She never spoke about her parents or about her sisters. She always mentioned her grandfather. She would say, 'A man of God in the full sense of the word.' "

"And did she have guilt feelings?"

"I guess so, but she never talked about it. She was very restrained. Once she said to me, 'What won't people do to earn a living?' She didn't express disgust or revulsion, the way we all do. She did her work every day without complaining about headaches or stomachaches. More than once I said to myself, *Nasha is strong, she's contemptuous of us.* It turns out I was wrong."

Hugo hears the voices, and as he listens, he sees the rushing water envelop her pure legs. What will be, and how will his life proceed from now on? He doesn't know. He imagines that toward evening Nasha will surprise everyone and stand in the doorway, saying, *The fisherman was wrong. It wasn't me. Here I am standing before you.* In the end she will tell them, *I was in Grandpa's church, and I went up to his grave. He took me in his open arms and called me "my daughter."*

Thus Hugo sits in the corner and dreams. Meanwhile, The Residence returns to its ordinary pace. The regular questions are asked, and the regular answers come in their wake. Suddenly an older woman's voice is heard: "How much should I make?"

"Thirty portions, no more."

"Sandwiches, too?"

"Of course."

Hunger torments him, and he waits tensely for Nasha's arrival.

Toward evening the closet door opens, and Victoria stands in the doorway. "What are you doing?" she asks, as though he was again caught doing something naughty.

"Nothing," he says, and stands up.

"Nasha drowned in the river, and you sit there as though everything is coming to you."

"I didn't know," he lies.

"Nasha drowned, and I don't know who they're going to put in her room. Not everyone will want to watch over you. It's risky to watch over you. You're endangering all of us. Do you understand?"

"Yes."

"If there are more searches, you'll have to get out of here. We can't keep you anymore."

"Where will I go?"

"To the forest. There are Jews in the forest."

"And who will watch over Mariana's clothes?"

"That's no concern of yours."

Later, Victoria brings him soup and meatballs and leaves. Hugo sinks completely into the tasty food. The terrors and fears that tortured him all day long depart. He recovers and says to himself, *If I have to run away, I'll run away. Now it's summer, and the nights are warm. There's fruit in the forest. The farmers won't identify me. I'm blond. I'm wearing a cross on my chest, and I speak fluent Ukrainian. In the forest I'll find Mariana, and we'll live together in nature, far from people and their scheming.*

32

The following days are tense: the women in The Residence quarrel and weep bitter tears. Nasha's death continues to shake their hearts.

"The evil fish ate her flesh," a voice of despair is heard saying in the corridor. Victoria's opinion is different: "Now Nasha is in heaven, and good angels escort her from place to place. There's nothing to worry about. She's in good shape now. If only we were, too." But she speaks to Hugo in a different tone of voice: "You have to run away. If you don't run away, we'll chase you away."

"I'm waiting for Mariana."

"There's nothing for you to wait for. She won't come. You have to go to the forest. There are still Jews there."

Hugo disdains the fear that has gripped him, but it is stronger than he is. At night he dreams he is with his parents on the express train that makes its way to the Carpathians. They are covered with snow. The train stops, as always, at the station that everybody calls "The Peak." Hugo clamps his skis onto his boots and skis straight from the platform. The skiing is smooth, and he feels his whole body soaring. His father, who is skiing behind him, calls out, "Hugo, you're skiing wonderfully. You've improved a lot since the last time we were here. Where did you learn? That didn't happen by itself." Encouraged by his father's words, Hugo increases his speed and soars over the snow. He says in a loud voice, "I've overcome fear. Now I'm not afraid anymore."

The next day Victoria speaks to Hugo sternly. "They're searching for Jews from house to house. You're endangering us all. You have a few more hours to get your knapsack ready, crawl out through the hole, and disappear. If you don't, the guard will deliver you to the police."

"And where will I go?" His voice trembles.

"I've already told you—to the forest. There are Jews in the forest. Don't be a coward. Take a risk and live. Whoever doesn't take a risk—fear kills him."

"I'll go tonight," Hugo says.

"If I open the closet tomorrow morning and find you, your blood is on your own head."

That is the verdict, and he pictures the guard dragging him.

In his heart Hugo decides that he'll leave the suitcase, the Jules Verne and Karl May books, and the arithmetic and geometry books. He'll take some warm clothes, the notebook, and the Bible. *If God wants me to come back here, I'll find everything in its place, but if He wants me to stay in the forest, there's nothing to be done.* The words roll about in his head. Later he realizes that this is Mariana's way of speaking, and he has adopted it.

For some reason Sofia, his parents' housekeeper, appears before his eyes. She stood in palpable contradiction to all the ideas that were prevalent in his house. Her country manners, her religiosity, her personal beliefs, and her arbitrariness bespoke a confidence in herself and her way of life. Doubts never clouded her spirit. More than once she had said, "The Jews are too thoughtful. I never saw a Jew give his anger free reign. Why don't Jews get angry?" Often, when she came back from church, Hugo would hear her say, "Why don't you go to a house of worship? I come back from church a new woman. The prayers, the music, the sermon bind me to God and His Messiah. Don't you long for God?"

"We long," his father would answer, half seriously, half facetiously.

"If so, why do you stay at home on the Sabbath?"

"God is everywhere, at home, too. Isn't that what they say?" His father tried to answer cleverly.

Hearing that, Sofia would wave her arm as if to say, *Those are just excuses.* Sometimes she would add, "The Jews are a strange nation. I'll never understand them."

Sofia was full of vitality, and his parents liked her. They used to buy her a present for every holiday, or they'd give her some money so she could buy something for herself. About a month before the German invasion, she had gone back to her village. Hugo's mother supplied her with clothing and severance pay. Sofia cried like a child and asked, "Why am I leaving you? You're better to me than my parents and my sisters."

"You can stay," his mother immediately responded.

"I swore to my parents that I'd come back. I can't violate that oath."

All three of them accompanied Sofia to the railroad station, and they didn't leave until she was seated next to the window.

Hugo rouses himself from his daydream. It's two in the morning. The lair called "the closet," where he has been imprisoned for about a year, now seems to him like a refuge that not only protected him but also nourished him with enchanted images. Every time he crawls down the opening near the toilet and goes outside, the darkness seems thick and full of hostility.

Time is quickly passing, but Hugo doesn't hurry. Mariana's clothes, filling the closet and covering its walls, are precious to him now, as though they belong to his inner world. If he is going to die, better to die here and not outside, he says to himself, without properly considering what he's talking about.

At four o'clock Hugo shoves the knapsack through the opening and crawls down after it. Darkness cushions the bottom of the fence and the tree trunks. Pale patches of light are already scattered in the sky. Hugo could easily climb the fence and reach the field, but his feet refuse to obey. He stands in place and doesn't move. Finally he goes into the woodshed and curls up in a corner.

33

Hugo sits and awaits the guard's footsteps. Once he saw him through the cracks; a tall, broad-shouldered man, he was reviling one of the women: "You're just what you are. Clear out and go to your room."

"I won't go. I don't take orders from you," she shouted at him.

"If I hear one more word, I'll crush you," he said, and he demonstrated with his fingers.

Hugo feels sorry for himself, because he's going to be crushed in the guard's powerful hands and he'll never see his parents again. But to get up and jump over the fence into the thick darkness—his legs refuse to do it. He takes the notebook out of the knapsack and writes:

Dear Papa and Mama,
Some time ago I left the closet. Mariana didn't come back to me as she promised, and the cook, Victoria, threatened to turn me in. I have no choice but to escape to the forest. Now I'm sitting in the woodshed and preparing myself to leave. Don't worry, I'll get to the forest and I'll find shelter there, but if fortune doesn't favor me, and I'm caught or I disappear, you should know that you were in my thoughts all the time.

Hugo returns the notebook to the knapsack and tears flood his face.

The sky changes hue, and pink rays break through the horizon. From the woodshed he can see the meadows and the house wrapped in vines. From Mariana's room, he saw only parts of them, and now they are revealed in full. *I'm beginning a new life,* he says as he gathers his strength.

While Hugo is standing at the entrance to the woodshed, preparing to throw the knapsack over the fence and then jump over after it, a desperate voice is heard calling, "Hugo, Hugo, where are you?" For a moment he's afraid it's an illusion, but the voice is heard again, with the same desperate tone.

"I'm here," he answers.

"I can't see you."

"I'm outside."

"Come back to me."

He approaches the opening and crawls back in. When he pokes his head out of the darkness, he sees Mariana kneeling.

"Mariana," he whispers.

"Good God, why did you go outside?"

"Victoria threatened to turn me in."

Even in the darkness he can see how much she has changed. Her face has become narrow, her hair is pulled back, and her eyes are sunken. The way she holds him in her arms is also different. "I've stopped drinking," she says, and lowers her head.

Hugo doesn't hold back and kisses her face.

"I had some hard days, and I decided to dry out and come back here. Here I have my own room, food, and a salary. Outside they abused me."

Hugo remembers her previous declines, but not one like this. Mariana tells him that for a week not a drop has passed her lips. Drying out depresses her, but she has no choice.

"I'll help you," he says.

"Without brandy, my life isn't worth living. All the joy and all the desire for life have abandoned me, but I have no choice. Outside they persecuted me like a mangy dog."

Hugo holds her hand, kisses it, and says, "Don't worry, Mariana. I'll do whatever you tell me to do."

"I thank you very much," she says in a voice unlike any he has heard her utter.

Mariana immediately starts tidying the room, mopping the floor, and returning the pictures to the shelves. Her image once again looks out from every corner—young and full of lust for life.

"What did you do during the days I wasn't here?"

"I sat in the corner and thought about you."

"I looked for someplace that would be right for us, but I couldn't find anything. I wandered from place to place, and everywhere they recognized me and persecuted me, the way that hypocrite Victoria was abusing you. What were you going to do?"

"Run away to the forest to look for you."

"My hero."

In the afternoon, Mariana runs a bath for Hugo and says, "Now I'll wash my man. I abandoned him for a long time, and now he'll be mine again." For a moment her old tone of voice comes back to her, and the light returns to her face.

That night Hugo sleeps with Mariana in the big bed. Her soft body and her perfumes surround him with sharp pleasure. "You're mine, you're all mine. Men are bullies and coarse in spirit, and only you are strong and sweet." Thus, with a wave of her hand, Mariana drives away the darkness, which just a few hours earlier was about to smother him.

34

But over the next few days, there is no light. Mariana keeps saying that without brandy she'll go out of her mind. The guests don't complain about her, but some of them say, "What's the matter with you? Where has the fire in you gone?"

Mariana is suffering, and Hugo can feel it in everything she does. She scrubs the room every day, and shakes out the mattress and the blankets. Hugo notices that her movements are fierce, and that when she lights a cigarette, her fingers tremble.

Mariana's guests are soldiers and officers, and Hugo soon learns that the war is going badly for them now. Many soldiers are being sent to the front. Once he hears one of them tell her, "Tomorrow they're sending me to the East. Take this ring with my name engraved on it. I passed the nicest hours of this cursed war with you."

Hearing his words, Mariana bursts into tears.

"Why are you crying?"

"I feel sorry for you," she says, and cries some more.

One evening she brings Hugo a bottle of brandy and says, "You'll watch over it. You won't let me drink too much. I'll sip a little before my morning sleep, and a little at night, when I don't have clients. You'll be on watch and say to me, Mariana, now you're not allowed to drink. You're smart and know exactly when I'm allowed to drink and when it's forbidden. I lose track. You'll be my bookkeeper."

Hugo knows in his heart that the job is a thankless one, and the day is not far when Mariana will say, *Don't mix in, don't tell me what to do.* But he does what she wants and says, "I'll watch over the bottle, and if it's necessary, I'll remind you."

That night Hugo dreams he's in a field full of flowers and trees, and his parents are sitting by his side. They used to take day trips to the Carpathians every season. Their favorites were the spring and the summer. They would explore and would wonder at the landscapes. Then they would sit on the ground and eat a light meal, speaking little. The wagon driver would wait for them next to one of the tall trees. He usually drank a drop too much and became merry.

On the way back, he would joke about the Jews, who don't drink and always retain their sanity. "Sanity, you should know, Doctor," he said to Hugo's father, "does not always help in life. Too much sanity spoils the flavor of life. You take three or four drinks, and you're immediately in a world where everything is good."

"Excessive drinking is harmful to your health," Hugo's father would respond.

"Even somebody who takes care of his health will get sick in the end."

"Lying in hospital isn't a pleasure I'd wish on myself."

"Sooner or later everybody ends up there," the wagon driver would crow victoriously.

Hugo's father liked the wagon drivers. He would listen to their wishes and their confessions, and sometimes he tried to deflate somewhat their baseless self-assurance. But of course nothing worked, and they stuck to their guns. They were planted like boulders in their way of thinking. At the end of the argument, they would say, "The Jews are stubborn, a stiff-necked people. You can't change their minds."

Hearing that, Hugo's father would burst out laughing and say, "You're right."

"What good does it do me to be right?" the driver would say, and then join in the laughter.

This time, in his dream, it's different. Hugo's mother looks at him in wonderment, as if to say, *Why won't you tell me what happened to you?*

Hugo recovers and says, "What is there to tell? I was in Mariana's closet."

"I know that. After all, I'm the one who brought you to her. But what did you see there, and what did you hear, and how did the days pass for you?"

"That's a long story," he replies ambiguously.

"Will we ever hear the whole story from you?"

"What is there to tell?" He tries again to evade her.

"Everything interests us," his mother says in a tone familiar to him.

"There were days as long as the underworld and days as short as a breeze," says Hugo, glad that he found the words.

"I didn't imagine I would be able to come here again," his mother says.

"It's impossible to forget summers in the Carpathians." Language returns to Hugo.

"Thank God we're together."

"Do you believe in God?" Hugo is glad he can ask questions, and not only be the one asked.

"Why do you ask?"

"In our earlier life, I never heard you say, 'Thank God.' "

"My mother, your grandmother, would sometimes say,

'Thank God.' Now I allow myself to speak in her words. Is that a sin?"

Here Hugo's father intervenes. He is dressed in his white suit, which gives a simple elegance to his height.

"One doesn't easily acquire beliefs or change them," he says. "I've remained as I was."

"I can't believe my ears," says Hugo's mother, and she raises her head.

"Did you change?" his father asks in a tone intended to relieve the tension in the air.

"It seems to me that we've all changed. You were in a labor camp for about two years, and you built the bridges over the Bug River. Hugo was with Mariana, and I worked like a slave in the fields. Could it be that all of this didn't change us?"

"I feel that I've grown older, but not that I've changed," replies Hugo's father.

"As for me," says Hugo, touching the cross on his chest, "this cross saved me."

That statement makes his parents fall silent, and they stand in astonishment at their son's words. It's clear they won't go on to ask what or why.

35

Mariana's torments as she tries to dry out extend through the whole day. Every morning, after breakfast, Hugo hands her the bottle, and she takes a few long gulps, saying, "You're my secret, you're my elixir of life, you keep me alive." For caution's sake, she splashes perfume on her body and clothes. "No one will notice that I drank," she says.

When Mariana is sad or depressed, it's hard for her to restrain herself. "Just one sip," she says, "and no more." Hugo hands her the bottle, and she drinks and whispers, "Hide the bottle fast, so that I won't see it." And when her friends discover that she has had a drink, they rebuke her. "Have you sinned again?"

"Just a sip."

"Be careful," they warn, "Madam has a sense of smell like a dog's."

Sometimes her friend Kitty comes into her room. Kitty is very short, and she looks like a girl who ended up there by mistake on the way home from school. She is charming and cheerful, and she amuses her friends. She has, it seems, customers who are hers and hers alone.

Kitty likes to tell about her experiences, and she sometimes talks about them at length and in detail. Mariana and her friends don't talk about theirs. Their impressions are usually summed up in a single word or a short sentence, *A beast, disgusting, horrid; what do you expect from an unbridled bull? I feel like vomiting.* Only rarely do you hear, *He brought me a box of candy, he told me about his house in Salzburg.*

Hugo learns from them that there is a special unit in the city that hunts down Jews. Every week they find a few. Mainly the Jews are executed, but some are interrogated and tortured until they reveal their friends' hiding places. The Germans intend to kill them down to the very last one, Hugo hears, and he shivers.

One day the closet door opens, and Kitty is standing in the entrance. "I came to see you. Mariana has told me a lot about you."

Hugo rises to his feet and doesn't know what to say.

"Good Lord, you're my height. How old are you?"

"In a little while I'll be twelve."

"I'm twice your age, even a bit more. What do you do all day?"

"Nothing. What is there to do here?"

"Don't you read? Jews liked to read, isn't that so?"

"I think, and sometimes I imagine things."

"Are you afraid?"

"No."

"Mariana told me about you. She likes you."

"And are you content here?" he dares to ask.

"This is my life," she says with a simplicity that touches his heart. After a pause, she adds, "I'm an orphan. I've been an orphan for twenty years. This is my home. Here I have friends."

"Don't you have sisters?"

"I'm an only child," she says and chuckles.

In the school where Hugo studied, there were some girls Kitty's height, with the same look. But Kitty isn't a girl. She reminds him, for some reason, of Frieda, who also had a girlish face. The last time he saw her, she was crushed among the deportees, waving her straw hat.

"Aren't you bored?"

"No."

"I would be bored. I need friends. You're a good-looking boy, and it's no wonder that Mariana likes you."

"I help her." Hugo tries to diminish his status.

"How?"

"In whatever way I can."

"That's good of you," says Kitty. "I'll come to visit you again. Now I have to go."

"Did I disappoint you?"

"No. Not at all. You're a good-looking, smart boy. I was curious and so I came to see you." She smiles and locks the closet door.

Hugo takes out the Bible and reads the story of Joseph. He immediately visualizes Joseph as a slightly built prince, dressed in a striped coat. His brothers are earthy and coarse of spirit, and their eyes disclose that they are out to harm him. Strangely, Joseph ignores their plots. He is immersed in his princely world. Every time his brothers speak, he smiles, as though he has uncovered their dark interior. In his heart he knows that his brothers would not hesitate to murder him, but he ignores them purposely, and in so doing he expresses his contempt for them.

Reading and thinking about what he has read restores to Hugo, without his realizing it, some of the life he had lost. Before his eyes he sees his German teacher, a converted Jew, who used to formulate ideas clearly. Franz and Anna were his favorites. But it seems to Hugo that the dark days in the closet have secretly taught him things that he lacked, and that when school resumes, he, too, will be able to express his thoughts tersely, without getting tangled up in pointless details.

That little discovery pleases him.

36

The harvest is over. Wagons laden with straw roll along the dirt roads. Hugo sits and watches them. The more he looks, the more he knows that he once saw laden wagons like that during a golden summer along the Prut, but where it was and under what circumstances, he can't remember. That forgetting pains him. Not long ago he saw his parents standing right next to him, at their full height, and now they are just passing shadows. Every time he tries to visualize them, they slip away or are covered with darkness. Their voices, too, which were bright and clear, have faded.

Mariana keeps saying—as always, with repressed anger—that her body can't withstand this pressure for long. She speaks about her body as a being that she has no control over. Once she says to Hugo, "My body has calmed down a bit. Apparently it's restrained itself." Mainly she reviles it and calls it "loathsome flesh." She speaks of her breasts as udders that have been milked without end. Once she surprises Hugo and says, "It's no wonder the priest says, 'Abandon flesh, for today it is here and tomorrow it is under the earth. Think about your soul and about the kingdom of heaven.' "

Every few days little Kitty comes in and asks how he is. Hugo's hidden life makes her curious. "What do you think about?" she asks, and apparently she expects a long answer. Hugo tells her something that he hasn't even revealed to Mariana. In the spring he saw his parents in his imagination, but now they have gone away from him. "What does that mean?" he asks.

"Don't worry. They'll come back to you," she says in a soft voice.

"How do you know?" Hugo asks, and immediately knows that he shouldn't have.

"Mine also went away from me, but now they've come back. Almost every night I see them in a dream."

"Do they come to you from the other world?"

"That's right. I'm happy to greet them."

Kitty doesn't probe too much. She tells him there are rumors that the war will be over soon. All the soldiers that were posted permanently in the city have been sent to the front.

"And they're not hunting down Jews anymore?" Hugo inquires.

"There is a small unit that has stayed behind and is looking for Jews. They always find one or two, shackle their hands, and bring them through the city streets. They look very miserable. In a little while the war will be over and the nightmare will be finished."

Hugo likes to hear Kitty's voice. Even though she's twenty-four, it reminds him of the voices of the girls in his school.

"And you're really a Jew?" She surprises him again.

"Correct. Why are you asking?"

"You look like one of us, just like one of us."

"I'm a Jew. It can't be denied," Hugo says, and chuckles.

Kitty looks at him fondly and says, "For years I dreamed I would have a brother like you, tall, with curly hair, and talking the way you talk."

"I'm willing to be your brother."

"Thanks," she says, and blushes.

Every meeting with Kitty leaves a kind of pleasure in him and becomes part of his imagination. Once he dreams he is strolling next to a river with her, and suddenly Kitty announces that she is thinking of fleeing from The Residence and living in the country. She's fed up with the fat guests. "If you want, we could go away together. I assume that you're also fed up with life in the cage."

"And what will I say to Mariana?"

"Tell Mariana that you're fed up with the cage. You're a boy like all the other boys. You didn't sin or commit a crime, and you're allowed to live outdoors."

"Won't the Germans hunt me down?"

"You're my brother, and you look like me." She laughs.

Hugo wakes up and finds Mariana sitting by his side.

"Give me a sip, honey. I didn't want to disturb you, so I waited for you to wake up. You sleep very beautifully. It's just a pleasure to watch you in your sleep. That's how puppies sleep."

"You should have woken me. You shouldn't suffer too much," Hugo says, and is surprised at himself.

"I wanted to know how long I could bear this torment."

Hugo hands her the bottle. Mariana takes a long swig and immediately takes another.

"Take the bottle and hide it," she says, and gets to her feet. "Let's hope there won't be any guests tonight. They're getting fewer, thank God, but there are some who come back here and don't forget to comment that my breath smells of brandy. I'm waiting desperately for the end of the war, and then we'll be free. You'll get out of the closet, and I'll get out of The Residence. It's better to hoe a cornfield than to be crushed night after night. My hero, why am I bothering your head? The day will come when you'll say to yourself, Mariana was as crazy as a coot."

37

The summer is dying. The fields that just yesterday were golden are now harvested, barren, and gloomy. The nights are cold, and Hugo covers himself under the sheepskins. Once a week Mariana washes him. That time is very pleasant, and it fills him with a secret feeling that stays within him all week long.

At night, when Mariana has no guests, she invites Hugo into her bed, hugs him, and says, "You're Mariana's. You're her man. All men are bastards. Only you truly love her."

When fortune favors him, he sleeps in her embrace the whole night. But on some nights an unexpected guest knocks on her door, and he must crouch down and creep into the closet. All the warm pleasure evaporates, as though it had never existed. Searing humiliation remains.

Between morning and evening light, Mariana is tormented. She lists her torments one by one. "The soldiers treat me like a mattress and make me do disgusting things. When I drank brandy, I could stand that humiliation, but without brandy, every limb of my body is despised and painful." Hugo can't grasp all of her feelings, but he sees the trembling of her hands. More than anything else, that tremor says, *It's impossible for me to bear all the men who follow one after the other. The time has come to flee, and it doesn't matter where.*

Hugo feels that he must save her. "I'll run away with you," he says. "We'll live in the country, just you and I."

"People will recognize me and beat me." Mariana reverts to her old fears.

"We'll run away to places where they won't recognize us."

"Are you sure?" she asks, as if he has the answer.

"My heart tells me that you need brandy. In the mountains, by ourselves and without threats, you'll be able to drink as much as you want."

"You understand Mariana, and you love her," she says, and gives him a quick hug.

Every time Mariana decides to leave The Residence, something happens that holds her back. A few days ago Paula fainted and was sent to the hospital. Her situation got worse, and Madam refused to pay the hospital bills. For its part, the hospital threatened to transfer Paula to the poorhouse, where abandoned people quickly died. There was a general mobilization. Everybody talked about saving Paula as a holy deed. They collected money and jewelry, and there was a great moment of reconciliation. A specialist was called in, and he brought Paula back to life. Everybody celebrated her recovery with drinking and song. Madam threatened to fire all the revelers. Everybody was drunk and merry and had sealed their ears to her threats, but when Madam announced that she was going to police headquarters, they sobered up and stopped.

That very day Paula's condition worsened, and she died that night. Gloom and helplessness fell upon The Residence, but there were no recriminations or calls for rebellion.

"Paula departed because we ignored her pain, and when we were roused, it was too late. People are no different from animals. They live only for themselves." Mariana spoke with a cold objectivity that terrified Hugo.

Hugo notices that when Mariana speaks about God and about His Messiah, she forms her sentences in the negative: "God doesn't love Mariana. If He loved her, He wouldn't torture her. He would show her the true path." Another frequent comment is: "Mariana deserves it. In all of her ways she is rebellious, as the priest says." And another: "I didn't know how to love my parents, as God commanded, and I became addicted to dubious pleasures. God sees everything and hears everything, and He punishes people for their actions. I bear a burden of shame. I haven't yet gotten a tenth of what I deserve."

Once he heard her say, "Jesus, take me to you. I'm fed up with this life." But when a guest was good to her, when he gave her extra banknotes or a box of candy, she forgot her trials. She washed, made herself up, put on a colorful dress and high-heeled shoes, and stood up straight in the center of the room. "How do I look?" she would ask.

"You're marvelous," Hugo would say, to flatter her.

"It's wrong to complain too much. Not everything is black," she would say in moderate tones. When Mariana is content, Hugo also comes out of his shell, and his world expands.

When the last of the guests have left the room, Mariana stays in bed and sinks into a deep sleep. Sometimes she sleeps until twilight. Hugo is tortured by hunger, but he's careful not to disturb her. When she wakes up, she hurries to bring him a hot meal, apologizing and scolding herself. "I neglected my heart's beloved. I deserve a whipping."

One day she told him, "It will be different when we're together in a secluded place. I have to gather strength. I need a little push, and we'll take off. Don't despair, Hugo, we'll do it, and in the nicest way. Nature is the most suitable place for

Mariana. People drive her out of her mind. It's hard for me to bear their hypocrisy and cruelty. I love birds. I'm willing to give my life for them. A little bird that pecks at bread crumbs in your hand is part of God above. For a moment you become weightless, and you can fly away with it." She then fell silent. It was clear to Hugo that those words weren't hers, but that someone else had put them in her mouth.

38

Thus the days pass. Hugo celebrates his twelfth birthday with Mariana. She takes a few swallows from the bottle and announces, "Today you've finally reached maturity. Today you're a man. But not like all other men. You, unlike them, will be a gentleman—generous and loyal to all those who love you. Remember, nature gave you the right height, a charming appearance, and a sensitive heart. Life, I feel, won't be hard on you anymore. You like to observe, to think, to imagine. Without a doubt you'll be an artist. It's right for an artist to be handsome. One day Mariana will appear in your imagination, and you'll want to paint her. You know her body and her soul. Don't paint her as a miserable woman. I don't want to be fixed in your memory in the image of a wretched woman. Remember, Mariana struggles like a lioness every night with wild men. Engrave Mariana in your memory as a fighting woman. Do you promise me?"

In recent days Hugo has felt an agitation in his body, and when Mariana hugs him, the pleasure grows stronger. It seems to Hugo that this is a feeling it's forbidden to express openly, but

when he is lying in Mariana's embrace in bed, he allows himself
to kiss her neck.

"What's happening to me?" The words slip out of his
mouth.

"You've matured, and you're a man. In a little while you'll
understand some of the secrets of life."

Hugo has noticed that Mariana looks at him now with a
certain smile, and every time he draws near her, she opens her
arms and encircles him.

The days of mourning for Paula do not pass easily. In the corridor and in their rooms they speak about Paula's mother, who
wanted to have Paula buried next to her daughter, and about
Paula's former husband, who got so drunk that he scratched his
face and shouted, "I'm a scoundrel. I'm worthless. I'm the
worst of the worst. I had a gift from heaven and I didn't know
how to keep it. In hell they'll roast me. I deserve it, and you
shouldn't feel sorry for me."

But more than anything, they speak about Paula's funeral.
Observing her friends who came to see her off to the world of
truth, the priest raised his voice and called out, "Wanton
women, return to your Father who is in heaven. God knows
man's soul and his frivolous mind. God, unlike human beings,
forgives. Return to Him this very day."

Paula's death leaves an impression that doesn't fade. The
women mention things in her name, speak about her devotion
to her mother, and constantly talk about her mortal illness.
Hugo hears it all, and the cemetery appears before his eyes with
its many crosses, the shouts of grief ringing in his ears.

One night Hugo dreams about his last birthday party at
home. He sees Anna and Otto, his mother, who with the last
remnant of her strength had tried to make the guests happy,
and the guest with the accordion who had worn a heavy coat

and had tried to coax music out of the reluctant instrument. The guests hadn't sat down, as was customary, but stood, with cups of tea in their hands. His mother went from person to person and apologized. At that moment it hadn't seemed like a birthday party, but like a silent assembly where everyone expected everyone else to open his mouth with ancient words of prayer. No one came forward, and no one prayed. The guests looked at one another, wondering whether they would see each other again.

The cold rouses Hugo from his dream. It's quiet. From Mariana's room friendly murmurs are heard. This time he isn't envious or angry. His sorrow at having been taken away from his home and his parents is stronger than envy and rasps him inside. Only after he rises to his feet and stands next to the cracks in the wall do the tears flood his eyes.

Mariana doesn't like it when he cries. She once criticized him about it. "A man doesn't cry," she said. "Only children and women cry." Since then he has stopped crying, but sometimes the tears overwhelm him.

Toward morning Hugo hears one of the women tell the guard, "Last night they caught a lot of Jews. They found them in a cellar and ordered them to crawl on the road. Anyone who didn't crawl right was shot."

"We thought there were no more Jews left," says the guard noncommitally.

"There are a lot. They're hiding."

"Nothing can help them."

"People fight for their lives as long as their soul is in them."

"The Jews love life too much," the guard says in a flat, metallic voice.

39

The closet door opens, and Kitty stands in the doorway with a small package in her hands. "I brought you a chocolate bar," she says, and hands him the gift.

"Thank you," says Hugo, rising to his feet.

It's afternoon, and the autumn light falls on her small figure. It brings out her pleasant features, and now Hugo notices again that she is his height.

"What do you do?" she asks, as she has already.

"Nothing special."

"Don't you miss your friends?"

Hugo shrugs his shoulders as if to say, *What can I do?*

"When I miss my friends, I take a little vacation and go to visit them," Kitty says, revealing the extent of her innocence.

"Is it far?" Hugo asks, wanting to give her a chance to talk.

"About an hour by train, perhaps a little less."

"I'm not allowed to leave here."

Hearing his answer, Kitty smiles, as though she has finally understood something complicated.

The other women speak about Kitty as a girl who hasn't matured or developed. The child within her dug itself in and refuses to leave. Most of the women like her and treat her like a young relative who must be protected, but there are a few women who can't stand her. She arouses uncontrollable anger in them, and every time they run into her, they curse her and call her strange names. Once Hugo saw one of the women attack her in the courtyard. Kitty was standing near the fence, bent over, and her expression said simply, *Why are you angry at me? What did I do?*

"You're still asking why? Get out of here. We don't want to see you."

Mariana also thinks that Kitty is out of place in The Residence. "She's innocent, and even her curiosity doesn't suit the place. She annoys the women with her questions. The Residence isn't a place for women like her. She should learn a profession, work, or get married. Her place is not here."

It's hard for Hugo to understand that tangle, but he has learned to understand Mariana a bit better. Most of the day she restrains herself and suffers, and when Hugo hands her the bottle, she drinks and says, "How good it is that I have you. You're my heaven." The praise embarrasses him, and he wants to say a few consoling words to her, but he can't find them.

During the past weeks Hugo has felt very close to Mariana. "You're maturing," she kept saying. "In a little while you'll be a sturdy, loving man." Nighttime in Mariana's bed was a giddiness of pleasures that stayed with him all day long.

While Hugo is deep in his imagination, the closet door opens and Victoria stands in the doorway. She is stunned and says, "Are you still here?"

"Mariana watches over me," the fear within him replies.

"You're endangering us all," Victoria says, the anger visible in her brow.

"I'll go soon."

"You already promised and didn't keep it."

"This time I will," he says, trying to evade her furious eyes.

"We'll see," Victoria says, and closes the door.

That's a threat, and Hugo knows it. The thought that Victoria will inform on him and that soldiers will come and surround the house becomes more palpable with every passing moment. Hugo is so frightened that he checks the escape hatch twice and sips a few drops from Mariana's bottle. He feels dizzy and immediately falls asleep. Toward evening Mariana comes to the doorway with a bowl of soup in her hand. Hugo tells her that Victoria has come to the closet, and that her words were harsh and evil.

"Don't worry. We're going to leave this place soon."

"Where will we go?"

"Anywhere, just not here."

Life here is tense and constricted, and Hugo wants very much to write the details down in his notebook. But the words, for some reason, aren't within his reach. It's now clear to him, though not with a clarity that can be garbed in words, that everything that has happened around him will be brought to light one day. And he is gathering it all up. Or, rather, things are being gathered up within him by themselves. Mariana apparently senses this, and she keeps saying, "Don't remember me as an unfortunate woman. Mariana has been battling on this front since the age of fourteen. It's a merciless front. I refused to be a servant in rich people's houses, and for that I was punished. If you ever remember this woman who was called Mariana, write that she fought to the end of her strength, and that in the end her heart's beloved freed her from prison."

"Who is that?"

"You, and none other."

Meanwhile, Mariana has another hard night. One of the guests shouts at her, calls her names, and keeps asking her to do things that apparently disgust her. He complains, and Madam scolds her and writes a warning in her account book. Hugo hears everything, and his heart tightens.

But the following night Mariana has no guests, and she invites Hugo to come to her. Mariana is soft and devoted. He feels her arms and legs exquisitely, and he has a strong desire to fondle her breasts.

40

And so the days pass—a mixture of disquiet, fear, and powerful pleasures. Hugo's earlier life slips far away from him, and it is now a pale patch that gradually evaporates and fades away.

Papa, Mama, where are you? He asks without meaning it. They are no longer within him. In vain he tries to raise them up from the depths of his memory. They refuse to dress in their image. They have also departed from his dreams. Mariana fills his dreams.

What will be, and how will his life go on? Hugo doesn't think about that. He has become part of this strange place and can easily identify some of the voices: that of the authoritative and venomous guard; that of Victoria, who complains that she works day and night and gets angry at a woman named Sheba, who gobbles food down without measure or proportion and leaves empty pots; and of course the thin, childish voice of Kitty. Hugo is sorry that he'll soon be leaving. In his heart he consoles himself with the thought that Mariana will be with him in his wanderings. And without her nightly obligations, she will be all his.

Hugo imagines his wanderings with Mariana in the Carpathian Mountains as a voyage of pleasure and contemplation—

like his golden summer vacations with his parents. But now all the responsibility will be upon him.

Hugo knows that his imagination is not impartial, but the desire to be with Mariana, far from other people, plants words in his mouth that he does not ordinarily use. Sometimes they sound frightfully hollow to him, and sometimes an unpleasant artificiality arises from them.

"Do you forgive me?" he says.

"For what?"

"Because I'm not expressing myself properly."

"What are you talking about?" Mariana says, and bursts out laughing.

But for now there is rain again, and cold. "Next week we'll leave," says Mariana, putting off their departure. The army of occupation is sent to the front, and only a small unit that is looking for Jews is left in the city. They, in fact, are the clients of The Residence.

Clearly the war is coming to an end. There is no longer any doubt that the Germans are in trouble. The guard, who always spoke in praise of the German army, has stopped doing so. Now he speaks with the same words of praise about the Russian army. They knew how to retreat, he says, cunningly tempting the Germans to plunge into the snowy plains after them. The Germans' end will be like that of Napoleon. The winter, not the tanks, will win the war.

The women hear this and are afraid. It is clear to everyone that those who served the Germans will be punished. The Russian army bears grudges and takes revenge.

"What will they do to us?" asks a young voice that Hugo can't identify.

"After every war, there are pardons. Sins like these aren't considered serious," says the guard in his authoritative voice.

That statement doesn't assuage the fears of the woman who asked, and she wants to know whether the pardon will also apply to her. The guard's patience wears out, and he answers without looking at her.

"You have nothing to fear," he says. "They won't rape you."

The guests have become very few. At night the women sit and play cards and reminisce. Sometimes a confession is heard, accompanied by tears. Mariana is tranquil. She drinks as much as she pleases. When Mariana drinks the amount she needs, her face lights up and out of her mouth come surprising comments. She sees the future in pink colors and promises Hugo that as soon as the weather improves, they will set out.

"You're big already," she says, "and you should know that The Residence is nothing more than a whorehouse."

Hugo has learned some of the secrets of the place, though there are things that remain more hidden than visible.

Now the women fight over each guest. But not Mariana. She has had enough of them, and she's glad she can sleep in her bed with Hugo. Hugo's joy is boundless.

"A person should bless every day and every hour." Mariana surprises him again.

"Why?" Hugo wonders.

"Because everything can change in a moment. A day without degradation is a gift from heaven, and it should be blessed. You have to learn this, honey. Nothing is self-explanatory. We are given over into God's hands. When He wishes to, He harms, and when He wishes to, He is beneficent."

"Does God watch over us?"

"Always. For that reason I'm frightened. God doesn't like these houses of sin. God loves married women who bring children into the world. He doesn't love women like me."

"I love you."

"But you're not God," Mariana says, and they both laugh.

Hugo opens the Bible again and reads the story of Joseph.

Hugo feels that he, too, like Joseph, bears within him a secret that will be revealed. He, too, for the moment, has to undergo many trials, but what the future will bring him, he doesn't know.

"You'll be an artist," Mariana keeps saying. "You have the right height and observant eyes. You think correctly, and you don't let sensitivity drown you. In short, you'll be an artist. That's what my heart says."

It's strange that she, who since childhood has known hardship and has struggled, does not deny that people can have both beauty and nobility. Where did she acquire that understanding? Hugo continues to wonder about this.

41

Mariana's religiosity surprises Hugo anew every time. He has noticed that when she's depressed, she doesn't talk about God but about herself and her sins, painting hell in fiery colors. But two or three swallows of brandy erase the gloom from her face. A new light makes her forehead throb, and she speaks directly to God.

"Dear God, You understand my heart better than any person. You know that my pleasures in this world were few and bad, my humiliations were many and bitter. I don't say that I'm a righteous woman worthy to go to heaven. I bear a burden of shame, and that's why I'll pay a forfeit when the day comes. But I never stopped longing for You, God. Even when I'm in the depths of hell, You are my beloved."

At night she allows him to touch her breasts. Her breasts are big and full, and they give off warmth and an inebriating smell. Mariana seems to like the way he touches her, because she says, "You're gentle, you're good, you love Mariana."

Again she makes Hugo swear. "Whatever happens between us is a secret forever and ever."

"I swear," he cries out.

Now that there are hardly any guests, the nights are filled

with soft darkness. On the rare occasions when a guest knocks at Mariana's door, she quickly tells him she's drunk too much and can't entertain anyone. The guest turns away and goes to the next door.

Mariana is now laden with brandy. Her mood is exalted, her brain is feverish, and from her mouth come glowing utterances. She tells Hugo that she has worked in residences like this since she was a young girl. They were all the same: a guard at the door, a thin and unbearable madam, and the hostesses. Among the hostesses there were good ones and mean ones. Most of them were bitches. This was no surprise: two or three hungry men every night can burn up even the sturdiest woman. "Since I was fourteen, they've been devouring me," she says. "Now I feel like lying in bed and hugging my big puppy and sleeping for hours and hours. There's nothing like an uninterrupted night's sleep."

Again she surprises him. "You should stay a puppy," she says. "Men who are puppies are sweet. When they grow up they turn into beasts of prey. I won't let you grow up. You'll stay the way you are. Do you agree?"

"I agree."

"I knew you'd agree. I know you by now."

One night she tells him, "There's nothing else to be said: Jews are gentler. They wouldn't abuse a naked woman. They'll always touch her softly, whisper a good word in her ear, always leave her a few extra banknotes. They know that Madam takes most of the cash for herself. Your mother was always good to me. During the hardest days, she remembered me and brought me clothes, fruit, cheese. What didn't she bring? She never forgot that the two of us once sat at the same desk, that both of us loved to play jump rope and ball. She never said to me, *Why don't you do respectable work?* I actually expected her to speak sternly to me, but I was glad that she didn't torment me.

"Like I said: the Jews are gentler. The Jewish students

always tried to get me to join the Communist Party. Once I even let myself be convinced to go to their headquarters. They discussed and argued over things I didn't have any idea about. To tell the truth, I wasn't suitable for them. I grew up in mud, and like a mud-animal, I didn't know any other atmosphere.

"You, thank God, grew up in a good home. Your parents let you observe, think, imagine. I ran away and went from place to place, always afraid and always ashamed. My father, God forgive him, used to beat me with sticks. It started when I was a child. He also hit my sister, but he beat me more bitterly. It's no wonder I ran away from home.

"He used to follow me, and when he found me, he would beat me mercilessly. I can feel his lashes to this very day. Those are scars that never healed. My flesh still remembers them. He was a fierce detective. He wouldn't return home until he found me. Sometimes he would look for me for a whole week, and when he found me, there was no limit to his cruelty.

"Why am I remembering him? It's impossible not to remember him. His lashes are embedded in me, to the marrow of my bones. I don't mean to disturb his eternal rest. Let him rest in peace in his grave, but what can I do? When I lie in bed, the scars wake me up and gnaw at me.

"My mother, of blessed memory, was better to me. She also suffered. My father didn't spare her, either. He was always angry at her: 'Why didn't you pick the cabbage? Why is the barn neglected?' The poor thing would apologize and ask for mercy and promise to do everything, but because she didn't keep her promises, he would scream at her and sometimes slap her face. In time, when she got sick, he would say, 'You're pretending to be sick. There's nothing wrong with you. You don't want to work. From lying in bed so much, you'll really get sick.' But in the end he died before she did."

Hugo hears all this and says, "In a little while, we'll be surrounded by nature, without people."

"But now it's raining," Mariana replies. "Better to stay here. Here there's a warm stove."

As the hours pass it rains harder. There are no preparations for nightly duties and no sudden visits from Madam. The women sit in the hall. They drink and sing. Hugo likes to listen to their Ukrainian folk songs. Sometimes a sob is heard from the hall, and everyone joins in. Only Madam isn't pleased. Hugo sometimes hears her voice: "Without customers, we'll have to close The Residence."

"And what will happen to us?"

"Everyone will go her own way."

Upon hearing her answer, the women sit in silence, and Hugo feels that the enemy is both outside and within. He wants to say, the way Mariana herself used to say now and then, *Don't be afraid. Fear is a shameful quality, fear is what brings us down to hell. You mustn't fear people.*

42

Winter comes before its time. Persistent rumors say that the German army has begun to withdraw. Trains stream from the front to the rear without stopping at stations. Even from the closet, it's possible to hear their muffled rush.

"Now it's impossible to leave," Mariana says. "Now we have to stay here until the fury of the rains has passed. This rain will bring hail and, finally, snow. A person with no house would freeze." Mariana is pleased to have no contradiction between her wishes and the conditions outdoors that force them to remain in The Residence.

If it weren't for the guard, they would all curl up in bed and sleep even more. But for some reason the guard has changed his mind and now is warning the women that the Russians will whip them to death.

"Whoever sold her body to the Germans won't be let off. You have to run away as soon as possible." His tone of voice has changed recently, and he sounds less authoritative. Victoria's advice is different: "You have to flee to convents and return to God."

"How can we return to God?" A young woman's voice is heard, but Hugo can't identify it.

"Bend your knees and say, 'Lord Jesus, forgive me for all

the sins I committed. From now on I swear that I won't sin or lead others into sin.' "

"Should we say it now or in the convent?"

"Now."

"It's strange to make an oath in this place."

"Why is it strange? The moment a person swears not to sin, God begins to listen to him."

Later he hears one of the women hissing, "A cursed life."

"Is married life better? My sister's husband beats her every day."

"Men desecrate us three times a night."

"Today, after ten years of desecration, I'd choose marriage."

"Now the Russians will come and whip us to death. What the Germans did to the Jews, the Russians will do to us. The Russians have no God in their hearts."

There are no more guests. There is tension and creeping fear. The girls sit in the hall, chat, drink, and play cards. They remember the guests who were nice to them, brought them boxes of candy, and didn't ask them to do anything disgusting.

"In a little while, the volcano will erupt," the guard warns them.

"Let it erupt. Our life is worth zero squared," replies one of them, and everybody laughs.

Mariana's mood is exalted. She drinks as much as she wants and regrets the days when she denied herself the marvelous potion known as brandy. You only live once, she says.

Hugo is also content. Mariana doesn't stop hugging him, and every few days she stands him next to the door, measures him, and says, "You've gotten taller. In a little while hairs will grow." When she drinks, she is free. She shows him the bottles of perfume she has in her drawers, the jewelry, and the silk stockings she received as presents. Hugo likes to watch her when she stretches out her leg and puts on a stocking. Sometimes she stands before the mirror wearing only panties and a brassiere and says, "Isn't it true that I haven't lost my shape? I'm just the way I should be, not fat and not thin. A lot of women have doughy legs or a swollen belly. And now we have to teach Hugo how to love Mariana."

"I love you," Hugo quickly confirms.

"Wait, wait. You don't know everything yet."

After repeated warnings, the guard finally runs away. Madam announces that she's now locking up The Residence. The kitchen will be closed, and everyone will have to take care of herself.

"And what will happen to us?"

"I can't support you. I've already spent what I had. For more than a month, there's been no income. I can't feed seventeen girls. The bakery won't give me bread, and the butcher won't give me meat."

"You'll be sorry. You can't close an institution. The German army will return and take revenge against everybody who spread rumors about its defeat and closed the institutions that served them," one of the women warns her.

"What can I do?" she says in a different tone of voice.

"Don't be hasty."

"I'm not being hasty," she replies. "I've been running this place for twenty years. Managing a residence like this is no small matter. I know what's possible and what's impossible. Now things have gone too far. The pantry is empty, and so is the cellar." She bursts into sobs.

There is silence, and Madam withdraws to her apartment.

Later Victoria comes out of the kitchen and says in a whisper, "I have supplies for another week, if we're sparing. After a week—God help us."

"Thank you, Victoria, may God preserve you." They bless her.

Mariana seems unaffected by the commotion. Since she began drinking again, her mood is steady—elevated, actually, but without any decline. Whatever happens hardly touches her. She tells Hugo about her childhood and early youth, and about the days when she was a girl in love with a boy named Andrei. He was handsome. One day his parents moved to a different village, and he forgot her. She cried a lot over him and kept looking for him. He disappeared and left her wounded.

"I won't abandon you," Hugo quickly confirms.

"Let's hope not," she says. Then she laughs and hugs him.

43

Now come the days they had all been looking forward to: everyone sleeps late, eats breakfast together, shares pleasant dreams, and keeps asking what good food is left in the kitchen.

Mariana doesn't stop drinking, obviously seeking to recover what she had lost during the time of her abstinence. She often speaks about her youth, about the moves from brothel to brothel until she arrived at The Residence. She talks and talks, but her words make no impression. Her friends look at her as if to say, *We've all been through that. What's so special?*

But when she says, "Now I want to introduce my young friend to you," everyone is silent. Most of them already know the secret, or have guessed. Hugo is stunned. His mind always pictured the women of The Residence in the image of Mariana. Now they sit in the hall around the table, seventeen young women, each with her own hairstyle, looking like girls at a class reunion. At first glance, they remind Hugo of Sofia's friends, young men and women who used to gather in their home on her birthday. They had come from the village and also went shopping while they were in town, thereby combining practicality with amusement. Hugo had been charmed by their way of speaking, their gestures, and their colorful village language.

After inspecting Hugo from head to foot, one of the women asks, "What's your name?"

"Hugo," he replies, pleased that he didn't lower his head.

"A nice name. I never heard of a name like that."

"It doesn't sound Jewish," another woman comments.

Kitty stands out in her childish clothing and with her big eyes. The others are wrapped in colorful robes, as though they just got out of bed.

"Shall we make Hugo a cup of coffee?" one of them asks.

"Hugo drinks milk," says Mariana.

Mariana's comment provokes loud laughter.

"What's so funny?" asks Mariana.

"He's a big boy. He's a sturdy lad, a boy for coffee and not for milk."

"Why don't you say something?" one of the women asks Hugo.

"What do you want him to say?" Mariana tries to defend him.

"I thought he was a child. It turns out I was wrong. He's a lad by any standard."

"You're wrong. He's just tall." Mariana protects Hugo again.

"I've learned the difference, thank God, between a child and a lad."

That argument displeases Mariana. She takes his hand and says, "Hugo's got a cold, he has to rest."

"He doesn't look as if he's got a cold," the woman replies provocatively.

"He's got a cold, and a bad one," says Mariana, extricating him from the women's covetous gaze.

Hugo has hardly entered the closet when he hears the women's laughter. His name and Mariana's rise from the laughter. The laughter keeps swelling, and for a moment it sounds like gloating, because they managed to raise the veil from Mariana's secret.

In the afternoon, Mariana prepares a hot bath and says, "Now I'll wash my puppy. My puppy's growing from day to day, maturing. In a little while he'll be Mariana's height. In a little while he'll be even taller than her. I'm looking forward to that moment. Don't be afraid, honey. Mariana's swallowed a good bit, but she's not drunk. I hate drunks."

When she puts the big towel on his shoulders, she says, "You're maturing. You're maturing very nicely. It's a pleasure to see you." Hugo hears a didactic tone in her voice, as though she were explaining something to him about the laws of nature. Then she rubs his body with fragrant lotion and says, "My puppy smells like first fruit." The phrase "first fruit" captivates him. He remembers another phrase, "bud and flower," that Mariana also uses sometimes.

Now Hugo sees that most of the clothes in the suitcase are too short for him, and in some of the outfits he looks ridiculous. Mariana inspects the clothes and says, "Mariana will get you some older boy's clothes. These clothes are simply too small on you. You've grown up properly."

That night, after the bath, is a whirl of pleasures and dreams that come one after the other. Hugo has learned that dreams aren't uniform. Pleasure is mingled with fear. Suddenly Mariana says, "Too bad we can't stop time: if only we could always live this way, Mariana with her puppy. Mariana doesn't need anything else. This is exactly what she needs. Hugo will grow up and defend her. The brave puppy."

In time Hugo will say to himself, *It was too hasty.* For that reason the experience wasn't absorbed in full detail. He regrets that the decorative bottles were lost. Sometimes bottles are no less important than their contents. Mariana's marvelous mouth always gives off a smell of brandy and chocolate, sweet to the palate, and the passage from her neck to her breasts is short and full of softness. "Delight, dear," Mariana keeps saying, "that's what a woman needs, the rest is dessert."

44

The next day Kitty comes in to visit him. The surprise in her eyes seems to say, *What sin did you commit that you've been given such a severe punishment? You're a sweet kid, and your place is at a desk in school, not in a dark, damp closet.*

Hugo had previously noticed that astonishment. *I'm a Jew,* he wants to say, *and Jews apparently are undesirable. I don't know why. I presume that if everybody thinks we're undesirable, there's a reason for it. I'm glad that you don't think so.* That's what he wants to say, but those simple thoughts refuse to garb themselves in words, and he replies with a shrug of his shoulder.

Kitty's gaze widens even more. "Strange," she says, "very strange."

Hugo has noticed that Kitty's attentiveness takes him back to his home and to the vocabulary he used there. He wants to use the expressions "let us assume," "most probably," and "there must be something to it," which were often heard in his house. But those words are meaningless here, as though they weren't really words but simply their remains.

"What school do you go to?" Hugo asks, and immediately realizes the stupidity of his question.

"I've been out of school for many years," Kitty says. "I finished elementary school, and I've been working since then."

She smiles, and the smile reveals her little teeth. The brightness adds a touch of youth to her cheeks.

"I've forgotten school, too," he says.

"Impossible."

"I promised my mother that I would do arithmetic problems, read, and write. I didn't keep the promise, and so I've forgotten everything I learned."

"A boy like you doesn't forget easily."

"That's true," Hugo replies. "You'd expect that a boy who had studied in school for five years, whose mother read to him every night and conversed with him—you'd expect him to continue to read, write, do arithmetic problems, but it didn't happen to me. I'm separated from everything I had, from everything I knew, even from my parents."

"You speak very beautifully. It shows that you haven't forgotten what you learned."

"I haven't progressed, I haven't progressed in any area. Lack of progress is marching in place, and marching in place is forgetting. I'll give you an example. In algebra we were about to begin equations, and we had started to learn French. Everything is erased from my memory."

"You're excellent," Kitty says, astonished by the torrent of words.

The things he told Kitty opened the seal on Hugo's memory. He now sees his house before his eyes—the kitchen, where he liked to sit at the old table, the living room, his parents' bedroom, and his room. A little kingdom, full of enchanted things—a parquet floor, an electric train, wooden blocks, Jules Verne and Karl May.

"What are you thinking about, Hugo?" Kitty asks in a whisper.

"I'm not thinking. I'm seeing what I haven't seen in a long time."

"You're very well educated," she says with a kind of authority. "Now I understand why everybody talks about 'smart Jews,' " she adds.

"They're wrong," Hugo responds curtly.

"I don't understand."

"They're not smart. They're too sensitive. My mother, if I may use her as an example, was a pharmacist with two diplomas, but all her life she gave to poor and suffering people. God knows where she is now and who she's taking care of. She was always running, and because of that, she always came home exhausted and sank, pale, into the armchair."

"You're right," Kitty says, as though she understands his words.

"It's not a question of being right, my dear, but of understanding the situation as it is." The moment that sentence leaves his mouth, Hugo remembers that it's what Anna used to say. It was hard for him to compete with her ability to express herself. Only Franz, the constant competitor, could equal her, and everyone else appeared to stammer, to pile up words, adding and taking away as needed and not as needed. Only Anna knew how to phrase an idea clearly.

"Thanks for the conversation. I have to go," says Kitty in her childish voice.

"Thank you."

"Why are you thanking me?"

"Because of my conversation with you, my parents, my house, and my school friends appeared before me. The months in the closet had deprived me of them."

"I'm pleased," says Kitty, and she steps back.

"It's a present I hadn't expected," Hugo says. The words choke in his mouth.

Hugo thinks of writing in the notebook and clarifying some of the feelings that arose within him after the conversation with Kitty. But he immediately senses that the words available to him won't do that.

Every time he writes—and he doesn't write often—Hugo feels that the days in the closet have dissolved his active vocabulary, not to mention the words he had adopted from books. After the war, he'll show the notebook to Anna. She'll read it, lower her eyes for a moment—a lowering of self-assurance—and say, "It needs, it seems to me, further thought, also reduction and polishing." She would always relate to a page of writing as if it were a mathematical exercise, removing all the superfluous steps. In the end she would say, "It's still not enough, there are still unnecessary words here, it still doesn't ring true." Sometimes Hugo would look at her work and feel inferior.

When he read a weak or careless composition, Hugo's German teacher used to say, "Is this all your thinking came up with? You've succeeded: not a single sensible word. A composition like this should never have been created. In the future, don't even hand in such a composition. You'd be better off writing on the top of the page or on the bottom, *I have not yet attained the level of a thinking creature.*"

45

The winter continues, and covers the fields and the houses with a thick veil of snow. Again the frost returns, but not to worry, Hugo is sleeping with Mariana. Every night he's wrapped in warmth and softness. They sleep like everyone else, until late. Sometimes, in her sleep, she draws him to her. He already knows what to do.

"I have food for another four days," Victoria keeps reminding the women. "After that, you can chew on the walls." Now every minute is precious, and everyone knows it. They drink, play cards, reminisce, and confess. Hugo sees a woman kneeling before a crucifix, crossing herself and praying. For meals, Mariana takes Hugo out of the closet, and he sits with everyone. They are a merry bunch, full of life, and they have received an unexpected vacation in the middle of winter. They enjoy one another's company and do whatever they please.

"Now Hugo will speak." One of the women halts the flood of happiness.

"What do you want from him? He's still a kid."

"He's been with us for a year and a half. It would be interesting to hear what's running around in his head."

Mariana intervenes. "You can't think about anything else," she says. "Always the same thing."

"Twelve-year-olds already know what sin is."

Hugo listens and enjoys the humor, the sassiness, and the insights. He has noticed that there isn't much difference between their thoughts and their words. Women speak about everything that gives them pleasure or pain, though not in the same tone of voice.

Victoria's repeated threat, that the supplies are steadily dwindling, no longer frightens them. "It's a good thing you're not threatening us with hell," one of the women says.

"I am threatening, but what good will my threats do for stopped ears?"

"Don't worry. One day we'll repent."

"I guess I won't live to see that."

"Mom, you mustn't lose hope."

"Look who's talking," replies Victoria, making a strange motion with her head.

The word "God" isn't uncommon here. The women often fight over it, and Hugo senses that if a priest or monk were to enter the room, the women would kneel silently in their places and ask forgiveness. "God is everywhere," he heard one of them explaining at length. "There is no place where He is not present. He is even to be found here, in this garbage dump. We have cut ourselves off from Him, not He from us."

"You're wrong. I think about Him all the time," another answered.

"If you thought about Him all the time, you wouldn't be here."

"I'm here because I have no alternative."

"That's an excuse. You can use that excuse on us, but not in God's ear. God knows exactly what's the truth and what's a lie."

Hearing those words, the women fall silent, but not for long. Suddenly one of them bursts into sobs. Hearing her weeping, other women gather around her and say, "Don't listen to that one. You know her. She looks for faults in everyone except herself."

Suddenly Madam appears. Since the guard left his post, she has been careful about what she says and doesn't threaten anyone. She is a handsome woman and could have been the mother of any of the girls here. She speaks in Ukrainian and peppers her words with German. Her appearance stuns Hugo. "How are my girls?" she addresses the seated women.

"We're unemployed, and our future is in doubt. Maybe you could advise us on what to do? You're our mother," says one rather young woman, who has drunk a great deal but isn't drunk.

"Advise? Me? You know life better than I do."

"We haven't had time to think. Three men every night make you dumb."

"Don't exaggerate. There were a lot of nights when you slept alone and even got served breakfast in bed."

"I can't remember them."

"I've got a list of your free nights."

"Interesting. My body doesn't remember them."

Madam has firm opinions. "A profession is a profession," she says. "If you chose it, don't look at it as a punishment, bad luck, or the devil knows what. Every profession has its disadvantages and its little pleasures." As for the men, she says, "Some are wild beasts who have to be put in their place, but most of them treat women gently."

"When's the last time you slept with a man?" one of the women asks impudently.

"I knew men before you were born." Madam gives as good as she gets.

"Maybe once they were gentle, but not today."

"People don't change. What was will always be."

Madam doesn't keep it a secret from them that a soft girl or one who's too picky are not for her. "Even in our profession," she says, "you can maintain manners and respect. But for that you need backbone."

Hugo goes back to the closet. *I've got to write down everything that's happening to me,* he says to himself, *so that I'll always remember what I saw and heard. Mama will read and flinch, and she'll say, Good God, but Papa will take it in good spirit. Strange and puzzling things always amused him. He'll say, Our Hugo, we must assume, is no longer the Hugo we knew. He's matured before his time. Is that a reason to hit him?*

46

The threat hangs over everything and is palpable at every meal. Supplies remain for only two more days; after that, everyone will be on her own. The house will be closed. It's actually better for it to be closed. The Russians are merciless. Whoever collaborated with the Germans will be hanged in the city square. That threat, which Victoria repeats with a trembling voice, makes no impression on the women, who are immersed in the freedom that has been given to them. "God in heaven," they say, "who took care of us until now, will keep on taking care of us."

"That was His care?"

"You mustn't be ungrateful. We didn't go hungry, and we didn't tremble with cold."

"True, we were just trampled."

Every word and every sentence receives a response. There are differences of opinion, but there are no bitter quarrels. Hugo sits and observes them: each face has its own expression. The women don't look gloomy or depressed. They are taking advantage of the respite that was granted to them. It's common for them to speak in the third person, and in that way they distance themselves a little from their lives.

"I hate myself," he often hears.

"Go to a convent, and there you'll be freed of yourself."

"That isn't as bad an idea as I used to think."

"It's hard for me to imagine you as an ascetic."

When Hugo is alone in the closet their faces come back to him, and he sees them one by one. Sometimes it seems to him that he has known the women for years, and only now have they removed the veil from their faces.

Suddenly Hugo is sorry that his mother doesn't understand him, and that he has to conceal these powerful experiences from her. In contrast to her, Uncle Sigmund, drunk and merry, repeats to the family, "Don't worry about Hugo. He's getting an excellent lesson. You're tested on algebra and trigonometry, and you forget it. It's a good thing he saw life in its nakedness while he was still young. Denials and words that reveal less than they conceal never helped anyone. The time has come to stop deceiving ourselves and our fellows."

The next day Hugo enters the hall, and what does he see? The women are down on their knees, and facing them, on a chair, is an icon of Jesus. Victoria is standing next to the kneeling women. She is reading, and they are repeating after her, "Good Jesus, forgive us all our sins. Because of our many sins and our pollution, we didn't see You. You are merciful and full of loving-kindness. Don't forget your girls and don't leave them to drown in a slough of sin. Save them with Your grace."

After a pause, Victoria calls out, "Get up, girls, and stand on your feet. From now on you are joined to our Lord Jesus. Turn away from evil and do good, and don't forget even for a moment that we are dust and ashes. Only by virtue of the soul, which is part of God above, do we exist. From now on, no more dealings of the flesh, but only the kingdom of heaven."

Victoria's face is pale, but fire flares in her eyes. It's obvious that the words are not hers, and that someone else is speaking from within her. The women understand that there's no need to comment or disagree, but just to accept the simple meaning of what she said.

Mariana, who didn't take part in the ceremony, is stunned. What happened in the hall wasn't like prayer. It was a mighty movement of the soul. Every night they would drink and sing folk songs and church songs. Victoria would admonish them that heavy drinking is a sin, and that they must overcome this temptation, but her efforts are in vain.

Meanwhile, one of the women attacks Kitty. Kitty is stunned, and the woman beats her even harder, screaming, "You aren't allowed to be here. You don't belong here. You're like a thorn in our flesh." Kitty doesn't open her mouth, not even when the blood flows down her face.

Some time passes before the women grasp the horror of what has happened, and when they do, the poor girl is lying on the floor unconscious. For a long time they try to revive her. At last Kitty opens her eyes and asks, "What happened?" The terrified women, who are kneeling over her, answer together. "Nothing happened, thank God, nothing." Everybody sighs in relief.

47

The guard's son sneaks in, and he has news. "The German army is withdrawing in disarray, and the Russian army is closing in on its rear." When he used to come to The Residence, his father would send him to one of the rooms. All the women were afraid of him, and they would scream when they saw him. He was as violent as he looked. Once his father sent him into Mariana's room, and Mariana hollered in fear, "Jesus, save me." He tried to overcome her, but she was hysterical and struggled wildly. In the end, he spat at her and said, "You don't even know how to be a whore."

Since they last saw him, he has grown thinner. His violence hasn't disappeared, but it isn't like before.

"You have to run away, and as quickly as possible," he says.

"Where will we go?" one of them asks.

"Anywhere, just not here."

His father and he collaborated with the Germans, turning in Jews and Communists. Now he feels the noose closing around him, and he has come to seek witnesses to testify in his favor.

"We're not qualified to be witnesses," one of them says.

"Why not?" he asks.

"Whoever works in our profession isn't believed. They say that she's lying or making things up."

"You won't testify on my behalf?"

"I'll testify, but the investigators will disqualify my testimony."

He apparently understands his situation, and when night falls, he clears out.

A woman's voice is heard. "All these years he's been turning in Communists and Jews. Now his time has come."

A snowstorm rages outside, covering the houses and the fences. Every time an obstacle stands in Mariana's way, she grabs her bottle and won't let it go. This night she outdoes herself. "Now let God be worried, not me. I can't stop the whirl of the storm."

Hugo isn't worried. The nights with Mariana are warm and pleasurable, and it seems to him that all this will continue without end. In the middle of the night, she catches fire, hugging and kissing Hugo and saying, "Now you're mine. Now no one will take you away from me." Hugo is astonished by the power of her softness, until her body and his are one.

More than once in his life, Hugo will try to reimagine that drunken night. He will call up the thick darkness that was infused with perfume and brandy, and the pleasure that was mixed with a fear of the abyss. But not a word passed between them, as if words had become extinct.

Victoria serves the last meal with restrained formality, and it's evident that parting is hard for her. Eventually she recovers and says, "Girls, you mustn't be afraid. Fear is a despicable trait, and we have to overcome it. God is in heaven, and He will preserve you."

Where will we go? their eyes ask again and again.

"There's nowhere to go," Victoria says. "A storm is raging, and we can only be by ourselves and pray. Prayer is our secret weapon."

"What will we eat, Mother?"

"I have some more corn flour, and tomorrow I'll give everybody a slice of corn bread." Victoria's voice is now full and not hesitant. The girls are attentive to what she says and not afraid of her. She can't feed them as she has done all these years, but she has abundant faith.

Mariana still has a quarter of a bottle of brandy. She is frugal, sipping a few drops at a time and saying, "What will I do when the brandy runs out? I'll lose my mind. Hugo, honey, guard the bottle. If I ask for it, tell me that I have to save the rest for an emergency. I won't get angry at you."

But the nights are uninterrupted pleasure. Hugo drinks the last of the brandy from her mouth, wrapped in her legs, hearing only whispers of love. "You're a wonderful puppy. All those months I longed for you. Now you're mine forever." Hugo hears and does what she wants. Sometimes sudden fear makes him tremble, but he overcomes it. *Mariana loves me,* he says to himself, *and there's nothing to fear.*

Everybody sleeps late, and in the afternoon Victoria brings out the icon, puts it on the chair, and the girls fall to their knees and pray.

"Prayer foils plots and changes fates," Victoria instructs them.

"What would we do without you, Mother?"

"It's not me. God sent me to you. God takes care of His creatures. There is no coincidence in the world."

What would we do without you? their eyes ask.

"I gave you what God told me to give you. Now the image of Jesus is engraved on your hearts, and you know in your bodies, too, that there is a God in heaven. You mustn't fear, and you mustn't despair."

"And what will happen with our sins?"

"If anyone confesses and promises not to sin again, his sins are erased."

Meanwhile, Madam has fled for her life. The women break into her apartment, and wealth and luxury abound in every corner. For a moment they are astounded. Then they begin to loot. They don't find jewelry or money, but there is a cupboard full of beverages and chocolates. "If there's no bread, we'll drink liqueur and eat chocolate," one of them says, and everybody cheers her. There's joy, as after a successful robbery. Mariana satisfies herself with five bottles of brandy, two bottles of liqueur, a lot of chocolate, and a big package of cigarettes.

At night spirits are high, and everybody goes back to loot some more. They find hidden corners, and in them are not jewels or gold coins, but a package of silk stockings and perfumes.

"Do not rejoice at the fall of your enemy," Victoria warns them. "You mustn't exult too much."

"Madam oppressed us night after night."

"God doesn't like gloating."

Over the past weeks, Victoria has changed completely. Her face has become narrow and taken on a deathly pallor. She no longer speaks like an ordinary person. Biblical verses tumble from her mouth, both clear and sharp verses and obscure ones. When something upsets her, fire lights up her eyes, and they blaze in fury.

48

Yesterday the blizzard seemed to be dying down, but it turns out to be just a pause. From hour to hour the winds grow stronger, and in the morning the yard and the fields are covered with snowdrifts. Not a living soul can be seen outside. In The Residence, everything is drunkenness, the gobbling of chocolate and cookies, singing, and declarations. "What we did for the Germans, we'll do for the Russians now. It's not for nothing that we call our profession the oldest one. Since ancient times, men have needed women. Everybody understands that in our line of work, one isn't choosy about one's clients. Whoever comes, comes. Today Germans, tomorrow Russians."

"The Russians are jealous."

"We'll serve them just the way we served the Germans— even better, because the Ukrainians and the Russians are brother nations." That is Masha's voice. It has a housewife's practicality. Because of her orderly way of speaking and because she is older, they call her "Our Masha."

Hugo can identify most of them, but not by name. Each of them has a nickname, except for Kitty. Since she was beaten, Kitty's face has turned yellowish blue, and her eyes have sunk into their sockets. She doesn't complain, but her bruised presence keeps asking, *What's bad about me that annoys the strong women? True, I'm not big, and I'm not strong. Do they have to hit me because of that?* Sylvia, the cleaning woman, takes pity on the weak and the stricken, and she makes applesauce for Kitty, saying, "This will strengthen you and make you healthy."

Every moment brings a new surprise. In the evening one of the women says to Mariana, "What a darling boy you have. Why do you keep him only to yourself? We want to pet him a little, too."

"You should be ashamed of yourself. He's just a child," Masha scolds her in a motherly voice.

"I didn't mean anything by it, just to pet him. Come, boy, come to me."

Hugo freezes in his place and says nothing.

Mariana responds with repressed anger. "Leave him alone."

"You're horribly selfish," says the woman with venom.

"Selfish?" Mariana's face grows tense.

"To keep him just to yourself. What is that, if not selfishness?"

"I ran a risk and protected him. Is that what you call selfishness?"

"Don't play the innocent. We know each other too well."

"You're mistaken."

"I'm not mistaken."

Masha intervenes. "Why fight?" she says. "He belongs to us all."

"I don't agree," says Mariana. "Hugo's mother was my childhood friend. I promised her that I would protect him until my last breath."

"Every woman needs a child. Every woman longs for her own child. Why keep us from a little stroke and a kiss? It's very natural," says Masha in her motherly voice.

"I know her well," says Mariana, without looking at the woman who asked to caress him.

"There's no need to fight. In a little while the blizzard will die down, and everybody will go her own way. Who knows when we'll meet again. Why not part in friendship? Life is short. Who knows what's in store for us?" says Masha, sounding like a woman worried about her family.

Masha was prophesying without knowing it. Suddenly the whirling of the blizzard stops, and everyone stands at the windows and looks out. They can't believe their eyes. Silent snow covers the houses and the fields. There is neither man nor beast, just whiteness on top of whiteness, and a silence you can feel through the windows.

"This period has come to an end," says one of the women, pleased with how the sentence has struck her mouth.

"What period are you talking about?" the question soon comes.

"My ten years in this place: the room, the hall, Madam, the guard, the guests, the vacations, all the good and the bad. In a little while the Russians will come, and everything will be destroyed. Now do you understand?"

"For me there's no difference. How does that change things?"

"There is a difference. The Russians will come and flog us. The guard said it clearly, 'Everyone who slept with the Germans will be sentenced to death.' They'll hang us in the city square, and the whole city will come and see our execution."

"You're exaggerating."

"I'm not exaggerating. I'm saying just what they said and just what my heart says: the Russians are already preparing the scaffolds. They know no mercy."

Victoria stands like a bastion. "You mustn't fear," she repeats. "Fear degrades us. God is our father. He loves us and He will have mercy on us. You mustn't give in to imaginings and false wishes. From now on, every woman must say to herself: As I sinned, so I sinned. Now I deliver myself to the hands of God. May heaven guide me. I'm willing to do just what they tell me to do from on high. People are evil, only God is pure."

Victoria speaks with religious devotion, but the women don't listen to her. They stand at the windows, wondering and trembling. Even after darkness falls and it is night, they don't move from the windows.

To her credit, Victoria doesn't let them wallow in their fears. "It doesn't matter what those in power do," she keeps saying. "What matters is what God does. Fear of people is a sin. Overcome fear, stand straight, and walk toward God. Our Lord Jesus did not fear when they nailed Him to the cross, because He and God were one. Whoever clings to His virtues wins the kingdom of heaven. Remember what I'm telling you."

They all look at her in astonishment. No one comments, and no one asks a question.

Suddenly one of the drunken women puts out her hand and says to Hugo, "Darling, come to me. I want to hug you."

"Leave him alone," Mariana says dismissively.

Immediately they all scatter, each to her own room.

49

Toward morning there was a great panic, and all the women fled. Mariana and Hugo slept through it all, and when they wake up, no one is left in the house except for Victoria and Sylvia, and they are dressed in their coats and about to set out.

"What's the matter with you?" asks Victoria.

"I was asleep and didn't hear a thing," says Mariana.

"There's no one in the house. The girls left most of their belongings. They didn't want to drag anything along. Too bad."

"Have the Russians come?" Mariana wonders.

"They are spread out through the whole city."

"Frightening."

"There's nothing to fear." Victoria doesn't forget her principles, even at this early hour.

"I'll take a suitcase. I can't live without brandy or cigarettes. Then I'll leave, too," says Mariana, as if it were a minor transition.

Mariana stuffs a few garments into the little suitcase, along with some shoes and the brandy and cigarettes. Hugo's knapsack is ready. "I don't need anything else. This is exactly what I need." Mariana speaks in her ordinary tone of voice.

The Residence suddenly seems like a big body whose soul

has been removed. Victoria hurries Sylvia along. "The house is full of ghosts," she says. "Come, let's get out of here quickly."

The sky is high and blue, and the sun is bright and dazzling. While he was in the closet, Hugo imagined his liberation as a winged run that couldn't be stopped. Now he staggers after Mariana with heavy steps. "Too bad we didn't get up earlier," says Mariana. She makes a sharp turn toward a grove of trees.

The grove is sparse, and the short, bare trees leave them even more exposed. Mariana doesn't feel comfortable in the open air. She changes direction and finally sits down under a tree and says, "We have to find a protected place. Here everything is wide open." Hugo knows that she will soon take a bottle out of the suitcase, have a swallow, and her mood will improve.

"Aren't you cold?" she asks, shivering.

"No."

Hugo loves the tilt of her head and the question that comes in its wake. Her body still radiates warmth and the smell of perfume. He takes her hand and kisses it. Mariana smiles, takes a bottle out of the suitcase, drinks, and says, "The sky is beautiful, isn't it?"

He sees her in daylight for the first time now and is astonished at her beauty.

"We have to find a house. We can't live without a house. I won't go to the convent. In the convent they slave away and pray all the time. I love God, but I don't feel like praying all the time." Hugo listens attentively to her mutterings. In them she always expresses her true heart's desires, and they are usually fantasies that have no basis in reality. Now he can follow them, because she's speaking slowly, sad and happy by turns, and in the end she sums it up for herself. "I've suffered enough, and now I'll live in the country, just me and Hugo. You understand me, don't you?" She turns to him.

"It seems to me that I do," Hugo answers cautiously.

"Don't hesitate, honey."

Hugo doesn't expect that response and laughs.

"You should know that hesitation is our undoing."

They are outside the city, in the heart of the snow-covered fields. From here Hugo can see the white church, the water tower, and some buildings that he can't identify. The months in the closet have distanced him from the city that he loved. Now, when he sees its edges, he remembers the long walks he took with his father along the river, in the alleys alongside the park, and in secret places that only his father knew.

Mariana guesses what he is thinking and says, "We'll always be together." She hugs him and covers his mouth with hers. He feels her tongue and the taste of brandy.

They could have sat there for a long while, enjoying the landscape and the closeness that warmed them both. But then an unidentifiable noise is heard in the distance—perhaps a tractor or a tank that is stuck and struggling to move. The sudden noise spoils their feeling of closeness.

"We've got to move on," Mariana says, and rises to her feet. "We mustn't be lazy."

They advance without speaking. Suddenly Hugo sees the closet before his eyes—the straw mattress, the sheepskins, and the jumble of Mariana's clothes. That was the home of his imaginings for a year and a half. For hours he would wait painfully for her to come, but when she did appear in the doorway, his despair would vanish like the morning fog.

"Strange." The word slips out of his mouth.

"What's strange, dear?"

"The bright light and the sky," he says.

"It's a sign that God is watching over us."

When Mariana drinks from her bottle, she sometimes utters sentences that make no sense, or whose logic is faulty. But they always have a tone of exaltation and wonder. Sometimes she utters an expression or a simile that surprises Hugo with its brilliance. Once, after she had drunk half a bottle and was foggy, she said, "You should know, my dear, that God dwells within you, even in your belly button."

While they are plodding along, a peasant suddenly appears before them. Mariana is frightened, but she quickly recovers and asks, "Have the Russians come yet?"

"They're at the outskirts of the city."

"And when will they get here?"

"Today, apparently," says the peasant in a subdued tone of voice.

"There isn't much time," says Mariana, unwittingly betraying her fear.

The peasant fixes his gaze on her. "Aren't you Mariana?" he asks.

"You're mistaken," she immediately responds.

"I was sure you were Mariana."

"People sometimes make mistakes."

"Is this your son?"

"My son? Can't you see that he's my son?"

"Mistakes keep happening," he says, and turns away.

"There are ghosts everywhere," she mutters as the peasant walks away. Hugo now realizes that the lives of all the women who lived in The Residence—who entertained Germans in their rooms, had sex with them, and partied with them all night—are in danger. In his imagination he nurtured the illusion that Mariana didn't belong to them. She only pretended she belonged to them. She was secretly always his, and now she really is all his.

50

They find shelter in a hayloft, abandoned but roofed. Mariana spreads her kerchief on the ground and puts a small bottle of liqueur and some chocolate-covered cookies on it. Hugo tastes the liqueur, and it pleases him.

The sun now stands in the middle of the sky and is reflected on the blanket of snow, which gleams with great intensity. When they traveled to the Carpathians to ski, Hugo's mother took care to wear sunglasses. He hears the sound of her voice, warning and fearful.

After finishing the strange meal, Mariana lights a cigarette and says, "It's odd that everyone is glad the war is over, and only I'm afraid."

"What are you afraid of?"

"Of the Russians. They're fanatics. They will kill anyone who was in contact with the Germans. How strange—life isn't so important to me, yet the fear still remains."

"We'll slip away from them," says Hugo, trying to pull her out of her distress.

"I'm not complaining. I feel good now. A night spent sleeping alone or with you is worth everything to me. Since my youth, I've been forced to work like a slave, night after night."

"I'll watch over you," says Hugo, looking into her eyes.

"You have to get sturdy and grow. Since you've been with me, you've grown, but not enough. I'll make sure you have enough to eat. Spring is around the corner, and when it comes, we can walk along the river, catch fish, and grill them."

Hugo wants to flatter her, but he can't find the words, so he says, "Thank you very much."

Mariana looks at him softly and says, "Friends don't need to say thank you. Friends help each other. It goes without saying."

"I was wrong," Hugo says.

"We have lovely days ahead of us," Mariana announces, and sips from the bottle.

Later, they keep their distance from the houses on the road. Mariana is in a good mood. She sings and jokes and imitates Madam speaking German. At last she says, "I'm not sorry I left The Residence. In a little while spring will come, the trees will be covered with leaves, and they will be our roof. Mariana loves nature. Nature is good to women. Nature doesn't threaten, and it isn't violent. A woman can sit on a riverbank and dip her feet in the water, and if the water is warm, she can swim. Do you agree?"

"Absolutely."

"You love Mariana, and you make no demands or criticisms of her."

"You're beautiful."

"That's what Mariana loves to hear. My father, of blessed memory, used to say, 'Beautiful women are a disaster. All troubles come because of them.' " She chuckles with the harsh voice of a crow.

The setting sun stands on the horizon. Frost is blowing in the wind, and Mariana rouses herself from her thoughts and says, "In a little while night will fall, and we have no roof over our heads. We've gotten too far from the houses, and now we'll have to go back to them." There is no panic in her voice. Hugo has noticed that when the bottle is within reach, her thoughts are clear and without gloomy clouds.

"The horizon is beautiful," she continues in a nostalgic tone. "When I was a girl, I loved to look at it, but many years have passed. I forgot how beautiful it is. I was sure then that if I walked for an hour or two, I'd get to it. Why are you laughing?"

"I thought the same thing when I was a child."

"I knew we had something in common," she says, and they both laugh.

They advance with short steps, and without hurrying. "I would give all the money in the world for a cup of coffee and some cheesecake," Mariana says. "I'm not hungry, but a cup of coffee and some cheesecake would strengthen the faith within me. What about you, sweetie? You haven't eaten all day. Mariana is very selfish, and she's always tied to her own belly button. Sometimes she forgets the people she loves. That's a flaw in my character. I doubt I can correct a flaw like that. But you forgive me. You always forgive me."

Meanwhile, night has fallen, and it has gotten colder. Mariana gives Hugo her thick sweater and the kerchief. The coat that he brought with him from home is short on him now, and it won't button. "Now you'll be warm," she says, and is pleased with his new look.

Suddenly, a cabin appears before them, a rather meager-looking hut with no fence.

"Let's ask. Maybe they'll let us spend the night," she says, and knocks on the door.

An old man opens it, and Mariana quickly tells him that they have fled from the front and are looking for a place to sleep—for payment, of course.

"Who are you?" asks the old man in a sharp voice.

"My name is Maria, and I'm a widow and a mother. This is my son, Janek."

"What will you pay me with?"

"I'll give you two packets of German cigarettes."

"Come in. I was about to go to sleep. A person doesn't know what the night will bring him."

"We're quiet, and we won't disturb you. In the morning we'll be on our way."

"Have the Russians come already?" the old man inquires.

"They've broken through the front, and they're rushing forward."

"Only God knows what the day will bring."

Mariana hands him the two packets, and the old man holds them in his trembling hands. "All winter long I haven't smoked," he says. "Without cigarettes, life is tasteless. I don't have the money to buy them. In the past my sons used to bring me tobacco, and I would roll my own cigarettes. This last year they haven't come. They forgot their father."

"They didn't forget. The war blocked the roads." Mariana defends them.

"If a son wants to see his father, he gets there. Now everyone is waiting for the father to die. An old father is a curse. After his death, they come and finger his possessions and fight over every pillow. That's it. Who am I to complain? Would you like some potato soup that I made?"

"Gladly, grandfather."

The hot soup fills them, and Mariana thanks him again.

"People have forgotten that we are commanded to help one another," the old man murmurs.

Later, they fall into bed and sleep like stones. Mariana wakes up several times and kisses Hugo hard on the neck. He sinks between her breasts and sleeps dreamlessly.

51

They awaken late and expect the old man to offer them a hot cup of tea or a hot herbal brew. The old man doesn't offer them anything. His eyes are filled with anger. "He's your son?" he asks.

"Indeed," she says.

"That's not how a mother sleeps with her son." He doesn't conceal his opinion.

Mariana is stunned by the old man's sharp comment and freezes in her place.

The old man shuts the door behind them without saying anything.

The morning is bright and quiet. From time to time the muffled thunder of cannon fire breaks through and then fades. Mariana sips from the bottle, curses the old man, and says, "In every old man there lurks a fornicator." Hugo doesn't know that word, but he imagines that it refers to something bad.

"What time is it?" asks Mariana, like someone who has suddenly lost track of time.

"Exactly nine-thirty."

"That's a good hour. A cup of coffee or something else hot would immediately drive away my thirst. My late mother used to say, 'Man doesn't live by bread alone,' and may I add, preferably with coffee. I wasted my life for nothing. If I had married a Jew, my situation would be different. A Jew supports his wife, takes care of her, and pampers her." The word "Jew," which they didn't use often in his home, now sounds, in the open field, like a mysterious term, cut off from time and place, hovering above the earth like a little hunted bird.

They advance, and Mariana continues to curse the old man. "There are ghosts everywhere. Sometimes they take on the form of Madam, and sometimes of an old fornicator. There's no cleanliness in this life. Everything is malice or filth." After a pause she adds, "Don't listen to Mariana's chatter. She's got to talk. If she doesn't talk, she'll explode."

Hugo has noticed that it is hard for Mariana to listen and not easy for her to speak in complete sentences. But when she drinks from the bottle, the words well up inside her, and she speaks about her father and mother and sister, and sometimes about the friends who haven't been loyal to her.

Suddenly she asks him, "Do you know what a whore is?"

"Not everything."

"Better that way."

Mariana goes on to talk about the pollution of the body and the urgent need to take a bath. "Without a bath, a woman is a chunk of pollution." But she immediately changes her tone and says, "I yearn for a big bathtub, just for us." Hugo likes this mood. When Mariana yearns for something, her yearning brings forth a picture: a broad bathtub full of fragrant suds to lie in for hours, buoyed by warm water, and then to doze off in. "A snooze in the bathtub is heaven on earth. Do you agree?"

They walk on without speaking. Hugo is hungry, and his head is spinning. Mariana suggests making a little fire, melting some snow, and adding chocolate to the boiling water. The idea brightens her eyes, and she says, "The world isn't only darkness. Madam gave us back a little of what she stole. What would I do without brandy?"

As they are about to break off branches and start a fire, Mariana notices a small hut. "A grocery store!" she shouts. "A grocery store in the middle of the white desert. Who would have believed it?" Mariana's senses haven't deceived her. It is indeed a village grocery store. An elderly woman stands at the counter.

"Good morning, mother."

"The morning has already passed, my daughter." The woman corrects her.

"I'm still holding on to the hem of its apron," Mariana jokes. "We came to buy a loaf of bread, and some oil, and if you can graciously add some onion, we'd thank you greatly."

"I have no bread. The war has impoverished us."

"We'll make do with rye bread or black bread, any kind of bread. We haven't eaten for two days."

"I have no bread, daughter. Potatoes and a little cheese is what I can sell you."

"Give it to me, mother, and I'll pay you."

"With what money will you pay me?"

"With German money."

"They say that the Germans have retreated. Who will want their money?"

"Take this bracelet. It's silver with jewels, and add on some smoked meat or sausage."

The woman is stunned by the offer, but she is immediately captivated by the charm of the glittering jewelry.

"Is it silver or tin?" She tries not to show her interest.

"Pure silver, on my word of honor."

"God knows the truth. I'll go see what I have." She bends down and takes a few potatoes from a crate.

"Be generous, mother."

"A person has to take care of himself, isn't that so?"

She takes a piece of cheese, a small sausage, and two onions out of the pantry. "I'll put it all in a sack for you." Her voice softens.

"God bless you," says Mariana.

They return to the fields. The sun stands in the middle of the sky, and it's warm. Water is already burbling beneath the snow. Here and there they can also see it running. The light returns to Mariana's face, and it's evident that the supplies she has just bought have made her happy. "In a little while we'll stop and light a bonfire and make ourselves a meal fit for kings. But not under the open sky. Mariana is looking for a tree with broad branches. Mariana doesn't like sitting out in the open."

Along the way they come upon trees, but not with broad branches. Finally, they find a tree that pleases her. They put their belongings under it and go out to gather firewood. Mariana puts a few papers among the twigs. Before long a fire is kindled.

"I love bonfires. They remind me of my childhood," she says, and her face is full of light.

52

They sit and look at the fire. The flames are thin and blue and give off a good smell of burning wood. For a long while they just stare at it. The potatoes in the middle of the fire take on a dark crust. It's pleasant to sit and not do anything.

"God knows what will be, but meanwhile we have something to eat. As long as there are supplies to stave off hunger, there's nothing to worry about. If the weather stays the way it is now, we can get to the mountains in two or three days, and there it will be easier for us. In the mountains they don't pursue people who have committed no misdeed."

The gleaming snow covers the earth, leaving no bare spots. Mariana is apparently apprehensive. "In the mountains, they won't pursue us," she repeats. "In the mountains they don't dig into a person's past. They respond to his deeds. I'm prepared to do any kind of work and to earn my bread by the sweat of my brow. They'll see that Mariana's not lazy," she says to herself. Suddenly she's silent.

The potatoes and cheese are tasty. Mariana melts some snow in a pot and prepares tea. The tea and the chocolate-covered wafers remind Hugo of the trips his family would take when the season changed from winter to spring. His mother loved the white snow flowers that would peek out of the earth that was suddenly laid bare, black and moist.

The vision of those distant and forgotten mountains dazzles Hugo, and he closes his eyes. Now he clearly sees his mother kneeling, looking with wonder at the white flowers, and his father, seeing her wonderment, kneeling as well. For a moment they marvel together without speaking.

This vision, buried within him, breaks through and appears before his eyes, stunning him. Tears catch him unawares and flood his face.

"What's the matter with you?" says Mariana. "A big fellow like you doesn't cry anymore."

"I remembered my parents."

"You mustn't cry. We're setting out on a long and dangerous journey. Who will watch over Mariana? A spoiled fellow cries, but a strong and brave lad mustn't cry. We'll have to climb mountains, cross rivers, and get our bread from the earth. A strong boy knows how to suffer and never cries." Her voice is determined, and Hugo feels that he has made a mistake, that he must overcome his weakness.

"I'm sorry," he says, and wipes his eyes.

"Crying is hard to forgive. All those years I wanted to cry, but I restrained myself. A person who cries announces to the world that he's lost and needs pity. A person who asks for pity is a sad sack. You can be anything, but not a sad sack. Do you understand?"

"I understand," Hugo says, and without doubt he does understand.

"From now on not even a single tear."

"I promise."

For quite a while they sit and drink tea. Mariana's face doesn't soften. She sinks deep into thought, and her eyes express dour seriousness. In his heart he knows that if he asks her pardon now, she won't be forgiving. He must wait and, when the time comes, prove to her that he's brave, that emotions and weakness have no control over him.

"I've been thinking about you," Mariana says, rousing him from his thoughts. "You've changed and matured, but you still have quite a way to go. Jews spoil their children, and they don't prepare them properly for life. A Ukrainian child works in the field, and if they hit him, he doesn't cry. He knows that life isn't a plate of strawberries."

Then she takes a few swigs from her bottle and stops punishing him. Hugo gathers some twigs and brings the bonfire back to life. "Come to me, baby, and I'll give you a kiss. It's good that you're with me. It's hard to be alone. Bad thoughts strangle you."

"Should I melt more snow?"

"There's no need. We've drunk enough. What time is it?"

"Three o'clock."

"In a little while we'll have to set out. We can't sleep outdoors. Let's hope that God sends us decent people," she says, and puts the bottle in the fire. Strangely, that motion, which had nothing superfluous about it, implants itself in Hugo's memory with great clarity. In time he will wonder: *When did the tears freeze in me?*

53

The sun sinks toward the horizon, glowing like a red-hot iron. Mariana doesn't stop marveling at the splendid sight. "If there is beauty like that, it's a sign that God is in heaven. Only God can create colors like that. My grandma used to say, 'God created goodness and beauty, and people only spoil what God created.' "

They walk on, toward houses that are scattered along the road. Mariana keeps thinking out loud. "I'm amazed at the Jews. An intelligent people, everybody agrees, yet most of them don't believe in God. How many times did I ask your mother, 'How is it that you don't believe in God? After all, you see His deeds every day, every hour.' "

"And how did she answer you?" Hugo dares to ask.

"To her credit it must be said that she didn't talk cleverly and say things beyond what my mind could grasp. She simply said, 'I lost my faith while at gymnasium, and since then it hasn't returned to me.' I'm sorry for your mother and for your uncle Sigmund, who lost their faith in God. I liked to laugh with Sigmund, laugh with my whole heart. I thought that if we married, I could lift myself and him up from drunkenness. But every time we would talk about a wedding, he would make a dismissive gesture with his right hand, as if to say, *I've already tried that. There's no point to it.*

"At first I thought that he didn't want to marry me because I'm a simple woman. Later I understood that he was a lost person. I was willing to marry him as he was, to cook his meals and wash his clothes, but then the hard days came, the persecution and the ghetto, and he told me something I'll never forget: 'I can't be saved any longer. Save yourself. The Jews have been condemned to death. You're still young.' Every time I remember that, I choke with pain. What a marvelous man, what a great soul."

Then Mariana falls silent and walks with her head bowed, sunk within herself. Hugo doesn't disturb her. When Mariana is silent, she's gathering her thoughts in order to reveal them to him later. When she's thinking, she's connected to other worlds. Sometimes she reveals a bit to him. Once she said, "Don't forget, there's an upper world and a lower world. We're mired in the lower world. If we're good, God will save us and take us to Him up above. I have no patience for all the little acts of deceit that we have to experience here. I want Him to redeem me now. He knows how much I've suffered here. I'm sure He will take that into account when He comes to judge me. I'm not afraid. Whatever He does, I'll accept with love. I feel great closeness to Him and to His holy son."

Suddenly a man comes out of one of the houses and strides toward them. Mariana is frightened and says, "Let's step aside."

Hugo has noticed that people who appeared suddenly frightened her. There were people she recognized from a distance and avoided. It's strange how many people she knows. Once she said, "I know that bastard, and also his brother, and also his cousin. I wish I didn't know them. Every time I remember them, my body weeps. Good God, what have I done to my miserable body? I'm a criminal."

Two days before they set out, Hugo heard Mariana say to

her friends in The Residence, "There's no sense in running away. They'll identify us easily. If the father doesn't, the son will." Everybody laughed. Then he heard one of the women say, "Whores and Jews are always persecuted. There's nothing to be done."

Night falls, and Mariana decides to knock on the door of a meager hut. An old woman opens the door and asks, "Who are you?"

"My name is Maria. This is my son, Janek. Our house is close to the front, and we're looking for a place to spend tonight."

"What will you give me in return?"

"A bottle of good drink. That's what I have."

"Come in. I don't want to waste the heat."

The hut is tidy and clean. The smell of starch fills the two rooms. "Sit down," says the old woman, and she serves them hot herbal tea. Mariana tells her that they have been on the road for days because the front is getting close to their house.

"The Russians are coming back?"

"They're coming back."

"Woe is me for those who were here and woe is me for those who are coming. The first are murderers, the second are heretics. God is sending us difficult trials."

Mariana takes an ornate bottle of liqueur out of the suitcase and hands it to the old woman. The old woman grabs it and says, "A pretty bottle. Let's hope the drink inside is worthy of the vessel that preserves it. In our times, everything is deception."

The bed is wide and soft, and they sleep in each other's embrace all night long. Hugo tells Mariana that the brandy in her mouth is sweet and tasty. Mariana is enthralled. In her great enthusiasm, she hugs him and says, "Kiss me anywhere you feel like it. You're my knight. You're better than anything I ever knew in my life."

Afterward, he sinks into her and into a deep sleep. In his dream, people are trying to snatch Mariana away from him. He grips her with all his strength and drags her back. In the end, they both fall into a pit and are saved.

54

Outside the sun is already high in the sky, a warm sun. The snow, which sparkled only yesterday with its poignant beauty, has already lost its crispness and turned into muddy slush.

"What's the matter with you, snow?" Mariana lifts her head and calls out. The sight of her raised head reminds Hugo of an animal whose master has abandoned it. "Now all the roads are open, and the Russians will advance as they please. Until now the snow and the storms protected us. Now all the fortifications have collapsed. The tanks will speed right through to us, but you'll protect Mariana. You'll tell them that Mariana protected you and loved you. Am I lying?"

"You're telling the truth," replies Hugo.

"Say it a bit louder."

Hugo raises his voice and shouts, "Mariana is telling the truth. Let everyone know that there's no one like Mariana. She's beautiful, good, and loyal."

Now a new spirit grips her, and she speaks of the different life that is in store for them in the mountains. "People in the mountains are quiet, they work in the fields and in vegetable gardens. We'll also work in vegetable gardens, and at noon we'll sit under a broad-branched tree and eat corn porridge with cheese and cream, and finish off with a cup of fragrant coffee. It will be warm and pleasant, and we'll doze a little. After our nap, we'll return to the vegetable gardens. Tilling the soil is good for the body and the soul. We'll work till sunset, and in the evening we'll return to our hut, and no one will find fault with us."

But meanwhile, they gather wood and light a fire. Mariana makes tea and is about to soar off again in her imagination when some bad luck appears, as though emerging from beneath the earth—a peasant. He fixes her with an angry look and says, "What are you doing here?"

"Nothing," she answers, stunned.

"Get out of here."

"What harm have I done?"

"You're even asking?"

Now it seems as though he is about to come over and hit her. Mariana rises to her feet and cries out, "I'm not afraid of death. God knows the truth, and He will judge me with justice. God hates hypocrites and self-righteous people."

"You're talking about God?" he says, and spits at her.

"You'll pay for that spit. God remembers every injustice. You'll get yours in this world and in the world to come. His account book is open, and He writes everything down."

"Whore," he hisses, and goes on his way.

Mariana sits back down, boiling with rage. Hugo knows he has to leave her alone now. When Mariana is furious, she falls silent and bites her lips, and then she curses for a long time, swigging from the bottle and mumbling. Hugo likes to hear her mumblings. They burble like running water.

Suddenly, as though just waking up, she says, "Mariana is too concerned with herself and forgets that she has a darling of a lad. We have to learn how to see the good. My grandma used to say, 'The world is full of His goodness, too bad our eyes don't see it.' Do you remember your grandma?" Again she surprises him.

"Grandpa and Grandma live in the Carpathians," replies

Hugo. "They have a little farm, and we go to them for summer vacations. Life in the Carpathians is very different from life in the city. There a different clock ticks, with different hands. You go out for a walk in the morning and come home in the evening, day after day."

"Are your grandparents religious?"

"Grandpa prays every morning. He wraps himself in a prayer shawl, and you can't see his face. When Grandma prays, she hides her face in both hands."

"I'm glad you got to see them."

"Everything there is very beautiful, very quiet, and wrapped in mystery."

"There are things that we see and don't understand, but in time they become clear. I'm glad you saw your grandparents praying. A person who prays is close to God. In my early childhood I knew how to pray. Since then, much water has flowed."

They heed their feet and move on. From the villages near the main road they hear the roar of tanks and the cheering of the peasants. They move away from the main road and are bogged down in the melting snow. The wetness penetrates Hugo's shoes, and he is sorry he left his other pair in the closet.

Once again he sees the closet before his eyes, and Mariana's room, and the hall where the young women gathered. The many days he spent there now seem as though they belong in a hidden world within him, a world that will be revealed to him in detail one day. For now, it's locked behind seven locks.

"What are you thinking about?"

"About the closet and about your room." He doesn't hide it from her.

"Better to forget that. For me it was a jail cell. The people and the walls only darkened my life. I thank God for freeing me from that prison and giving you to me."

As they slog through the snow, another mood grips Mariana. "You'll forget me," she says. "You'll grow up, and you'll have other interests. Women will chase you. I'll be remembered as a strange woman in the flow of your life. You'll be successful. I have no doubt that you'll be successful. Your success will be so great that not even for a moment will you ask yourself, 'Who was that Mariana, who was with me in The Residence and in the open fields?' "

"Mariana," he dares to interrupt her, "I'll always be with you."

"It's customary to say that."

"I love you," he says, and his voice chokes.

"So you say."

"I'll go with you wherever you go. Remove doubt from your heart."

Mariana chuckles and says, "It's not your fault, darling. It's man's rotten nature. A person is just flesh and blood, enslaved to the day and to the needs of that day. When she doesn't have a house, and she doesn't have food, and she doesn't have a living soul, she does what I did. I could have been a laundress or a servant in the house of some rich people, but I went to The Residences. In a residence, you're not yourself. You're a chunk of flesh that they roll and turn over, pinch, or just bite. At the end of the night, you're bruised and wounded and you bury yourself in the pit of sleep. Do you understand what I'm trying to tell you?"

"I'm trying."

"Mariana doesn't like the word 'trying.' Either you understand or you don't. 'Trying' is a word for spoiled people, for people who don't know how to decide. Listen to what Mariana is telling you, don't say 'I'm trying'—do it!"

55

The day, which began with a clear, bright sky, suddenly clouds over, and a fierce rain beats down on them. While they are looking for a tree to hide under, they notice an empty storage shed, and Mariana, in high spirits, immediately proclaims, "God preserves the innocent. God knew that we had no house and He provided us with a roof over our heads."

Mariana doesn't pray often, but she frequently announces that God is in heaven and that, because He exists, there's nothing to fear. If troubles come to you, examine your deeds and accept the troubles with love.

Mariana is inconsistent in her faith. Often, when she was in distress, despair overwhelmed her. Once Hugo found her pounding her head against the wall and shouting bitterly, "Why was I born? What is my purpose in this world? Only to serve as a mattress for soldiers? If that's it, I'd rather die."

Now her spirits are high. She is singing and joking, and she calls the Jews good and delicate creatures whose lives were spoiled by mental confusion. Even Sigmund, who was as addicted to his liquor as a Ukrainian, even he didn't know how to shake off niggling thoughts. *Now I won't think,* he would say to himself. *Now I'm giving myself over to the caprice of my heart.* "More than once I begged him, 'Sigmund, call out loud, God is in heaven. You don't know how much good that will do you.' Hearing my request, he would burst out laughing, as if I'd said something foolish. He never agreed to admit that God exists. He kept saying, 'How do you know? If you give me one little proof, I'll start to believe.' 'The soul,' I kept saying, 'doesn't your soul announce to you that God exists?' And what was his answer? 'Even the existence of the soul needs proof.' That's why I say, the Jews can't live without proof.

"But you, my sweet, you already know that there's no need for proofs. You just have to direct your soul in the correct manner. Faith is a simple matter. If you believe in God, you'll see a lot of beauty. And another thing, don't use the word 'contradiction.' Sigmund used to say to me sometimes, 'There's a contradiction in what you're saying.' I loved every word that came out of his mouth, but not that word. I often tried to uproot that strange word from his head, but he stood his ground. I hoped that at least in his drunkenness, he would discover and admit that God exists. But all my efforts were in vain."

These reminiscences don't make them sad. Mariana and Hugo make love as though they were in a wide double bed, not an abandoned storage shed. Hugo again promises that he will always be with her, in good and bad times.

"In a little while your mother will come and take you away from me," Mariana says.

"The war isn't over yet."

"The war will be over soon, and they'll do to Mariana what they did to the Jews."

"You're exaggerating." He allows himself to correct her.

"Realistic predictions don't exaggerate, they show you what will be. You have to be alert and listen to them. Don't be afraid, darling, Mariana's not afraid of death. Death isn't as horrible as it's described. You pass from this world to a better one. True, there is a heavenly court, but you should know that it takes not only deeds into account but also intentions. Do you understand?"

The rain, which seemed to be determined and angry just a while ago, stops all at once. The sun comes out again, and the fields are spread out, flat and broad. The isolated trees in the heart of the plain look like forgotten signposts from another age.

Later Hugo falls asleep. He barely hears the last words that Mariana says. He sleeps and dreams many dreams, but all he remembers is his mother's face. His mother was in the pharmacy, completely absorbed in the effort to decipher a prescription that had been handed to her. It was noon, just before the pharmacy closed for lunch. At that hour the pharmacy was usually full. His father was in the adjacent room, mixing a prescription for a customer. That familiar picture, of which Hugo knew every detail, made him happy. He expected his mother to notice him and be surprised. But although she was apparently aware of him, she didn't pay him any notice. For a long time Hugo stood and wondered why. Finally he decided, *If they're ignoring me, I'll be on my way.*

The sun is setting, and again the nagging question arises. "Where will we sleep?" Mariana knocks on several doors, but no one is willing to let them stay the night. In the tavern, she is immediately recognized, and everyone mocks and curses her. Mariana isn't silent. She calls them adulterers and sanctimonious men who lord it over the weak. "The time will come, and it's not far away, when God will punish you. God doesn't forgive adultery or self-righteousness. He adds punishment upon punishment."

Again they are in the depths of darkness. Mariana is full of brandy and calls out loud, "I love the night. The night is better

than people and their houses." Hugo rushes to gather twigs.
They light a fire, boil water in the pot, and put some potatoes
in the fire.

They eat the remainder of the cheese and a piece of the
sausage, and Mariana gives her imagination free reign: "I foresee days when we'll have plenty; poverty doesn't suit us. I see a
small house, a vegetable garden, an orchard. We'll milk the
cow, but we won't slaughter her. We'll spend most of the day in
nature, and in the evening we'll come home and light the oven.
I love a lit oven, when you can see the flames in it. That's all,
nothing more. Wait a moment, I forgot the main thing—
a bathtub. In our house there has to be a bathtub. Without a
bathtub, life isn't life. You have to lie in the bathtub for two or
three hours every day. That's the kind of life I foresee. What do
you think?"

Thus they pass the first part of the night.

56

After midnight, when they're already half frozen, they find an empty tavern whose owner agrees to let them sleep there. Mariana is drunk, and she keeps blessing the proprietor, who is not impressed by her blessings and demands payment. Mariana gives him a banknote, and he demands more. She gives him more and asks for a blanket. Hugo's feet are as cold as ice, and Mariana rubs them briskly. In the end they wrap themselves in each other and fall asleep.

They wake up early in the morning and set out immediately. An overcast day is preferable to a moldy alcove, Mariana maintains. Fortunately they find a tree with broad branches and prepare to make a fire.

The snow is melting, and the black earth that was hidden all winter is revealed. Thin smoke rises from the chimneys atop the houses. It's a tranquil, innocent morning. Mariana looks particularly beautiful. Her large eyes are wide open, and her long neck becomes her.

After finishing her tea, Mariana takes a few swigs from the bottle and her heart opens. "My life was ruined from the start," she says. "I don't want to blame my father and mother. I used to blame them and hang all the bad things that happened to me on them. Now I know, it was my youthful restlessness. I was young and beautiful, and everybody was in love with me. I didn't know then that they were predators, that they only wanted my flesh. They taught me to drink and smoke. I was thirteen, fourteen, stunned by the money they gave me. I was sure things would go on that way all my life. I didn't know they were poisoning me. At fourteen, I already couldn't manage without brandy. My parents shunned me. They wouldn't even let me into the house. 'You're lost,' they told me, and I was sure that they were evil and would relent. After that—from whore-house to whorehouse, from madam to madam. Why am I telling you all this? I'm telling you so that you'll know that Mariana's life was ruined from the start. Now it's impossible to fix it."

"Why?"

"Because a large part of my body has been ravished. The wolves ravished it. I don't expect mercy or who knows what. The Russians say that if a woman slept with the Germans, her blood is on her head. I assume that God won't stand by me, either. I ignored Him all those years."

"But God is greatly merciful and forgiving." Hugo interrupts her.

"Yes, to those who are worthy, to those who walk in His ways and do what He asks of them."

"You love Him very much."

"It's a late love. For many years I rebelled against Him."

How right she is becomes clear that very day. People attack them wherever they go. They throw stones at them, call them bad names, and sic big dogs on them. Mariana protects them from the dogs with a stick, and she curses the people loudly. They call her "servant of the Germans," and she calls them "hypocrites" and "bastards." They wound her neck, which heightens her anger and frees her tongue.

Now it's evident they have to leave, and soon. Hugo bandages Mariana's neck with a handkerchief, and they set out.

"Too bad I don't have iodine. I had a lot of it in my room, but who ever thought I'd be wounded?" she mutters to herself.

That night they walk quite a bit. Mariana is angry at herself, because she has no idea where they are. "After all, I was born in these parts. I wandered around here during my whole childhood. What's the matter with me?"

"We're walking toward the mountains." Hugo tries to comfort her.

"How do you know?"

"I feel it." He is drawn out by her words.

"We're groping like blind people. In every corner, there's a pitfall or a trap. Who knows where Satan is dragging us. He's a cheat, and he's cunning."

57

Morning breaks through and lights up the darkness. To their surprise, Mariana and Hugo find themselves standing at the foot of a mountain. On its side there are small houses surrounded by gardens. "We got there, thank God," says Mariana, as if they had reached a different continent. She immediately sinks down onto the ground.

Hugo hurries to gather wood and light a fire. Mariana announces out loud, "From here, I'm not moving. I don't have the strength to lift myself and walk even one more step."

"We'll rest. There's no hurry." Hugo speaks like an adult.

Then a large sun comes out and lights up the mountains and the plain. Thin mist rises from the moist earth. Not far from them a river meanders. It's peaceful, as after a mighty battle that ended in a standoff.

Mariana puts the suitcase under her head and falls asleep. Hugo feels that he has now been freed from his bonds and can step out into the outdoors. His previous life, crammed and restricted in the closet, seems distant to him, rooted in darkness.

Mariana sleeps until noon, and when she wakes and sees Hugo at her side, guarding her sleep, she is very moved. She holds out her arms and hugs him. "I slept, and you watched over my sleep, my good soul. You didn't sleep all last night, either."

"Do you feel better?"

"Certainly I feel better."

There are a few potatoes left and some sausage. They make a meal that, in her great enthusiasm, Mariana calls "a princely feast." Fatigue and nervousness have vanished from her face, and she is entirely given over to Hugo, as though she has just discovered him.

"What are you going to want to do in the future?" She surprises him.

"To be with you," he answers right away.

"The war is over, and soon your mother will come and get you."

"Let's see what happens." He tries to give his voice the composure of an adult.

Mariana again gives free reign to her imagination. "Mariana was a beautiful, tall woman. She could have been a singer who traveled from city to city and moved people, a devoted housewife who raised her children like the Jews, going with them on long summer vacations and coming back suntanned. If I had been a kept woman, my lover would have taken me to sunbathe. But I'm a simple whore. I don't want to conceal anything from you. To be a whore is the most contemptible thing in the world. Nothing is more contemptible."

Hugo has learned that every one of Mariana's moods has different words. Fortunately for him, her moods come and go, and so it is this time, too.

The sun is at its fullest, and spring is bursting from every blade of grass. Cows and horses have been taken out to graze. Mariana announces that this place is the loveliest imaginable and that it's forbidden to waste this precious time. "All my life I was shut up in rooms," she says again, "working at night and sleeping during the day. I forgot that there was a sky, plants, animals, and green beauty like this. Those poplars, look how tall they are. Now they're naked, but soon they'll be covered with silver leaves, and they'll be even more beautiful.

"Now I'm sitting and contemplating everything. Contemplation brings tranquility to the soul. 'Everything we see and hear is God,' my grandma used to say, 'because God dwells everywhere, even in the lowest weed.' I was a child then, and I was attentive to what she said. But I went astray very quickly."

Then she shuts her eyes and says, "The sun is warm and pleasant. I'm going to close my eyes. If informers come to arrest me, don't follow me. Run away. You're not to blame for my fate. You were good to me."

Hugo wants to say, *You're wrong, it's not true,* but Mariana immediately sinks into sleep.

Hugo sits and stares at the fire and the landscape. Memories don't disturb him. Instead, the sights of spring appear before his eyes. He imagines life from now on as pleasant— wandering along rivers with low trees on their banks, observing flowers of every hue, watching birds peck at seeds in the palm of his hand.

Mariana awakens and says, "Again you didn't sleep?"

"I'm not tired. I was contemplating the landscape."

"Come to me, and I'll give you a kiss. Who knows how much time I have left to be with you in this world."

"Always," he responds immediately.

58

The following days are clear and bright. The fire burns day and night. Hugo is sure that Mariana's fears will subside as they advance toward the wooded, uninhabited areas.

"Come on, let's get moving," he keeps saying.

"To where? Who knows what's swarming around out there."

To overcome his secret despair, Hugo fans the flames of the campfire and assures Mariana that collaborators won't reach them there. The place isn't populated, and it's far from the main road.

Meanwhile, their supplies have run out, and Hugo decides to go up to one of the nearby houses to replenish them. Mariana equips him with two silver rings and is pleased by his initiative. Before he sets out, she says in a voice that he hasn't heard before, "Please come back right away, and don't delay."

Fortune favors him, and for one ring he gets potatoes, a wedge of cheese, and pears. Mariana runs to him with open arms and calls him a "hero." Hugo knows that it's easy to change her mood. A small success restores the light to her face. She admits that depression is her enemy and knows that she mustn't give in to it. She must always look at the bright side of life and not sink into melancholy.

Later Hugo spreads out a shirt in the water. Luckily, he catches three fish. They clean the fish and grill them on the coals. In her joy, Mariana hugs and kisses Hugo and tells him he's in danger—she's simply going to gobble him up.

That night she teaches him two pleasant Ukrainian folk songs, singing each one several times. They fall asleep next to the fire, intertwined. Hugo dreams about his violin teacher, a short, irritable man who used to demand relaxation and quiet from his pupils. "Relaxation and quiet are the preconditions for good violin playing," he used to say. "For some reason," he once told Hugo, "my parents wanted me to be a violinist. I'm irritable. Irritability doesn't suit that instrument. Only a calm quiet brings out the required clarity and tempo."

The next day they set out. "It's a shame to leave this marvelous place," Mariana says. "I've gotten used to this little hollow and the campfire and the tall trees that sway in the wind. Why should we wander when we can sit?" So she speaks, but in her heart she knows there's no choice. The nights are cold, the earth is wet, and even a big fire only heats small parts of the body. They must have a roof over their heads.

They climb a hill from which the villages, the outlying areas, and parts of the city can be viewed. It turns out that they haven't gone far. Mariana is thrilled by the landscape. "Look, dear," she cries out, "at what God created. What beauty. What tranquility. Horses and dogs know how to live right. Only people, the crown of creation, as they say, make a commotion with everything they do. My grandma used to say, 'Flesh and blood—today quiet and drowsy, and tomorrow a murderer.' You have to be brave."

"What must I do?"

"Don't fear. Fear debases us. A debased person isn't worthy

of living. If you're going to live, then live in freedom. That simple thing was what I didn't know. All my life I lived a debased life."

"I'm not afraid."

"That's just what I wanted to hear from you. It's better to die than to live a debased life."

Later, for no discernible reason, Mariana bursts into tears. Hugo kneels and wipes her eyes, but her weeping does not subside. "Mariana's going to die, and no memory of her will be left. If I stayed alive, I could reform, but now I can't. In hell they'll roast me. Rightly, they'll roast me. You, my dear, take care of yourself. When the informers come to take me, don't go after me. They'll take me straight to the gallows, or who knows what."

"How do you know? There are no people here, there are no informers. There's a splendid landscape and great tranquility."

"With my own eyes I saw them."

"What did you see?"

"I saw three soldiers handcuff me and march me off."

"That was a bad dream. You mustn't believe in bad dreams."

"The dream was the truth," she says in a whisper.

But when the sun descends to the horizon, and the lower part of the sky turns purplish-red, Mariana calms down. She takes a few swallows of brandy, and the dark visions fade away.

Suddenly she says to him, "Why don't you read me some poems from the Bible?"

Hugo takes the Bible out of his knapsack and reads her the first psalm.

"It's very beautiful, even if I don't understand it. Do you?"

"I think so."

"That phrase pleases me a lot, 'like a tree planted by the rivers of water.' Do you like the Bible?"

"Mama liked to read it to me, but since then I've barely opened it."

"I forgot. You're not religious. But since you've been with Mariana, you've changed a little. Mariana loves God very much. Too bad I didn't walk in His ways. I always did the opposite. You have to promise me that you'll read a chapter or two every day. That will strengthen you and give you power and courage to overcome evildoers. Evildoers swarm everywhere. Do you promise me?"

"I promise."

"I knew you wouldn't refuse me."

They find shelter with an elderly couple. The old people accept German money and serve them hot vegetable soup. When Mariana asks whether the Germans have already retreated, the old man answers with assurance, "The German army is the best in the world. An army like that can't be defeated." The old man's words fill her with hope, and she suddenly feels that she has been given a reprieve.

Their room is wide, and there is a large bed in it. There's even a sink in the corner. After many days without a house, without washing, and without a toilet, the place seems like a splendid inn.

"We're in good shape here, right?" Mariana says.

"Very much so."

But Hugo's sleep isn't quiet that night. He sees his mother among a mass of refugees, and her face is dark and thin. She goes from person to person and asks whether they have seen Hugo. A woman refugee asks distractedly, "Where was he?" His mother is embarrassed for a moment, but she recovers and replies, "With a Christian woman."

The refugees are consumed by their hunger and don't take the trouble to answer her. They look to Hugo like the people from the ghetto who were waiting to be deported. In great despair he bites the handcuffs that shackle him. The massive effort does indeed free his hands, but instead of going down to the refugees and to his mother, he falls into a deep pit.

"What's the matter?" Mariana wakes him up.

"Nothing, a dream."

"Don't pay attention to dreams," she says, and draws him to her breast.

59

The next day the elderly couple offers them cups of tea. They accompany them to the gate and wish them a successful journey. Moved by the gesture, Mariana hugs and kisses the woman, and they immediately set out.

The following days are quiet and pass without surprises. They go from hill to hill, light campfires, and buy potatoes and cheese from the peasants. Hugo fishes successfully. Every day he catches three or four fish in his shirt.

Mariana's fears are not assuaged, but they have lessened and are no longer outwardly expressed. From time to time she says, "You, my dear, must watch out for yourself and not try to defend me. Everyone has their own fate. That's life." Hearing her words, Hugo freezes where he is and doesn't respond. But sometimes the words form in his mouth, and he says, "We'll always be together, that's God's will." His words bring a wry smile to her face.

Sometimes he reads psalms to her. Mariana encourages him and says, "Read, honey, you have a marvelous voice. I don't understand the poems, but they exalt my soul. Do you understand them?"

"Not everything is understandable to me, either."

"If we find a priest, he'll explain them to us. Sometimes they leave the church and stroll along the river."

While they are on the road, Hugo adopts Mariana's way of speaking. When something succeeds for him, or when Mariana overcomes her depression, he says, "Thank God." Mariana feels that she has transferred something of her inner self to Hugo. "Take the inside of Mariana and throw away the shell," she says to him. "What's inside her is faith in God on high, and her shell is depression. Depression is what always tries to drag her down to hell. If it weren't for that illness, her life would have been different. Beware of depression as of the plague."

But there are also days of laughter and drunken pleasures. "Isn't it true that Mariana is still young and beautiful?" she would say.

"Very true."

"If we get to a safe place, I'll take care of myself, and all my beauty will be yours."

"Thank you," says Hugo, because he can find no other words.

"We're like a pair of birds. Did you ever see a bird thank another bird? They hop from branch to branch, pleased with each other, and when evening comes, they fall asleep from having chattered so much."

"Too bad the water in the stream is so cold," she says at one point. "We could go into the stream and swim like two fish. When I was a little girl, I used to swim in the river. Since then I haven't. I have a strong desire to swim. It seems to me that swimming would ease my depression. When a person swims and comes out of the water, he immediately walks erect. His eyes see splendid colors. Am I wrong?" Hugo loves that sudden wonderment. At such times he feels she is connected to mysterious forces within her. Her expression changes, and she is under influences that are not her own.

"It's wrong that people kill animals and eat them," she says after a while. "That's a disreputable trait. Animals are so much like us that the killing of them cries out to heaven. Papa, of blessed memory, would slaughter a pig before every Easter. The memory of it gives me chills to this day. When I was young I swore in my heart that I wouldn't eat meat. Of course I didn't keep that oath."

"Our family is vegetarian."

"I didn't know."

"Just fruit and vegetables and dairy products."

"I always said the Jews are more sensitive. But what good did their sensitivity do them? They were persecuted even more cruelly. Don't ever forget that the members of your tribe were cruelly killed in the streets just because they were Jews."

"I won't forget."

"The Germans drove them into the ghetto and sent them who knows where, just because they were Jews. God can't bear injustice like that. He will bring a flood upon their persecutors. Don't forget, you mustn't pass over injustice in silence."

But there are also days of total silence. Mariana would sit down, sunk in her thoughts, and Hugo would keep drilling into himself: *I must plant every detail of this journey in my memory.* When Mariana is deep in thought, a strange light appears on her face, her forehead expands, and her hair stands up on her head. Sometimes it seems to Hugo that her lovely being is being eaten away by her dejection. But, not to worry, when she is once again filled with wonder, her face lights up with beauty.

"Forget my sadness and irritation and remember only the light that was between us," she says to him distractedly.

A peasant woman sells them a few eggs and a jar of cream, and they sit down on the ground to eat. After the meal, Mariana says to Hugo, "Of all the people who were with me, only you are mine."

"You're very beautiful." He can't restrain himself.

"I'm very glad that I please you. A woman without an admirer is a sealed well. Life is stifled in her, and her beauty withers. Now, thank the Lord, I'm far from all those who tormented me. Now I'm my own woman, and I am only with you."

"I don't mind sleeping outdoors. I can make campfires and they'll warm us up."

"That's very nice of you, but don't forget, it rains in the spring, and sometimes very hard."

"I can build us a temporary shelter."

They sit and talk that way until they run out of words, and then they lie down together and fall asleep.

60

What Mariana guessed would happen finally happens, but a bit differently from how she had imagined it. While they are sitting under an oak, drinking tea and contemplating the fire, three short men suddenly appear. They are dressed in old leather coats. "Get up, woman, and come with us," one of them orders.

Mariana is stunned. "Why?" she asks. "What did I do?"

"It's an order," he replies.

"I refuse to obey this illegal order."

"Why be stubborn, woman?" He speaks in an intentionally relaxed way.

"I never did harm to anyone. Why should I go with you?"

"You can make your arguments to the authorities. Meanwhile, get up and come with us."

"I refuse to go. I have a son, and I have to watch over him."

"I repeat what I said. Get up and come with us. The interrogation will be short, and afterward they'll let you go. Why are you being stubborn? It's not helping you."

"Why?" She raises her head, as though she has just woken up.

"There's no why. This is an order."

"What is my name, if you've been sent to get me?" She musters her courage and cunning.

"Mariana Podgorsky," he answers, and shows her the piece of cardboard in his hand.

"I won't go. Evil tongues must be answered with contempt."

Even to that the man responds with moderation and says, "If I were in your place, I wouldn't be stubborn."

"But I am being stubborn."

"If so," says the man, and he pulls a pistol from his belt, "we'll have no choice but to shoot you. Our order is to bring you in alive or to kill you. It would be easier to kill you and put an end to the whole business."

Hugo sees the three men up close. They are short, sturdy, and indifferent. He wants to approach them and beg for Mariana's life, but he is so frightened that the words freeze in his mouth.

The pistol and the coldness that accompany the man's last words apparently convince Mariana, and she rises to her feet.

Now it's clear—she's a head taller than they are.

"Walk, and we'll follow you," he says without raising his voice.

Hugo and Mariana start walking. The men don't hurry them. After a few minutes of walking, without turning her head back to them, Mariana asks, "Why do you need me? I'll thank you if you tell me the truth."

"You have nothing to be afraid of. The Russians aren't like the Germans. With the Russians, nothing is arbitrary. Every innocent person will be freed. You'll be freed, too. After all, you didn't kill anyone."

"I didn't commit any crime, and I didn't murder." She clings to those words.

"You have nothing to fear." He continues talking in a moderate tone of voice. "They'll investigate and examine, and in the end they'll let you go. You need some patience, that's all."

"Where are you taking me?"

"To the headquarters."

"They've hardly arrived, and they're investigating already."

"A week has passed since the region was liberated. Now they're checking into everything, and in a little while new life will begin."

"Since my childhood, I've supported myself. No one helped me." Mariana brings a new tone into the conversation.

Hugo feels as if he's in a dream, constricted and bound. Even to reach out and take her hand, even that small gesture, is not within his power.

"Mariana," he whispers.

"What, honey?"

"Where are we going?"

"You heard," she says curtly.

It turns out they were very close to the city, and right near the river. Hugo remembers clearly the long walks he took with his father. Those were always times of contemplation, mindfulness, and love of nature. He had especially liked the summer walks. On Friday afternoons, on their way home, they would meet bearded Jews going to synagogue. Seeing those Jews, his father would fall silent. In answer to Hugo's question as to whether those were the real Jews, his father would give a long reply that would confuse things more than it clarified them. Hugo remembers his father's slight embarrassment and the silence that accompanied it.

"Are we going to walk through the city?" Mariana asks, again without turning to face them.

"The headquarters are located on the outskirts of the city. We're not far from there."

"Why don't you let me go, brothers?" She addresses them without imploring.

"We're on duty, and our duty won't permit us to do things like that."

"We're brothers, we're all Ukrainians and the children of Ukrainians," Mariana says. "What if you tell them that you couldn't find me?"

"We've already been looking for you for three days. We can't come back empty-handed."

"I'll pay you double."

"We're Communists and believe in Comrade Stalin."

"We're Ukrainians and believe in God and Jesus His Messiah," Mariana replies. "Leaders come and go, but God is eternal." There is strength in her voice.

"Communism has done away with the old beliefs." He isn't swept away by what she says.

"I would be careful about defying God," Mariana says. "God is in heaven, and He hears everything. On Judgment Day, we'll all stand before Him."

"Are you threatening us?"

"I have no pistol to threaten you. I wanted to remind you that Ukrainians didn't lose their faith in God even in the dark days."

"What do you want? We're just on duty and doing what we've been told to do. If you have any complaints, raise them at headquarters. There they will clarify everything. There everything is in order. They'll hear you out and free you."

"I want to remind you that I'm a loyal daughter of our tribe. None of us is the height of perfection. I was in the underworld with the God of our fathers. I never abandoned Him, even for a moment."

"In heaven you'll be found innocent," he says curtly.

"I hope that you'll also find me innocent, if only for the sake of my son, who doesn't have a living soul in the world."

"Where's his father?"

"God knows."

"Tell them everything in headquarters. They'll listen to you and let you go."

"They're Communists. They don't believe in God. If I were in your place, I would let the woman go. How much are they paying you for me?"

"We're Communists. We do everything because of our faith," he says, rejecting her request.

They reach the outskirts of the city, and Hugo immediately recognizes the area. The place is full of poplars; they appear in every yard and on every sidewalk. His father had a Ukrainian childhood friend there, a man whom they would sometimes visit on their way home after a walk along the river.

All of a sudden shouts are heard, shouts that shatter their tranquility. At first they sound to Hugo like expressions of wonder or condolence, but soon it becomes clear that they are the sounds of fury before an attack. In no time at all they are showered with stones. Mariana hugs the suitcase, trying to protect her face. The guards grin. "The people have recognized you. How do they know you?" one of them asks, hoping to provoke her.

"They've gone crazy," replies Mariana, as though it didn't concern her.

They walk on in the green tranquility of spring. What happened to them a few minutes ago now seems like an unrelated outburst, and Mariana repeats her request. "Leave me be. Let me go home."

"To what home?"

"My mother died. I'll go to my sister's."

"Your sister won't be happy to see you."

"How do you know?"

"We spoke to her at length."

"My sister is subject to moods." Mariana tries to dismiss the unfavorable impression.

But when they emerge from a long, quiet alley, people once

again recognize Mariana and throw stones at her. This time the guards are quicker and they shout at the stone-throwers to stop. When that doesn't work, they fire shots into the air. Then it stops immediately.

"You did well," says Mariana, breathing a sigh of relief.

They aren't far from the headquarters. Mariana keeps muttering, but the guards don't respond. They are tense, and if anyone dares to throw a stone or blunt object at them, a guard threatens the person with his gun. It's apparently important to them to bring Mariana to the headquarters neither beaten nor wounded.

In the months that follow Hugo will think a great deal about that painful trip. He will try to remember everything that was said and everything that was implied. Mariana knew what awaited her. She tried to get herself out of it, but everyone was against her, and not even her courage helped her.

Even now, her self-control and her tall beauty do not escape Hugo's eyes. Not even humiliation dampens her bright expression. "God, protect Mariana," Hugo says, and he feels his knees go weak. Meanwhile, they arrive at the headquarters.

"We're here," says the man with the pistol, pleased that he has succeeded in bringing the captured woman to the entrance of the cage.

Mariana puts the suitcase on the ground. "Watch this, honey," she says. "I'll be back soon. Don't go anywhere." She kisses Hugo's forehead. Then she walks unhurriedly toward the low gate, bends down to walk through it, and disappears.

61

Hugo stands there without moving. This is his city. He knows its streets and alleys. He has even passed through this not-very-splendid area a few times. He looks for someone familiar, but he sees only Russian soldiers dressed in long winter coats. Peasants carry firewood on their shoulders, and hungry dogs roam the streets.

An hour passes, and Mariana doesn't return. The thought that she is being interrogated about her connections with the Germans, that she will be accused of treason, hits home to Hugo only now. As though through a veil, he remembers her shouts and weeping when they would abuse her at night, and Madam's threats in the morning. He didn't absorb these details then. Now, as he stands alone next to the guard at the gate, expecting her to come back, it's as though the riddle has been stripped of its clues.

After standing for two hours, Hugo gets tired. He sits down on the ground and opens the suitcase. To his surprise he finds a little more cheese and bread. He eats, and his hunger abates. When he looks up, he sees the cook Victoria, accompanied by two guards. Her appearance stuns him, and he wants to approach her, the way one approaches a familiar person in an unfamiliar place. But then he remembers that she didn't like him and claimed he was endangering the women in The Residence.

"What do you want from me?" she asks one of the guards.

"At headquarters they'll explain everything to you," he replies impatiently.

"I'm not a young woman anymore," she says, and smiles.

The street fills with local people. The refugees stand out in their long, tattered coats.

"Who are you?" one of them asks Hugo.

"My name is Hugo." He doesn't conceal the fact.

"Are you Hans and Julia's son?"

"That's correct."

"Come to the square. They're giving out soup," the man says, and goes away.

That sudden attention and the mention of his parents' names help to lift Hugo from the dread in which he was mired. Now his father and mother appear before him—not as refugees who dash about in panic through the streets, but walking slowly, as if they were going to meet friends in a café.

One after another, the women from The Residence are brought to the headquarters. They are accompanied by guards and greeted by shouts of contempt. Even Sylvia, the old cleaning woman, is brought in. Astonishment freezes her small, wrinkled face. *This is a mistake,* she seems to be saying. *I'm old, I was just a cleaning woman.* The guards don't say anything. They stand tensely with the detainees in front of the locked gate. The women are crammed together in front of the gate, making it possible for the mob that has gathered to express its vindictive joy. That vulgar satisfaction is expressed not only in shouted insults but also in obscene gestures. The guards do nothing to silence the crowd.

It's good that Mariana has already gone in and was spared all this, Hugo thinks to himself.

Hugo recognizes most of the women, but not by name. As

always, Kitty stands out. Her face is also full of surprise. Here she looks more like a child than she did in The Residence, and her perplexed eyes keep asking, *What is the reason for this uproar?*

The arrested women express neither resentment nor resistance. They are just surprised that the gate won't open. If it opened, they would be saved from the curses and contempt that fall upon them from every direction. Hugo approaches and gets a better look at the women: they are still pretty, and some of them remind him of Mariana. But as a group they appear miserable and abandoned.

Hugo wants very much to say something to them, but the burly guards don't let anyone come close enough. Things continue that way for a long while, and at times it seems that the women will simply stand there until they are released. One of them, a tall woman who closely resembles Nasha, the one who drowned, turns to the guards and asks, "How long must we wait here?"

"It doesn't depend on us."

"Then on who?"

"On the camp commander. He calls the shots."

Suddenly Masha approaches, escorted by two guards, and all eyes turn to her. It's as if she were not their companion in suffering but a savior. The women nearby hug her, and the ones farther away reach out and touch her. "There's nothing to worry about," she says. "We won't hide a thing. We'll say openly, we were forced. If we hadn't obeyed, our fate would have been like that of the Jews."

"True," the trapped women agree.

"Both Victoria and Sylvia will testify that we were forced, and if Madam is against us, we'll say explicitly that she was the collaborator, not us." So she stands and prepares the collective defense brief. Her resolute words apparently make an impression on the crowd, because they stop cursing, and among the arrested women there is slight relief. Evening falls, the gate opens, and the women are taken inside. The gloating people scatter and go their way. A sudden silence falls on the place.

In the square, the refugees crowd around a large army pot full of soup. They eat the soup while standing, everyone keeping to himself. There's haste in their movements, like animals who have been hungry for days, and now, when they have obtained what they want, no longer have any interest in their fellows.

Hugo is thirsty. He's afraid to leave, in case Mariana is released and fails to find him. The thought that in a little while she will be freed, and that they will set out again, arouses new hope in him. With great clarity, Hugo remembers the blazing campfires and the fish they grilled on the coals. For Hugo, it is as though Mariana has been sculpted from that wonder. In vain he tries to remember one of her marvelous sentences. But, as though to spite him, nothing comes to mind.

"Mariana," he calls out, wanting her to appear to him.

The street grows quieter, and the refugees who surrounded the pot of soup also disperse. Only a few people remain, leaning against the walls, smoking cigarettes and talking. Hugo is thirsty and decides to approach the pot. He takes a metal bowl out of the suitcase, pours some soup into it, and sits down.

A refugee comes up to him. "Who are you?" he asks.

"My name is Hugo."

"And what is your family name?"

"Hugo Mansfeld."

"The pharmacists' son?"

"Correct."

"In the morning they give out tea and sandwiches here," the man says, and goes on his way.

Only now does he grasp what is going on: some people have been liberated and others are being sentenced behind the walls. The liberated ones run from place to place, looking for something. Hugo works up his courage, approaches one of them, and asks, "What's going on here?"

"Nothing. Why do you ask?"

"It seems to me that everybody is looking for something."

"You're wrong. Everybody has gathered here because there's soup. There's nothing like hot soup for a thirsty body," he says, and smiles.

Hugo returns to his place near the gate. The short conversation with the refugee, which revealed nothing, leaves him uneasy. For a moment it seems to him that the man bears a horrible secret within him, and that all of his words and movements are meant only to distract people from his secret. Now the man is leaning against the wall of a building and smoking hastily. From Hugo's corner he looks tall and broad-shouldered.

Later, the guard at the gate asks him, "Who are you waiting for?"

"For my mother."

"Where is she?"

"She's inside. Will she be there for a long time?"

"Who knows?" says the guard, and turns his back.

62

All night long Hugo waits tensely for Mariana's return. His expectation gradually fades, and toward morning he falls asleep. In his dream he sees his father, tall and sturdy, wearing a long coat, and looking like one of the refugees who are standing next to the pot of soup.

"Papa," Hugo calls out, and goes up to him.

The man turns a stranger's face to him. "Who are you looking for?" he asks.

"Sorry," replies Hugo, and withdraws.

"From now on, be careful," says the man, and turns away.

Hugo wakes up. The refugees aren't strangers to him. But the expression on their faces and their movements show that they have undergone an inner change that is difficult to explain. Hugo recoils from them. Instead, he approaches the pot, pours himself some soup, and takes a sandwich. Then he sits down.

Mariana is always late. She sometimes forgets that people are waiting for her, he says to himself. Now Hugo clearly remembers the closet and the thick darkness that pervaded it most of the day. But he also recalls how much light there was in Mariana's face when she stood in the doorway and apologized.

"I forgot my darling. Right away I'll bring him something to eat. You'll forgive me, yes?" And he did indeed forgive her.

Now Hugo imagines her return in similar fashion.

Meanwhile, several refugees have gathered around the pot. They seem withdrawn and don't speak. The soup is hot and it warms him. He pours himself another bowlful and finds a corner from which he can see the gate.

The gate doesn't open. Hugo once again visualizes the journey he made with Mariana after they left The Residence. It now seems long to him, and colorful, as though it lasted not weeks but months. Mariana wasn't optimistic, but she was prepared to delude herself into believing that in the mountains no one would find them.

From hour to hour, her expression changed, first earthy and infatuated with herself, and then all wounded longings for God. Throughout his life, Hugo will remember Mariana often. *She is with me wherever I go,* he will say. *Many years have passed, and she is still with me, as she was when I saw her in the doorway of the closet.*

During the long, dark nights in the closet, Hugo would dream that he had been liberated from that prison cell he had been locked in and was running home. That dream would recur often, and in different versions. Now here he is sitting a few streets away from his house, not far from the pharmacy, a ten-minute walk from Anna's house and almost the same distance from Otto's house, and he doesn't move from his place.

"What's your name?" A woman refugee speaks to him softly.

"My name is Hugo," he tells her.

"I wasn't wrong. You're the son of Hans and Julia."

"That's right."

"I've known your parents since I was a child. What are you doing here?"

"I'm waiting for the woman who saved me."

"Take care of yourself. There are horrible people here."

"I'll watch out," he says, trying not to prolong the conversation with her.

"I knew your parents very well. I even worked in their pharmacy for a while. You were three or four years old, so you don't remember me. My name is Mina. I studied with your parents at the university. I didn't finish." She speaks with intense brevity, cramming a lot of information into a few sentences. Hugo is distracted. He is afraid to look away from the gate. He doesn't ask her anything, so she says, "In a little while the people responsible will come and show us our temporary quarters. Don't go away."

How strange, Hugo thinks to himself, that gentle woman who spoke to him pleasantly and in his mother tongue also left him filled with disquiet.

Meanwhile, the guard at the gate has been replaced. Now an old soldier is standing there, dressed in a long coat. It seems to Hugo that the old man will listen to him and will tell him something about the interrogation going on inside.

"My mother's inside. How long will she have to be there?" Hugo overcomes his hesitation and asks.

"It depends on the interrogation. Now they're sentencing the whores who slept with the Germans."

"Will they give them a severe punishment?"

"The degree of punishment will be according to the severity of the sin," says the guard, pleased with his words.

Hugo is tired after an agitated night. The people and the sights that surround him got mixed up with his nightmares. He tries to clarify what was the nightmare and what is reality, but fatigue overcomes him, and he falls asleep.

63

When Hugo wakes, the sun has already set. The old soldier is still at his post. His unassuming presence encourages Hugo to ask, "Is the interrogation finished by now?"

"Apparently not." The guard is stingy with his words.

"How long do you estimate it will continue?" Hugo speaks like an adult.

"I've stopped asking myself questions like that," the guard replies, without bothering to look at Hugo.

Hugo returns to the square. Two young soldiers are filling the pot with fresh soup. The refugees observe them tensely. Hugo, too, stands and observes: the refugees are speaking German, using all the words he heard in his home, but they are not like his parents. Their way of standing shows that they have been in hiding places, and they move with caution. Before taking a step, they carefully look all around, like hunted animals.

"How long shall we stay here?" he hears one of the refugees ask another.

"I, at any rate, don't intend to stay here long," the man replies.

"And where will you go?"

"Anywhere, just not here."

"I'll wait," says the first man cautiously. "They say that not everyone has returned."

"Whoever hasn't come back so far isn't going to," the other replies. His words cut like a knife.

Hugo partly grasps the meaning of their conversation. He is torn by his desire to wait for Mariana and his desire to leave this place. To separate himself from the refugees who surround him, Hugo gives himself over entirely to his imagination. He pictures Mariana and himself together in uninhabited green places similar to those where they had been before they were caught.

Suddenly a woman bursts into bitter tears. Everyone gathers around her, but it's impossible to understand what she is saying. She mutters broken words and half-sentences that are incomprehensible. Finally she spits out, "I'm all alone. I have no one left in the world."

"All of us are alone. Stop wailing."

That reproach only increases her weeping.

Eventually they walk away from her. For a long time she cries bitterly, speaks about her parents and her sisters, and announces that there's no reason to live without them. Her crying finally subsides, and gray perplexity freezes on her face. For a moment Hugo thinks of leaving the suitcase and the knapsack with the guard and returning home. His house isn't far away—ten minutes at a run, and he'll be there. He'll go in, see if everything is in its place, and immediately return. The thought excites him, but then he remembers that all of Mariana's worldly goods are packed in the suitcase. If it were lost or stolen, Mariana would never forgive him. While he is given over to his thoughts, a truck arrives and aims its rear at the gate. People immediately gather in the street. A priest, wearing a gilded hat and with a gleaming cross hanging from his chest, heads the group.

It is clear that something dreadful and momentous is about to happen. The people surrounding the truck watch the gate, but it doesn't open. The priest begins a prayer, and those assembled join him. The prayer resounds and shakes the earth. More people gather and join in the prayer. Hugo gets the impression that they will stand there until the gate is opened and the imprisoned are freed.

As the praying continues, soldiers suddenly appear. They open the gate, storm the onlookers, and fire their guns in the air. There is a commotion, and Hugo grips the suitcase and the knapsack and pulls them to the side. The street empties out, and only the elderly priest remains on the sidewalk, praying determinedly.

Then the gate opens again, and women prisoners, wearing brown sackcloth dresses, emerge and are ordered to climb onto the truck. This isn't easy for them to do, but they help one another. Some of them trip and fall, but in the end they all get on.

Hugo immediately recognizes Mariana and calls out loud, "Mariana." People gather again and desperately call the names of the women who are standing in the truck, holding on to its bars. The priest waves his cross and raises his voice. "Jesus, save them," he prays, "they have no help or savior beside you." Hearing his supplication, everyone begins to pray again. The young soldiers are ill at ease for a moment, but then the order comes to shoot into the crowd. Now the prayers are mingled with sobs of pain. The women grabbing the bars of the truck look stunned by the sobbing and the shooting. Then they raise their arms and shout, "Jesus, we love you, you are the beloved of our heart forever and ever." The driver starts the truck, and it leaves without delay.

"They were forced. They're not guilty," people shout. A few of the wounded lie on the ground, and others kneel and tear up their shirts to bandage them. Because of the wounded, the women prisoners are forgotten for a moment. Then Hugo hears someone say to his friend, "My poor sister, my good sister, she gave everything she had to her family. Now she's on her way to death."

"How do you know?"

"Don't you know? The tribunal sentenced them to death by firing squad."

64

The people gradually disperse. The wounded, after they are bandaged, sit leaning against a wall. Bewilderment settles in their eyes. Some of them curse, and one woman pounds her head with her fists. As always, after such a horror, there is anger and gnashing of teeth.

A small group of women sit on the ground and keen. "Why did they kill them? What harm did they do? Whom did they injure? They were young and beautiful, and they brought a bit of light into our dark world." Later they change their tone and address heaven. "God, accept those young souls with love. You are merciful and forgiving, and You know that their souls were innocent and sought goodness. Fate was cruel to them. Now they are on their way to You. Don't judge them severely, spare them."

Hugo stays where he is. He feels that the words coming from the mourners' mouths are powerful and aimed in the right direction. His whole body wants to weep, but his tears are frozen. One of the refugees is watching the women. "They know how to pray," he says. "They address God the right way. Why are we mute? Why has prayer been taken from our mouths?"

"Are you still asking?" says his friend, who is standing next to him.

"Aren't I allowed to ask?"

"A question for its own sake is stupid."

Night falls. Everyone is tired. They sit by the fire and stare into it. No one asks what they are supposed to do or for whom they are supposed to wait to show them the way. Some of the men exchange banknotes and objects that appeared to be luxury items. There is great silence, as after a huge battle.

Hugo goes over to the guard at the gate and asks about the fate of the women who were taken away in the truck.

"What do you want to know?" The guard's patience has worn out.

"Where are they?"

"You're better off not knowing."

"Is it impossible to go to them?"

"You're apparently dumb," he says, and turns his back.

Only now does Hugo realize that Mariana knew exactly what was coming. But in the green tranquility that surrounded them, her words had sounded to him like either hallucinations or irrational fears. Once she told him explicitly, "If they kill me, don't forget me. You're the only person in the world whom I trust. I buried some of my soul inside you. I don't want to depart from the world without leaving you something of mine. I have no silver or gold. Take my love and hide it in your heart, and from time to time say to yourself, Once there was Mariana. She was a mortally wounded woman, but she never lost faith in God."

That evening she went on to say other marvelous things, of which Hugo grasped only a little. Most of them were whispers that were swallowed up inside her. Now her words are returning to him with an intense clarity.

Hugo realizes that the guard at the gate is not only ignoring him, he is also contemptuous of him. Before long, he expresses his revulsion in two words: "Go away."

Hugo returns to the square, to the refugees. The bonfire burns, and people surround it on all sides. The pot is full of soup, and everyone keeps refilling their bowls. Years of hunger take a while to satisfy. One old man claims that vegetable soup is a good thing for them to eat. The body has to get used to new conditions slowly, and it's wrong to burden the digestive system with heavy foods. Vegetable soup is the correct food at this time. The others look at him with amazement, as if he were saying things to them that they had never heard.

People approach Hugo and say, "You're Hugo, right?"

"Right."

"My name is Tina," one of them says, "and I am Otto's aunt."

"Where is Otto?" Hugo is frightened and rises to his feet.

"God knows. I'm waiting for everyone from my family. Where were you?"

"With Mariana."

"Poor thing. The sentence was horrible."

"It didn't apply to Mariana." The words escape from his mouth.

"I'm glad."

After a pause she adds, "I'm desperate to know what happened to my family. The news is confusing and contradictory. People here told me that they saw Otto's mother. But others say that she wasn't his mother, only a woman who looked like her. I've decided to wait. I won't move from here. We mustn't lose hope. There's no reason to live without hope. As long as we live, we have to hope. That's how God created us, whether we like it or not." She speaks in a torrent, as though she were reading or reciting. It's clear she isn't in control of what comes out of her mouth. The words pour out in a flood. "I won't go away from here. No power can move me. I'll wait here until the last moments of my life." She puts her hand on her mouth, but that gesture doesn't stop the flow of words. In the end she says to him, "Excuse me. Now I must be by myself." She turns away and is swallowed up in the darkness.

65

That night Hugo sleeps deeply. Scenes from his home and images that had just now passed before him creep into his dreams. In that mix Mariana stands out—not only her statuesque body but also the things that she says. She speaks about God and about the need to be close to Him. The refugees look at her and don't believe their ears. Her blowsy appearance contrasts with her pious words. Most of the refugees don't recognize her, but those who do say, with a smile, "If Mariana is talking about God, that's a sign that the Messiah is about to come." That, of course, is a barbed comment. Mariana simply amuses them.

Then she addresses them with a theatrical gesture and says, "You all know Hugo. But you only think that you know him. This is a different Hugo. What he managed to learn since I took him in cannot be measured. I planted everything that I had in his soul. I presume that certain people will have reservations about some of the things I taught him, but don't worry, I equipped him with a lot of faith. Now he knows that God dwells everywhere. That should be no small thing in your eyes. Opposition to the existence of God is so strong that even a little faith costs people a lot. That's why I said that Hugo has changed not only externally. He is going to surprise you."

Hugo wakes from his dream. The refugees lie curled up in their coats. It doesn't appear as though they have heard Mariana's words. Maybe they heard and now are waiting for her second appearance.

Hugo rises to his feet and sees for the first time that this part of the city has not changed at all: it is filled with two-story buildings. Families live on the upper story, and stores and workshops are on the ground floor. Jews did not live here. The stores and workshops are not yet open, and the tranquility of early morning still rests upon the houses. It's evident that the Ukrainians have not been driven out of their homes; even during the war they kept up their daily routines. There are no architectural treasures or notable buildings in this neighborhood. Everything here says: a house is simply a house, divided correctly and open to the garden. Decorations and ironwork are for the rich. Hugo absorbed an appreciation for that sort of simplicity in the past, and he remembers it.

Later new refugees arrive. Hugo vaguely remembers some of them but most are strangers to him. Perhaps because of their extreme emaciation, it is obvious that something within them has died. And the part that is left can't explain what has happened to them.

"We've changed," one of the new arrivals jokes.

"So it appears," responds his friend.

In addition to the pot of soup and the sandwiches, someone put up a new stand, where they serve drinks and hand out cigarettes. The German army left behind storehouses full of supplies, and the refugees arrive with full sacks. A woman with unkempt hair, wearing a military coat whose buttons have been torn off, prepares a pot of coffee and speaks to the refugees as if they were her brothers and sisters, and as if they had just awakened from a troubled sleep. "Drink, children, drink," she says to them softly. "I've prepared excellent coffee for you. There are goods in abundance. I'll cook whatever you want." She has apparently had a few drinks, and she is in an exalted mood. The refugees approach her, and she pours generously for them and blesses them. It's evident that she wants to give them something of her own to make them happy. The people are embarrassed by such a display of devotion.

Hugo observes the new refugees. They resemble his parents, but some are older. It's hard to know what they have undergone. Their gray faces are expressionless. They barely speak.

Later Hugo says to himself, *I'll go and see the city*. This was what he would sometimes say to himself after he had finished his homework and light still flickered in the windows. He liked that hour. Toward evening the city used to take on a new life. The sound of music playing could be heard from open windows, and people sat in coffeehouses, enjoying themselves and releasing the tension from a day of labor. Sometimes Hugo would meet Anna or Otto, and they would go into a coffeehouse and order ice cream. There was ice cream in almost every good coffeehouse, but the Alaska Café was famous for theirs.

At one of those relaxed meetings, Anna told Hugo that she intended to become an author. Her piano playing had indeed improved, but she couldn't stand the thought of the exhausting practice sessions and all the performances she would have to give over the years. Anna was outstanding in all subjects, but her compositions were famous throughout the school. They were read out loud not only in her class but in other classes as well. Everybody praised her rich vocabulary, her powers of description, her subtle humor, and of course her abundance of ideas.

"How to you intend to become an author?" Hugo asked her cautiously.

"I'm reading the classics."

"Flaubert?"

"Among others."

At that time Hugo was reading Jules Verne and Karl May, but Anna had other ideas.

It now seems to Hugo that everything that happened to him since leaving his home was a personal trial over which he had no control. His real life is being lived now, in this city. Here he knows every corner, every bend in the road, the broad avenues along which the trams travel.

Almost without realizing it, Hugo grips the suitcase and the knapsack and sets out. He advances slowly, as though he fears encountering a sight that will surprise him, but there is nothing surprising in what is revealed to him. Everything happens at a slow pace. Old people sit in the doorways of their houses, and wagons full of wood roll lazily down the street. That relaxed atmosphere, which Hugo remembers from his childhood and which now appears before his eyes, confirms his belief that what happened to him when he left his home was only a personal trial. Now he is emerging from the tunnel, and he walks on stable ground. Here nothing has changed. His fear that the city had been destroyed by bombing or looted by the German and Russian armies was for naught.

Hugo carefully examines everything that he comes across: nothing has changed, everything is as it was. There is Cyril's ice-cream stand. It's open, and Cyril stands inside, carefully dressed, as always. There is nothing exceptional in his demeanor. On the contrary, he looks at ease, and confident that customers will soon arrive.

Hugo sits on a bench on Acacia Avenue, the most modest of the city's avenues. He has a good view of the city, from the poplars alongside the river to the stores and coffeehouses. He used to sit here with Anna. Once he sat here with Franz, who tried to prove to him, with long and complex words, that science was advancing by leaps and bounds, and that everything that seemed stable and well grounded today would be thought of as childish in ten years. Franz was a genius. Conversation with him was always tiring and dizzying.

Forgotten images appear before him, among them images from school. Not everything was enjoyable there. After school, bullies used to pick on the few Jews who attended, and some of the teachers embarrassed the Jewish pupils who didn't come up to Anna's or Franz's level. But most days things proceeded without disturbance. Hugo is sorry that the war cut him off from his parents and from school; now he would have to start everything all over again. He stands up with the intention of going to the school, but the impulse that gets him up also keeps him in his place. He is afraid to advance, afraid that things will appear that he hadn't imagined.

66

Hugo overcomes his apprehension and sets off. On Acacia Avenue stands the tavern where Uncle Sigmund used to spend days and nights. Sometimes, as he walked by, Hugo would see him arguing with someone or sunk in thought. Hugo would stand there, hoping Sigmund would notice him. That never happened. Near the bar is a cheap café where Frieda always used to sit. He would meet her there occasionally. Unlike Uncle Sigmund, she would notice him promptly, hug and kiss him, and tell him that she was his mother's first cousin. She intended to visit the family, she would say, even if she wasn't invited.

His feet move slowly, as though unsure of their direction. Everything is familiar to him and has hardly changed. Here and there a tree has been uprooted and a sapling has been planted in its place. Some of the stores are open and some are shuttered. Near the tavern where Uncle Sigmund used to sit, there had been a dry goods store owned by a religious Jew. His mother sometimes went in to buy mill ends for her needy people. It was a gloomy kingdom, full of tunnels and many shelves of cloth. Little children with earlocks and ritual fringes raced around the aisles. The owner of the shop, a pleasant man, adorned with earlocks and a beard, would serve the customers patiently and spice his words with proverbs and jokes, all in

German mixed with Yiddish, which his mother understood well. Hugo, who had been raised on the purity of the German language, found it hard to understand. Now he envisions the interior of the shop, as though it were illuminated, even though the shop itself is shuttered.

In Uncle Sigmund's tavern people sit as always. The proprietor, whom Hugo recognizes immediately, is standing in the middle of the room and giving a speech full of self-importance, and everyone laughs. How strange, Hugo says to himself, everything here is unchanged, only Uncle Sigmund is missing.

He puts the suitcase and the knapsack down on the ground. Momentarily freed of his burden, Hugo does notice some changes: the homes of the Jews who had lived above the shops have been taken by Ukrainians. At the windows and on the balconies stand women and children, chatting and laughing. A different wind blows in the air. Hugo tries to identify it but doesn't succeed.

When he would walk along these streets with his mother, people greeted her, blessed her, and sometimes asked her for advice about some medical issue. In that respect, Hugo was more like his father. He wasn't involved in school matters, and, like his father, he preferred being by himself.

Now he wanders in the city of his birth like a person who has returned to it after many years. No one recognizes him, and no one greets him upon his return. Cold surrounds him on every side and makes him shiver. He grips the suitcase and the knapsack and resumes walking.

The school stands where it always has been. Classes aren't being held in it, but the main entrance is open, and near the broad stairway stands, as always, Big Ivan, the all-powerful janitor of the school.

"Hello, Mr. Ivan." Hugo addresses him as everyone always did.

"Who are you?" Ivan fixes him with his gaze.

"My name is Hugo Mansfeld. Don't you remember me?"

"I see that the Jews are coming back," he says. It's hard to know what he means by that.

"I'm going home to see whether my parents have returned. When does school start?"

"I'm the janitor, not the government. The government announces the opening of the school."

"I'm glad to see you," says Hugo, and indeed he is glad to find a familiar soul.

The janitor smiles and says, "Rumors circulated here that the Jews had been killed. False rumors, it turns out. Where were you?"

"I was hiding."

"I'm glad."

Ivan's wife appears in the entrance, and he quickly announces to her, "The Jews are coming back."

"Who said so?"

"Here's Hugo. Don't you remember him? He really got taller."

It's strange to see the school in its silence. This is how the building looked when he returned from summer vacation, but then he had returned thirsty for his friends and his city. Now he fears every corner.

Hugo continues on. In this part of the city he can walk with his eyes closed. The familiar sight of Ivan next to the stairs instills in him the feeling that the city hasn't changed. If Mr. Ivan is standing next to the stairs, that means that school will open soon.

The sight of the pharmacy changes everything. The elegant building, which had always been well maintained, has become a grocery store. Inside, the tall and gleaming cabinets, the marble counter, the vases of flowers—all have been uprooted. At the entrance stand crates of potatoes, red cabbage, garlic, and onions. The smell of smoked fish and rotten cabbage hangs in the air.

The pharmacy was one of Hugo's favorite places. His parents felt complete fulfillment there. Their love flourished. Some customers would say, "Hugo is like his mother," and others would put their hands on their hearts and say, "Hugo is a perfect copy of his father." Only now, standing before the ruins, does he absorb what has happened: what was will never return.

Now his step is heavier, more like a shuffle. Hugo remembers that sometimes his mother would return home early to prepare parcels for the needy. Hugo, already home from school, would see her approaching from a distance, dressed in a flowered dress, more like a girl than like his mother.

Suddenly, enchanted pieces of his childhood come back to him, as vividly as when he first experienced them. Whenever his mother saw him from a distance, she would call out his name in excitement, as though he had been revealed to her in a vision.

Hugo's mother also knew how to be affected by things that didn't immediately strike the eye. His father used to say, "You can learn how to be moved by Julia." His mother's response came promptly. "Make no mistake," she would say, "in Hans's eyes, being moved isn't regarded as a praiseworthy trait."

"You're wrong, my dear."

Hugo's feet bring him home.

The house stands where it always was. On the pleasant, broad balcony that looked out onto the city hangs blue laundry. The windows on the side are bare, and people can be seen inside. The big chandelier in the living room still hangs from the ceiling. For a long time Hugo stands there and looks, and what he had felt upon arriving at the city center now hits him with full force: the soul has fled from this precious place.

Evening falls and darkens the sights. Hugo wants to go back to the town square that he left that morning. He takes a shortcut through a Ukrainian neighborhood. There's no electricity, and the houses are lit by big kerosene lamps. People sit at tables and eat. The tranquility of nightfall descends upon the street and the houses. That's how it always was there, Hugo recalls. And it's still the same.

As he's about to leave the neighborhood, an old man calls out to him, "Who are you?"

"My name is Hugo Mansfeld," he answers.

"What are you doing here?"

"I came to see our house."

"Get out of here. I don't want to see you again," says the old man, waving his cane. Hugo quickens his steps, and before long he is back in the square, among the refugees.

67

When Hugo reaches the square, it is already night. Near the soup kettle and the food stands that have been set up, pots of coffee steam, and the murmur of people withdrawn into themselves is heard. A tall man wearing old army clothes hands Hugo a sandwich and a cup full of coffee. He does it cautiously and attentively, as though he knows that for hours no liquid has passed Hugo's lips. Hugo sits at some distance from the bonfire. The sandwich is tasty, and the hot coffee warms him. The sorrow he experienced during the day fades slightly. He's glad he came back to this place.

A woman approaches. "What's your name, young man?" she asks.

Hugo looks into her eyes and answers.

"You're Hans and Julia's son, right?"

"Right."

"They were wonderful people. There wasn't a poor person in the city whom they didn't give something to in their generosity." She wants to add something, but her voice is choked. Hugo wants to ask her where they are and when they will be coming here, but seeing that her face has suddenly closed up, he doesn't.

"Do you have warm clothing?" She changes her tone. "I'll bring you a coat. It's cold at night here." She goes over to the pile of clothes that lie off to the side, fishes out a coat, and hands it to Hugo. "Put it on," she says. "It's cold here at night." Hugo puts on the coat, and to his surprise he immediately feels comfortable.

"Thank you. What's your name, if I may ask?" The words escape from his mouth.

"My name is Dora. I used to go into the pharmacy sometimes. It was a model pharmacy. Everybody was welcomed with a smile."

The commotion in the square increases, but it doesn't become an uproar. It's evident that people here are careful of one another. The quiet talk reminds Hugo of a house of mourning. When his grandfather Jacob died, many people came to their house and surrounded them with loving silence. Hugo was then five years old. The quiet mourning seeped into him, and for many nights he dreamed about the people who had sat in his home without uttering a word.

"Why are the people so quiet?" he asked his mother then.

"What is there to say?" she replied, and said nothing more.

Hugo looks around him and becomes aware that some of the refugees are keeping a secret. People turn to them and ask them to reveal the secret to them, but for some reason they stubbornly refuse. A sturdy, overwrought woman with wild hair falls on one of the secret-keepers and vehemently demands that he tell her what happened at Camp Thirty-three.

"I don't know. I was outside of that camp." The secret-keeper defends himself.

"Your face says that you know exactly what happened, but you've decided not to reveal that knowledge."

"Nobody knows."

"But you were there, and you know. Why are you denying me and the people like me clear knowledge of what happened?"

"I can't," he says, and his voice chokes.

"So you do know." The woman doesn't relent. "I felt that you knew. You can't leave us in a fog forever. Just tell us."

"I can't," says the man, and bursts into tears.

"Why are you torturing him?" A man standing to the side mixes in.

"Because I have to know. My father and my mother, my two brothers, my husband, and my two children were there. Don't I deserve to know? I have to know."

"But he already told you that he can't." He continues defending the weeping man.

"That's no answer, it's concealment. Let him tell me what he knows. I deserve to have him tell me."

The man's weeping grows stronger, but the woman doesn't relent. She seems to believe that the weeping man could bring her dear ones back to life, and for some hidden reason he is refusing to do it.

Finally people separate them.

That night many secrets are revealed, but there is no weeping. The silence grows. The refugees sip mugs of coffee and glasses of brandy and numb the sorrow within them. Hugo feels fear. He's afraid that Mariana will come and fail to find him near the gate, so he decides to go back and sit there. But at that hour the gate is surrounded by many soldiers. From time to time the gate opens, and an officer announces something. The soldiers are quiet, expressing no resentment.

Later one of the refugees, an unpleasant-looking man, tells Hugo that the field court has been sitting for days, judging collaborators and informers. As for the whores, there's no doubt, they were condemned and executed that very day.

Hugo hears, curled up in the long coat, and closes his eyes.

Before his eyes Mariana rises to her full height, wearing a flowered dress and standing in the doorway of the closet. "Why don't you read me some poems from the Bible?" she asks. And when she approaches him, Hugo immediately notices a gaping hole in her neck, a hole with no signs of blood. The flesh around it is burned, and it is gray.

Hugo awakens. The bonfire is blazing in full force. The refugees sleep, wrapped in their coats. Potatoes and chunks of meat they laid on the coals have become charred.

68

Hugo remains awake. *I'll remember this night, too,* he says to himself. The passing hours fill him till there's no more room, but at the same time he feels hollow, as if he were being plundered from within.

He opens the suitcase and there before his eyes are Mariana's two flowered dresses—one mostly dark red and the other mostly sky blue. Both of them suited her. Both of them enhanced the light that filled her face and complemented her long neck and arms. There are also two pairs of shoes, both high-heeled. They made her taller and emphasized the beautiful outlines of her breasts. Sometimes she would say, "There's nothing like high-heeled shoes. They were created for Mariana." There are also two folded corsets. Mariana had a complex attitude toward corsets. Sometimes she complained that they made it hard for her to breathe, but when she was in a good mood, she would admit that the corset molded her figure. She spoke about her breasts with pity. "My poor breasts," she used to say, "what hasn't been done to them." There are also silk stockings, a few slips, bottles of perfume, lipsticks, powder, and a bottle and a half of brandy. From those few objects, Mariana is sculpted. "I don't need much," she would say. "I just want people to leave me alone."

Hugo doesn't forget even now how self-involved Mariana was. There were days when she forgot him, and he almost collapsed from hunger. But the light that glowed in her face would erase all the little injustices.

Years will pass, and Hugo will continue to wonder what libation she poured into his soul, and under what circumstances she was taken from him. If she has been within me until now, he would say, that means that one day we'll meet again.

Hugo closes the suitcase carefully and looks around. The bonfire now burns quietly. The refugees sleep, but some of them lie there with their eyes open. The woman with the wild hair who demanded immediate information has also sunk into deep sleep.

Flames leap out of the bonfire, and a man rises to his knees and begins to whisper. At first it sounds like a prayer, but soon it becomes clear that the man has come to the conclusion that those who haven't yet returned are not going to. In vain he has deluded himself and the others.

No one responds to his whispering. The people lie huddled under their coats like children. It occurs to Hugo that the man didn't intend to speak to the people's wakefulness, but to pour his secret discoveries into their sleep.

A short woman emerges from the darkness with a carton of sandwiches, a pot of coffee, and some mugs. She approaches one of the refugees and offers him a sandwich and a cup of coffee.

"Why aren't you sleeping?" the man asks in surprise.

"I don't need sleep," she says apologetically.

"You won't be able to keep it up. A person has to rest."

"I may be a short, thin woman, but I am very strong. You can't imagine how strong I am. Another woman in my place would have collapsed. I don't feel any weakness. I have the strength to undergo more."

"You're going to work like this all the time?"

"That's what I've been doing since I left the hiding place and learned what I learned."

"Have you no other plans for the future?"

"I do this willingly. If only I could do more. Take, please."

The man takes a sandwich in one hand and a mug in the other and promptly starts drinking.

Before long the woman stops next to Hugo and offers him a sandwich and coffee. Hugo takes the gift without saying anything. "You look familiar to me, son," she says.

"My name is Hugo Mansfeld."

"Good God," she says, and kneels. "You're Julia and Hans's son. How did you end up here?"

"I'm waiting for my parents."

"You mustn't wait for them," she whispers a bit louder. "We have to leave here. Whoever hasn't come by now probably won't come soon. We have to leave here, together, so that we can all watch over one another."

"Won't my parents come?"

"Not now. Now we have to leave."

"For where?" Hugo asks hesitantly.

"We have to leave together and watch over one another. Brothers don't say, I've already given. Brothers give more, and we have, thank God, a lot to give. One gives a cup of coffee and the other helps a woman bandage her wounds. One gives a blanket, and the other raises the pillow of a person who's having trouble breathing. We have a lot to give. We don't know yet how much we have."

She speaks in a flood of words. Hugo doesn't understand everything she plucks from her heart, but her words seep into him with the hot coffee. In time he will say to himself, *This was like a field hospital—people and blankets and burning pain.* The small woman goes from place to place, bandaging wounds, driving away bad thoughts, and serving coffee and sandwiches.

A man shows her the stump of his hand and asks, "Better?"

"Much better," she says, and kisses his forehead.